T0244011

FEELING KERALA

Celebrating 35 Years of
Penguin Random House India

FEELING KERALA

AN ANTHOLOGY OF CONTEMPORARY MALAYALAM STORIES

Translated from the
Malayalam by **J DEVIKA**

PENGUIN
VIKING

An imprint of Penguin Random House

VIKING

USA | Canada | UK | Ireland | Australia
New Zealand | India | South Africa | China

Viking is part of the Penguin Random House group of companies
whose addresses can be found at global.penguinrandomhouse.com

Published by Penguin Random House India Pvt. Ltd
4th Floor, Capital Tower 1, MG Road,
Gurugram 122 002, Haryana, India

First published in Viking by Penguin Random House India 2023

ISBN 9780670098118

Typeset in Sabon by Manipal Technologies Limited, Manipal
Printed at Thomson Press India Ltd, New Delhi

www.penguin.co.in

Dedicated to the memory of M. Gangadharan,
fellow free-spirit and lover of Kerala

Contents

Translator's Introduction

The idea of this anthology struck me as I was mulling over writing a book about the place I love best, Kerala. I have devoted much of my life to understanding society and culture in this part of India as an active participant in the collective exercise of reimagining it under the significantly different global and national scenarios of the twenty-first century. Anyone who wishes to learn about Kerala has no dearth of sources to choose from. From academic writing to statistics to journalism, information resources about this society are plentiful now. It is, of course, possible to introduce Kerala through numbers—through all that is reducible to quantitative proportions, measurable and comparable. But that project is not uncommon at all; indeed, the dominant narratives about Kerala are all about that.

Yet one necessarily has to turn to literature if one is to get a feel of the sensuous, living reality of this society beyond the platitudes dished out by a range of commentators from development experts to travel writers. That is, I believe that anyone seeking the uniqueness of a region must necessarily tread beyond indicators that enable comparisons with other regions. Literature alone may capture social processes in all their complexities in a regional culture swept up in rapid social change since the 1990s. For example, the manner in which social inequalities skyrocketing since the 1990s have altered the lived lives of individuals—of different social locations, economic status and cultural endowments—in Malayali society is best documented, in my view, in the works of Kerala's literary writers. The changing contours of family relationships, intimacy, consumption, community, faith, bodily experience—it is impossible to speak about contemporary Kerala without these. Surely, this is a daunting task and not all aspects can be covered equally. I choose, therefore, to focus on lived life in Kerala, and not on, say, the life of Malayali Non-Resident Indians (NRIs).

The short story is a particularly powerful medium in this respect. The aim of this book is to bring Kerala—as a living, pulsating entity changing in front of our eyes—to the reader through its short story writers. Contemporary Malayalam short stories are often astute and illuminating comments on social life. As a form, the short story thrives in Kerala and there is a whole new generation of sensitive, brilliant storytellers here, men and women, who are engaged in the invaluable task of building lenses that defamiliarize the ordinary and the everyday, revealing the subtle play of power and the hidden architectures, the hierarchies and layers, that structure them. Some of them have been translated and read in English and other languages; others are just beginning to emerge in Malayalam. Their words allow us to experience this world in its fullness. This book, then, is an important event in my life as a translator, a moment in which I bring together two strands of my life—that of the social researcher and historian, and that of the literary translator.

Choosing stories for this volume has not been easy. Most of these stories are by younger and relatively less translated authors, though seniors and much-translated writers are also included. The seniors in this group are writers who began to publish in the 1980s, and the youngest are those whose stories appeared in the past decade. It needs to be emphasized that this collection is not meant to be an adequate representation of the finest literary talent in short-story writing in Malayalam. That will surely require a much larger book—such is the abundance of talent in the form in Malayalam today. While I am certain that the authors chosen are all brilliantly talented members of this new generation, and I believe that each of the stories I have chosen is a fascinating read, they do not exhaust the galaxy of talents for sure. I have not included in this volume some of the finest Malayalam authors, for example, N. Prabhakaran, whose work has endlessly fascinated me.

The stories here have been chosen, rather, with the previously stated end in mind—that of providing a tour into the heart and soul of contemporary Kerala. They cover the different landscapes of Kerala, including the highland, the coastal areas and the growing urban centres. They move in and out of homes and take the readers into older spaces—the derelict homes of female-headed families, churches, panchayats, beaches that are homes to fisherfolk—and the new spaces of the capital—airports, tourist resorts, the cavernous mansions of the nouveau riche. Each story is preceded by a short introduction so that dreary footnoting can be avoided and the reader is familiarized beforehand with the worlds that each author opens up. In these stories, the lives of frustrated college lecturers, upwardly mobile non-resident men, insecure traditional elites, people struggling endlesslessly against caste oppression, menial workers, tribal people, predatory politicians, angry young women struggling against patriarchy and poverty, and home nurses who are always in transit, jostle for space as they do in Kerala.

I want to emphasize that this volume aims at getting past the twentieth-century characterizations of Kerala—for example, as defined by communist egalitarian spirit or matrilineal families. The Kerala of the present is certainly moving away at high speed from these. As a historian and researcher of contemporary social life, the attempts to reinforce such images seem to me to be clearly powered by vested interests that seek to sell a certain image of the region in the first world (or increasingly, to north Indian elites), suitably exoticized.

But it is true that Kerala is in many ways a unique place. Widespread literary, internet and cellphone prevalence, the heightened experience of migration and transnationalism have indeed ensured that there is not a dull day in this tiny sliver of land tucked away like a shockingly green banana leaf between the Sahya mountains and the Arabian Sea. Everybody, even those who seem completely disempowered, has a strategy, even a plan. That sets Kerala of the twenty-first century apart from other societies, for starters.

I want to thank all the authors in this volume who trusted me with their work as well as Premanka Goswami, Moutushi Mukherjee and all the others at Penguin Random House who took a keen interest in this project. Special thanks to A.J. Thomas, who introduced me to the writing of Prince Aymanam.

J Devika

The Angry Young Woman

The early twentieth century might well be characterized as the Age of the Angry Young Woman in Kerala. Everywhere, young women radiate astonished anger at the ease with which promises have been broken, rosy futures, once pointed to, have been denied. The late twentieth-century decades saw the large-scale entry of Malayali women into higher education. The 1990s were the heyday of 'women's empowerment' here: young women began to migrate to national educational metropolises; women began to enter into, and excel at, almost every new avenue that opened up at that time; the national economy boomed, promising women jobs and independence; after globalization and liberalization, the media explosion and later, the Internet and social media expanded young women's horizons unprecedentedly. In other words, the generation of college-going Malayali women of the 1990s—more in numbers compared with their predecessors—are strongly individuated. The ongoing conservative backlash that condemns women's aspirations as depraved and inimical to Malayali culture cannot corral them back into conservative spaces to serve as machines of procreation.

Nevertheless, the struggle is extremely taxing. Especially in families in which the young woman is made to carry the burden of family honour. Dowry in marriage was once upon a time limited to a few communities in Kerala and regulated by custom. During the course of the twentieth century, almost every community here accepted dowry payments at the time of weddings—which is a one-way flow of wealth from the bride's family to the bridegroom's, one which does not guarantee the bride safety or dignity. In present-day Kerala, where dowry rates have reached stratospheric proportions, despite all her achievements in education or employment, the girl is still the burden, the honour of her family is incumbent upon her and her alone, and 'settling' her in life implies bearing great expenses for her wedding ceremony and depletion of her family's wealth. The son, however incompetent he may be, promises to fetch a dowry of a few lakh rupees; the brilliant, individuated daughter can only be a drag on family resources.

It is not difficult to see why young Malayali women are often furious, burning with rage. Highly educated yet stubbornly undervalued and leashed to the male-centred family, she has to conform to domestic ideologies and limit the energies that arise from her individuation in service of the patriarchal family. Women's labour force and work participation rates in Kerala have been generally abysmal; there are signs that women may have even stopped seeking work. At the point at which the strong individuation of the young Malayali woman meets her undervaluation in the family and the labour market, the Angry Young Woman is born. Conservatives may think that this anger is fanned mainly by leftists and feminists. But this anger is structural—it comes from fundamental political, socio-economic and cultural shifts. It can present itself as liberating public anger; it can also be repressed and perverted.

Yama, one of Malayalam's most promising literary voices of the present, writes the following story filling it with the throbbing rage of the Angry Young Woman. That it is finally soothed by love does not make it any less searing.

The Funerary Palm

'Chudalaththengu'

Yama

The ants—trapped in the blob of mucous fallen on the hollow, termite-eaten windowsill—stopped struggling. She was weeping, chin pressed against arms crossed on the ledge; once or twice, her mother's curses fell on her ears like meteors—falling, helpless, exploding. It wasn't clear who she aimed them at. It seemed from the racket that the misshapen pots and pans in the kitchen were changing shape again. Her thin hands must be searching desperately for unbroken things now. Her mother, cursing death that slid away without bowing to her. Life, like a sharp spike of iron that the years could not corrode or waste away. Their relatives knew well how to keep a safe distance so that they would not fall on it . . .

At the tip of the branch of the moringa tree grown emaciated, thin and tall from the summer's drought, a fruit hung—a mature one, dry and ready to burst. The seeds grinned, pushing out through the parched shell, threatening to expand the race of moringas. She stared at it and felt as if a suicide bomber was unleashing an attack inside her brain. Inside the house, an unquiet silence had grown tall, a fortress which burst through the tiled roof and reached sky-high. The impenetrable frustration made her snarl.

'I'll kill them all! What's the point of living? FUCKing what?' Caught under her teeth, the words that tried to escape her mouth tore and bled. Amma must have heard her spit out that *theri-*, that cussword. Once, it used to be 'a rap on your *kiri* for every little theri'. The thumb and forefinger that once joined together to aim a rap on her lower lip were now weak and arthritic.

She searched for and found a piece of a shaving blade from the pile of books on the table. It was her brother who bought shaving blades. For his beard. But the piece of blade reminded her of well-sharpened pencils. Long back, in school, someone had told her that the lead in pencils was highly poisonous. So, she had stored away pieces of lead from pencil stubs in the hope of ending her life. For many reasons, she was not light enough at heart to laugh at that memory.

What the hell am I thinking about? Think too much, and you want to live. But there was not a damn thing that could get you back to the thought of living. No open grounds or fields to go out and walk in. The borderless nights, not hers. She knew well by now that buses may have fancy information boards, but they all have to inevitably stop somewhere. As a child, she thought that all buses ran on towards the ever-receding horizon. Now, it was this life which was running, without a clue about where it was going. To get to death, somehow. That was it. She raised the piece of blade to cut the vein that bulged on her left wrist. Her nerves writhed for a moment in the expectation of the blade slitting the skin's surface and entering like lightning. She noticed that the blade which tarried shakily over the blue-violet spread on her wrist was rusty. Rust can cause sepsis.

The face of Arya, who had died of a fever back in upper primary school, rose in her mind. That girl was so stingy with smiles. Her long, abundant, black, oiled hair, which fell nearly to her buttocks, would always be neatly braided. People said that she began to smile all the time a few days before her death; that was no exaggeration. In the classroom, she was the only one who had reached menarche; she had begun to bloom like a young, graceful tree. The evil eye took her, her mother had wailed, hugging her lifeless body. Raji often felt guilty: was it she who had cast that covetous eye on her?

As she lowered her head on the windowsill, she looked intently at the ants that had come to eat her tears and had ended up dead in the mucous. She swept off the dead ants with the blade's edge. Tearful moments hung heavy inside her.

'So, you won't give . . .?'

Had her brother started all over? She felt fearful again.

'*Daivame*, good God! Oh, your old man's put sooo much money in the bank when he popped off! Fine, take it!'

'I didn't ask about what's in the bank, I asked for that gold chain! You're kidding, aren't you? You're going to get that girl married with this lousy chain? I am grovelling like this only because it'd be easier for me to move around if I had a bike! Will get you another when I make some money!'

'I've no hope of marrying her off with this . . .' Amma's voice was fraying in sheer helplessness. 'It's just that . . . if one of us here falls ill . . . this is all we have to pawn . . .' The house seemed to be catching fire from her feverish heart. 'This is the first little bit of gold my Ammachi bought me. She's dead and gone. I won't sell this till I die . . .'

These humans . . .! Raji was overpowered by a terrible rush of disgust. She cussed the God who'd gifted them with brains that could ban all dreaming. Now they are all able to deny the slightest care for another. The race now is to prove who supports who. In their accounting of the emotions, cheap counters are deemed priceless. Even the account of the medicinal oil that had to be bought when Amma sprained her foot and had to be taken to the Ayurveda hospital was pulled out and brandished.

God, only if I could love someone. Only if someone loved me. I need to run away . . . somewhere. But where to? Where to run in this world where bottomless abysses lie in wait with jaws open at either ends of the land? What hell is this life in which one cannot live even a moment without adding up for tomorrow?

The degree exams were just over. The results did not matter, really. She knew well that further study was impossible, no matter how much she yearned for it. Even in the graduate course, she didn't get a chance to read all the textbooks properly. By the time she reached the Department Library, it would have been picked clean by the smart ones in her class. She used to wonder in frustration, how did they manage to do this so thoroughly? She never complained at home though, out of the fear that they would just tell her to drop out. And she knew that if she didn't step out of the house at least during the daytime every day, she would go raving mad. That house was like a cell with self-destructive characteristics, ready to explode. Houses must be the cellular tissue of society growing in the length and breadth of the street, she mused. Cells, with walls separating them and regulating mutual flows. Walls of concrete that now rose between houses that were once separated by small partitions of mud, which hid their view only by half. Each house had developed secrets and private things big enough to hide. An ordinary man's house today is a closed heart of mystery and intrigue.

Her brother and mother did not even know that there were such things as exam fees and semester fees to be dealt with in college. Neither had she tried to tell them, knowing fully well that it was useless. She managed to pay the exam fees working as an usher at events, work secured for her by some friends through an event management company. They'd kill her if they found out, that too she knew. Amma worried that blue-film racketeers were out there hunting for young girls. If Amma got to know that she had gone somewhere without her permission, she would certainly count it as a man-seeking misadventure. Her brother failed the tenth standard exam and then was too proud to attempt it again. But he was certain that he would be wealthy, some day. He was not ashamed to declare it frequently, puffed up with that baseless optimism.

Now he was a sidekick to some big real estate honcho. He thought he could take advantage of some fortuitous moment to sneak into that world and mint money. His tactics to this end included dressing well, being ever ready to socialize, and also throw some minor events and parties. Anyway, what he wrung out from the house was more than whatever he managed to earn. The little gold jewellery their mother possessed, he had taken away on the pretext of one business venture or the other. When they all sank without a trace, her jewellery shrunk to one small chain around her neck, an *arimani* chain, its beads shaped like grains of rice. The loan against the house property remained unpaid for months now. Where will the money come from? Who was there to help?

Maybe because they feared a cry for help, none of the relatives even pretended to notice them. She had noticed the rose apple tree in her uncle's house groaning under the weight of fruit, but she dared not step in there. Her maami—mother's brother's wife—would be standing there, staring out at the road, body pressed firmly to the wall—but seeing her in the distance, she would quickly retreat into the house. Her mother's brother's son would have been her bridegroom—according to custom—and there was such a young man in that house. Maybe that was the fear that made her aunt recoil—maybe the prospect of a marriage proposal loomed threateningly? And Amma, quite shamelessly, never failed to send them sweetmeats even when she had to borrow to buy the ingredients, when there was not a paisa left in the house. Just that Amma alone did not know that everyone else knew what she was calculating. Either she was unaware that the world had changed and customs too or she was pretending not to know, just to suit herself. For people who have nowhere to turn, what's the use of bothering about what's done or not in society?

Now their neighbours and relatives are acting like they weren't noticing this new art that was being performed rather regularly in this house these days. It was as though when the ruckus in the house grew worse, the attention of the neighbours became feebler and the distance between houses expanded. The old man was a drunk; he kicked the bucket at home and made life hell for the woman and the children. The only boy of the house had gone and pawned off the house and there was little hope of marrying off that girl who had come of age. Such were the apprehensions making their way around the locality: theories and concerns about people bereft of even an LIC policy.

From inside came a grating sound, of something being dragged on the ground. And a scream: *Help, murder*! As she leapt up from the chair, a nail that was sticking out sideways from it pierced her leg deeply. Paying no attention to the pain, she rushed into the kitchen. The sounds of lives shattering. Notes that only women's throats—their wails of sorrow—can reach.

When she went in, her mother was on the floor bleeding from her head, groaning. Her brother was trying to help her up.

'He killed me!'

'Raji, get some water . . . I didn't mean it . . . I swung my hand and she fell on her back . . .' His voice and hands were shaking. He pulled her hands to his chest and held them tight, utterly fearful. Her mother's eyeballs went round and round as though they were going around the world itself. In that horribly still scene bereft of sound and colour, two people clung to the love for life like fools. She ran and got some water and poured it into her mother's open mouth. It did not reach Amma's throat; the water mixed with saliva seeped out and streamed down the side of the arimani chain that had tightened around her neck. The TV that had been turned up loud to drown out the sounds in the house was playing a new item number that now accompanied death. Death, right next to male and female bodies entwining each other and thrusting

lustily. She was able to muse, impassively, that the dosa
and chutney that Amma had eaten for breakfast that
day would be digested by the furnace that would soon
consume her body. The dosa was made from the batter
that Amma had herself ground the evening before. In
the rest of the batter kept aside for the evening, that
woman's labour was already beginning to ferment.

Though they knew that she was gone, the two
siblings kept trying to shake her awake. Her body that
was limp from death shook in remembrance of life and
to the beat of their wailing. Raji slapped her head and
ran out howling. Society, just enough to conduct the
death feast, gathered there as was customary. When
footsteps were heard near the front door, her brother
slipped out through the back door. The locals gathered
in and around the house, sighing, hands on chins and
chests, and actually looking relieved that the turmoil
in that house had finally ended. Some even wept. The
TV, which had been screaming at full blast till then,
was turned off.

All this while, her poor mother who had held fast
to her life like she held that gold chain now continued
to bleed even though she was lifeless. Raji opened her
eyelids. The eyes of a young girl who romped merrily
on a hillslope—light years ago—stared back. The
fingertips, parched and cracked from labour, stretched
out towards butterflies. Corpses, unlike human beings,
are not beyond prediction. If they fall out with life,
they do not wake up. The spark of life stifled and
bruised and infected and confined in that little box of

stone and concrete shook off the pus-filled cells and flew away into the far distance.

She counted the tiny holes that were all over her mother's house-gown—traces of her engagement with kitchen fires and cooking. Before she counted ten, some people who were fired by the sudden revelation that the girl's mental state was affected helped her up and took her back inside, getting her to lie down there. The police arrived and asked her many questions. She answered, slack-jawed, staring. Their khaki was so well starched and ironed, she noted. There was not a single stain! She did not know when they took her mother's body for the post-mortem examination. When someone did tell her, she rushed to the place where the body had lain. The blood stain on the frame of the cot had dried by then; it blended into the wood.

The funeral went well. When her uncle came up to ask if he could sell Amma's necklace worth one-and-a-half *pavans* of gold for the expenses, she stared blankly at him. He was wise enough to take it as her consent. She thought—maybe this is what Amma meant when she said that this was all that was left for an *adiyantharam*—an emergency—or a feast?

The day after the post-mortem examination, Amma's body was cremated at the electric crematorium. She watched with disbelief as the corpse turned into a flaming torch in a rocket launcher explosion of sorts. Whose corpse burned in the furnace before my mother's? Some people had been standing around, glum and weary from loss. The oleander petals that had been strewn around her mother's body lay on the floor still, forming the shape of a narrow-necked bottle. The workers there might get rid of the shape before the next corpse arrives. At the end of all ceremonies, there comes a moment of indecision on which falls a pall of gloom. Be it a wedding or a festival, the end comes not when people go their separate ways. The end is when the next begins. Till then, the feeling lingers, like broken bits of balloons—once held by children—that lie desolate on the temple grounds after the festival is over and the festoons are brought down.

The wait for the ashes gave the women a chance to vent grief in quivering tones and the men a chance to smoke. When they returned in the car stuffed with relatives, she saw, through half-lowered windows, the cement chimney of the crematorium towering above the weeping willows; the smoke was still billowing from it.

Suddenly, a thought struck her—did they come away before her mother's body was fully consumed by the fire? Or was it that they cremated somebody else's body immediately after? Her mother was no longer Amma; she was a handful of ash and some swirls of smoke. Once we turn to ash and smoke, we are the same as everything else in the world. What worry must have filled Amma's mind when she was boiling the coffee and beginning her day the morning before? Would she have imagined eternal sleep at the day's end? So many plans that had slipped from her dying hands now sat in the corners of the house—grumbling, frustrated. The car raced in the opposite direction of her desire. The sight of a tragic life melting into thin air became more and more distant as the car picked up speed.

For two days, her aunts kept her company at night. Some women, her kin, shed genuine tears thinking of the sad future that awaited the girl who had become pale, ghost-like. Three weeks after the death, some of them still brought her food. Soon her aunts began to talk about their many responsibilities and endless labour, giving her subtle reminders of the value of their time. She finally told them that she was not scared to sleep alone at night. She cooked some gruel from the rice left in the copper pot and drank it. Her uncle gave her some notes wrapped in a sheet of white paper— ten thousand rupees—money left over after the funeral ceremony was conducted.

She hoped futilely that her mother's ghost would visit her at night. Her fears did not gift her an imagination strong enough to resurrect the dead woman's ghost. The windows opened and banged shut fruitlessly. Only the darkness stepped in. She felt sheepish about switching the lights on. She groped in the dark through the spaces where, once, the sense and nonsense of an ordinary family lay interwined. She searched for the piece of candle from among her mother's possessions and gently swept out the lower shelf of the almirah where she had kept her personal things.

A purple-coloured wedding sari wrapped in a sheet of newspaper. Photos in technicolour, of slim, fair Amma, from her golden days. Most young fellows must have been after her, the girl thought. Studio pictures of Achan and Amma. In some, her brother appeared too. A very well-dressed family. These people in the photos who gazed out at the world with such confidence, when did they turn into a bunch of crazies foaming at the mouth and raving? She picked up and opened the ration card in which her father and father's mother were still present though they were dead for ten years. A family of five. Just one of them left now, she alone. She thought of the ration dealer who wouldn't cut off the names of the absent family members—two dead and one absconding—so that the wasted life of the fifth would recover. Maybe from now he'll avoid her face, lowering his balding head when he poured the share of ration rice into her bag. These illicit shares will remain for the insects to eat up at the end of the month.

The inquest and investigation were all done but the police could not locate her brother. Let him escape, stay away, she prayed. What a life his must be now, she worried. Will those legs on which he escaped ever find rest? Maybe he'll return and surrender to the police. Suddenly, maybe because loneliness had pervaded her life completely, she was seized by an intense desire to see him. She walked about in the dark like someone condemned to solitary confinement in the world teeming with people. The awareness that a dawn awaited at the far end of the night truly troubled her. Whole night long, she flipped through TV channels. The cable bill was unpaid for months; 'Why haven't they cut the service yet?' she wondered. She used to feel that the young bill collector who came now and then wanted nothing but a glimpse of her. The soundless images on TV kept reflecting light into the darkness. She did not feel like taking her eyes off it. People who cried and laughed and rolled their eyes in surprise in exactly the same way. They continued doing it over and over even after she fell asleep, very late.

In the morning, she took a piss, went to the kitchen, made herself a cup of black tea. She counted the money wrapped in paper that her uncle had given her. A few 100-rupee notes. The stirrings of life began to be heard from the neighbouring houses. The aroma of breakfast wafted from their kitchens. The bathrooms seemed to stir joyfully in response to the cheerful sounds of people washing themselves. She wanted to live.

But she was unable to engross herself—except in watering the funerary coconut palm sapling planted on the place they had buried Amma's ashes. She drew water from the well near the little bathing shed. The walls of the bathing shed were of clumsily tied plastic sacks, which were now in tatters. The girl of the house can't bathe in the open, Amma had said so, but her brother paid no attention. So Amma had herself made a shed. She bathed in the privacy of that makeshift shed of plastic and wire that Amma had somehow built. The churidar-kurtas were all mostly unwashed and soiled. She chose one that didn't stink. Then she secured the house with the weak-looking lock—its hook so thin, it would surely offer an intruder no resistance. She noticed just then how breakable it was.

When she stood at the bus stop at the junction by the road, many people frowned.

'How many days since your Amma died, eh?' asked Vasu who worked at the Secretariat. People liked to count the days after the death, it seemed. People who didn't care for Amma's life when she was still alive, or her death. She did not reply; it was like she had decided not to answer all questions. Besides, the bus was approaching.

She got in, bought a twelve-rupee ticket to the last stop. The bus kept moving. She felt, maybe when she returned, Amma would be at home, sweeping the front-yard. Or making cotton lamp wicks for the *Vilakku* ceremony at Tekethil . . . or some other chore . . . she would be immersed in some task or the other. There's nothing to stop the possibility that time might have flowed backward by the time she returned home. As the stops passed, passengers were fewer. Amma's lifeless body and the loving memories of her that still lingered moved along with her in the bus. She kept feeling that Amma would emerge suddenly from the lively buzz of life on the road outside.

But the sight that met her eyes unexpectedly—it made her stagger inwardly. That man—tired, stubbly face, slipping through the crowd—surely that was her brother? What to do? Scream aloud? Whom did his eyes hiding behind a growing beard seek in the faces thronging the streets? She rang the conductor's bell. The bus stopped. Vehicles behind braked abruptly; drivers swore. As she leapt out, the conductor complained loudly.

'Where the hell from, this type? Leaping out as they please? Why am I sitting here then, eh?' There was a flurry; horns blared. Her attention wavered for a moment. She searched frantically, tearing down the footpath. He had vanished. Was it an illusion? She felt horribly let down.

The sun grew stronger. She felt that the hair on her head was scorched to the roots. The agitation had worn her down. Going into a small local Tamil teashop, she had a dosa and a cup of tea. She sat there for some time after she was done eating. It was the first time in her life that she was walking around freely with some cash in hand. A job had to be found—didn't matter if it was permanent or not. Better to live free, without permanent attachments, like a beggar on the streets. She had seen several signboards by the roadside asking for salesgirls. She signed up in a shop for nine thousand rupees a month and promised to start the next week; went to a photocopy shop, had a copy of her election ID card made, and gave it to the manager. The manager frowned at the photo, which bore no resemblance to her at all.

'Now its all terrorists and cheats—*comblete*! Can't be sure of anyone.' He kept pressing his lower lip with his fingers, clearly suspicious.

'Anna, no idea why they make you take that photo! My wife's photo in this card looks like that Sobha . . .'

'Sobha . . . who?' asked the manager.

'The one that killed Rajiv Gandhi? That one . . . Or was it Nalini? The one whose picture was all over the papers. My wife's photo looked like a faded picture of that one . . . She goes crazy when she sees it.'

That was from a salesman in the shop. She had no idea what he would be to her if she joined the place, but now, clearly, he was trying to help. The manager asked her to start from next week.

'Won't you get some other better work, *koche*?' he still asked. 'You are educated?' She did not respond.

The sun was overhead now. Though it was blazing hot outside, she stepped out and walked on. The cheap rubber sandals grew hot and began to stick to her feet. There were shops selling gold jewellery on either side of the road. That part of the city looked like an island of gold showrooms. The gold ornaments in the AC shop looked dull against the glowing yellow of the hot sun outside. Suddenly, she felt feverish and rather dizzy. She lurched towards the door of a nearby gold showroom. The doorman opened the door into the air-conditioned room and said something; she did not hear. She slid in and sat quietly with eyes shut in the coolness as though meditating. She wanted to sleep, but soon opened her eyes. Salesmen and customers moved slowly in the cool room.

'Hello, ma'am—may I help you? What do you wish to buy?' A very gentle voice. A good-looking young man in a spotless white shirt tucked into well-ironed black pants smiled at her.

'Gold or diamonds?' he asked.

'Gold,' she said quickly. A flash of lightning passed over her head. Thunder rumbled. 'Good God, where am I?' she asked herself.

'Here, ma'am, come here please.' The pleasant young man called her.

Will they be irked if I get out saying that I need nothing? What a tangle! She turned towards the door. The young man was now calling her in a louder voice, 'Ma'am, here, ma'am!'

She had less than ten thousand rupees in her bag, including the change of the hundred-rupee note after the bus fare and the meal. Poor Amma's beaded necklace. This money is going to be spent. But it must buy her something, for Amma's memory. That necklace was given to Amma by her mother. And if it was given to her by someone else, that necklace surely had the imprint of generations. She said:

'A nose stud. A small one. My budget is not more than one thousand and five hundred rupees.'

The young man pulled out two panels in which nose studs were arranged in rows. 'The ones that are for less than one thousand five hundred have stones on them . . . but you'll lose money if you resell them . . .'

'No, I won't sell this one.'

She decided to get one with a blue stone. When the salesman turned to pack it, a man and a buxom woman came over and sat near her. 'We'd like to change this,' the man said, placing a paper packet on the table. 'We want a small necklace in the latest design and a pair of anklets.' The woman added details. Raji did not hear any of it. Her eyes were on the beaded necklace that was now peeking out of the paper packet. She was still breathless.

It wasn't her mother's necklace—she knew that well. But the very sight of it was too much. The young man placed the chain and the two bangles that were in the packet on a weighing scale, noted the weight and put them back on the table.

'Madam, one thousand one hundred and eighty-five rupees,' said another young man, almost bowing.

'What?' She woke up from the reverie, not comprehending.

'The price of the nose stud.'

She hastily gave him twelve one-hundred rupee notes.

'Wait here please, madam. I'll bring the change.'

The pleasant-looking chap was now showing the couple the latest designs in small gold necklaces.

She was sweating. The beaded necklace was on the table, within her reach. It was a much-worn one. Like her mother's. One that was loved across generations. The grains of gold that had rubbed off it were the truly priceless ones. The beauty of adornment that had disappeared into the abyss of forgetfulness along with the dead limp cells of the body.

Only the mind can rein your body's nimbleness. But sometimes the mind will kick away the body's logic. Perhaps that's why it took eons for the memory of that act to get impressed in her brain.

'Is this yours, madam?' The young salesman stood before her with a small packet.

'Yes.'

'Madam, you haven't pierced your nose yet? We have a piercing gun here.'

She didn't know what it was. But she said, 'Yes, I must.'

They are going to catch me after I get the piercing done, she thought. The good-looking chap standing next to her is going to say: 'I knew it when I saw her—such a cheap slut. But then no matter what sort of whore, we've to call them all "madam", right? That's the job, right?'

'Close your eyes please, madam?' someone told her. She closed her eyes. Ah! Who cares what happens in this world now? She took a long breath. Someone gently turned her face to one side. She tried to sink into the hands that held her face. It slipped away. A tiny dot of pain, like an ant bite, on the nose.

'Open your eyes, madam,' the young man stood before her holding a square-shaped mirror.

'It suits you well, madam.'

She looked at her face in the mirror. Though badly sunburned, it looked beautiful to her. A small nose stud, from amma's *arimani* necklace. It will stay on my body till I die, she thought.

How long is it going to take for the gold bomb in her bag to explode? No one seemed to have noticed till now. Did no one know? She thanked the young man hurriedly and went out. No, she ran. Her legs were still running as she stood inside the bus. I have been running since centuries, she felt. She thought she could still hear the sounds of the feet of those who were pursuing her—even after she reached home. Her calves shook. She entered the house, checked whether all the doors and windows were bolted and secured. Going to the kitchen, she opened the lid of the water pot, lowered her head, and drank. The water got sucked into her nose and left her gasping for a few moments; she sat down on the floor, panting. Then stretched out there and fell asleep.

She woke with a start, hearing footsteps outside. It had grown quite dark there. She leapt up and went from room to room trying to see who was outside. Her foot hit many things in the darkness and ached. She tried to give shape to the darkness. Someone was pacing out there; just one person. If it were the police, there would be more than one? She considered running away; but the fear was like a dagger thrust into her belly, stuck there. She pricked up her ears to listen. The only sounds she could hear were of the leaves and stalks that the summer had wilted. They fell, drawn by the earth's love. No, there was someone there. Pacing. She was certain. Opening the window of the front room just a little, she scoured the darkness.

By the road, beside the funerary coconut sapling planted in her memory, sat Amma, groping her bare neck, weeping.

She swam up in the dark, took the necklace out of her bag, got out of the house, and went towards the sapling. Amma had disappeared beneath her funerary palm. There wasn't even a trace of the moon in the sky.

It was pitch-black. She dug up the base of the sapling, deposited the necklace there, covered it with soil. It was midnight and the road was deserted, but now a motorbike sped past. She hugged the ground to avoid its beam. And fell asleep there.

From next Monday, she began working at the shop. There were two other girls working there. She would wake up early in the morning, make breakfast and some lunch, pack it. She would eat half of the breakfast and run to catch the bus. Then, returning from work, she would eat the rest of it for dinner, wash the pots and leave then inverted to dry. From that time till she fell asleep, she sat by the window staring at the funerary palm, watching Amma sit under it and smile as she caressed her necklace. This was her routine throughout the entire month. But one day, suddenly, she began to feel that someone was following her. But who? Her feet made double the usual noise when she walked. Her heart pounded two times faster. Someone's searing gaze was burning a hole on her back. Her fear increased each day. But who was she to tell? One night she tried to go to Amma's funerary palm and tell her. But Amma was too engrossed in her gold chain and didn't even notice. She ranted at Amma, but Amma went right back into the sapling without any protest. The next day she had a fever when she went to work. There was a flu going around, so the manager sent her back home telling her to return after two days.

Her eyesight quivered as she stood at the bus stop. Then, in that bus stop that seemed empty—she saw him—the young man—through the flames that leapt from her eyes. No, she was wrong. It was he who was burning. The fire was inside his eyes. He rushed at her and pushed her hard. She fell down.

'You thief!' He snarled. 'Oh, look at her . . . so innocent—'

She looked at him as she lay on the ground. He was the same young chap who had helped her choose the nose stud in the jewellery showroom.

'Had begged endlessly for that job! Gone now!' He bent down close and hissed. She looked around for help. There was no one. How could the city be so empty? She was anxious. She closed her eyes that were sunken from the fever.

When she opened her eyes, she was lying on the floor of the veranda of the General Hospital; they were giving her a drip. That young man was still there. She stared blankly at his face.

'You have a number to call your folks? I'll call. I have no time to stay here. Where's that necklace? I'll go away if you give it to me.'

'There's no one to call,' she closed her eyes. Tears from the fever flowed out of the corners of her eyes. She tried not to sob.

When she was strong enough to sit up, he took the prescription from the nurse and went out. He came back after a little while, in an autorickshaw. They did not speak till they reached her house. By that time, the fever had abated; her body was cool. The neighbours sat inside the little cells that were their houses watching the boy and girl step out of the vehicle after dark; they cupped their chins in hands and sighed. The girl opened the door, went in. Not finding anyone else there, the boy stayed outside. She made some black tea and brought it out for him.

'Give me the necklace and I am leaving,' he said. 'Not to get the job back, just to throw it in their faces. They called me so many names before turning me out. True, I wasn't careful enough.'

She did not speak. Just sat with her head bowed, listening.

'I'll gain nothing from dragging you there,' he said.

The full moon drew milky shadows that danced slowly on the ground.

'You don't have current here?' he asked about the electricity. No answer came.

The neighbours were simply unable to sleep. They peered at the Boy and Girl through the cracks in the walls of their own houses, which festered like infected wounds. They adulterated sight to see what they wanted to see.

Girl and Boy sat on the edge of the ground in front of the house trying to give form to a formless conversation. In between she got up and went to the tree, removed some soil from under it, and took out the necklace. Her mother sobbed below. It is common for souls interred beneath the earth to weep. They weep because they know well—no matter how human beings may try to illuminate a dark night; the world is still dark. When she handed him that mud-stained necklace, she could feel a tempest brewing somewhere. He was troubled by the fact that when he put the necklace in his pocket and walked away, his mind, instead of accompanying him, was actually hurtling right back there. Mother-Palm began to quiver in a sharp, untrammelled gale that blew from somewhere. She now shook her locks loose dancing like an oracle, for seeds that were yet to open their eyes to the face of the earth. In the moonlight, Palm turned into shadows; sorrow and misery were now summoned inside the potent space of exorcism that She drew. Sorrow and Misery shrank and collapsed. Girl sat by, watching.

The Fearless

G.R. Indugopan's 'Elivaanam' brought to me memories of fieldwork. Specifically, the image of a ninety-two-year-old ex-sanitation worker of Tamil origin in a city slum in Thiruvananthapuram came back to me. Taken out of school at six, he began to help his father, a scavenger under the municipality. But he became a communist, a trade unionist. I sat in his tiny, dilapidated home—obviously, life was still full of material hardship—and listened. He shared memories of organizing a class of workers stigmatized beyond belief—in unblemished, perfectly formal, almost literary, Malayalam. 'I studied a little English, too,' he told me, eyes flashing, 'when Party school required the study of the works of D.D. Kosambi, D.N. Jha, and others . . .'

Clearly, trade unionism did not end poverty or stigma fully, but this is not the whole story. Something invaluable had been added despite all disappointments—a quiet, rooted sense of dignity, a clear-eyed understanding of the broken promise

of social justice and equality, too political and
compassionate to collapse into resentment, and a way
of speaking truth to power.

Such people still exist in contemporary Kerala. I
mean, you may meet many of them—if you try hard
enough. Yes, the present generation of Malayali
workers live in a very different Kerala, one in which the
discourse of the revolutionary proletariat is heard no
more. A place in which those who live through physical
labour are often painted in lurid shades of fear and
loathing, even by those on the political left. Increasingly
informalized—and yes, increasingly migrant—the
labourer faces exploitation by capital, exclusion by
the state, and stigmatization by mainstream Malayali
culture.

Indugopan's is a brave gesture, therefore—making
a non-Malayali who speaks fluent Malayalam and
lives here in the heart of his tale. The space that the
story unfolds in holds within it the two extremes
of contemporary unequal Malayali society: elite
aeromobile bodies, representing the openings,
freedoms, wealth and pleasure that the globalized
economy and neoliberal growth offers, and low-
status, low-paid workers. Muniyandi and his friends
are at its very margins and yet their labour—devalued,
stigmatized, suspect—is central to its functioning.

Yet he looks at power in the eye. Muniyandi
reads; he has taught himself English. He discerns the
workings of inequality that make the literate, articulate
poor look like troublemakers, and not citizens, in the

eye of power. Even his love for the work he does, which is almost aesthetic—rooted in memories of childhood—and his evidently skillful aim, does not impress power; police interrogation does not cease. But Muniyandi's deep compassion does disarm power, however temporarily. Muniyandi is a 'bird-scarer'—a safety worker, actually, who drives birds away from runways at airports to prevent accidents from birds hitting planes. We suddenly see the work of scaring away birds through a different lens. It does not look like low-status work. Rather, it is the daily practice of compassion. We learn that self-empowerment is more than learning English, reading newspapers, and gaining knowledge; it is also about making one's life and work meaningful in a world that dismisses it. The police officer sees it, too.

Skyrocket

'Elivaanam'

G.R. Indugopan

The airport manager had come out there to check something on the runway. Just then a skyrocket swooshed up close, like a missile. Bang! It blew up. The man got a real scare.

Hot, scorching sun. Muniyandi was seated in a corner at the place where the runway ended, buried in some political discussion with his colleague, Suku. A security guard came up to them.

'Manager Saar has summoned you . . .'

Muniyandi looked at his watch. Half an hour to the next flight. He had enough time.

He was not irritated by the wait in front of the manager's room. It was pleasant to step into air-conditioned space from the searing hot sun. But he did not have to wait for long; the sepoy came to get him.

There was a police officer—a subinspector—sitting in the manager's room. He wasn't waiting too long, either; his tea was barely sipped. He turned, scrutinized them from top to bottom. Then he hummed grimly and turned to the manager and asked, 'Actually, what is the work that they do?'

'Bird-scarers,' replied the manager. 'They scare away birds from the runway. Not very skilled, but this is a kind of traditional occupation at airports. We are just retaining it.'

Muniyandi butted in: 'Not like that, Saar. There are at least forty butcher shops in a radius of three or four kilometres from here. Lots of eagles around, Saare! Do you know how many flights we save?'

The SI fixed him with a pointed stare. 'I'll ask the questions,' he said. 'And then you'll answer.'

'Ooh . . .'

Muniyandi withdrew. But he was still mumbling.

'What, man?'

The SI sounded angry.

'Nothing, Saare . . . just thinking of our ill-luck! If there's a bird-hit on a plane, we'll lose our jobs. If there's no bird-hit, no one notices our work!'

'Who's Muniyandi?' the police officer asked unsmilingly.

'This chap . . .' the manager intervened.

The SI got up and asked him, 'Did you send a report against the manager to the newspapers?'

'Saare, that was as the secretary of our union,' said Muniyandi.

'Did you threaten the manager in his cabin?'

'My dear sir . . . I entered the cabin with his prior permission. We'll have to keep off work if our wages aren't increased. That's because we have no other way out . . . Do you know how much our daily wages are?'

SI went close, really close to his face, and asked.

'What was the flight that left last today?'

'Dubai Emirates.'

'Who lit the skyrocket after it took off?'

'I did, Saar . . .' Muniyandi admitted to it.

'Ah! Fine!'

The SI turned towards the manager as though he had discovered something.

Muniyandi explained: 'There's a mela going on in the maidan near here. Food festival and all. All the eagles in the city have moved here! The Airport Authority ought to pay more attention.'

'Just respond to what you are asked,' snapped the SI.

Muniyandi said: 'Six skyrockets were lit before the Dubai Emirates flight; and six after.'

'And which of those veered towards the airport?'

'One of them did not fire. Not sure which one. Its bottle slanted, that's why. Not done on purpose!'

'Yes, and it came exactly towards the airport manager's forehead . . .'

The SI now turned towards Suku.

'What's your role in this, eh?'

He trembled like a bunch of coconut palm flowers. 'I don't know anything, Saar,' he prayed, folding his palms.

Muniyandi said again, 'It slipped from my hand, Saar, don't rag him.'

'Who the hell are you to say that?' the police officer snarled as he raised his hand menacingly.

'Please, not here,' the manager objected.

Muniyandi turned to him and said, 'Saare, if you didn't want to raise our wages, you could've just said that. This dirty game was unnecessary.'

'Shut up!' roared the SI. 'I'll make arrangements for you to speak at length—just wait till we get to the police station!'

'This guy's their leader,' the manager pointed to Muniyandi. 'Has a real gift of the gab. And you know what, he even reads the English newspapers!'

'Is that true, you . . .?'

Muniyandi did not answer.

'Where do you get the English newspaper from?'

'They come and dump lots of English newspapers at the airport . . .'

'Ah! So you are a thief as well, uh? Come 'ere . . .'

Muniyandi was in a stuffy, narrow little room in the police station.

The SI asked him: 'You are aware that you are in the police station?'

'Yes, Saar,' he answered humbly.

'Uh! But you aren't sufficiently awed!'

'I am kind of numb by now, Saar . . .'

'Why's that, you . . .?'

'From living and more living . . . not scared of dying in custody, Saare. The daily wages I get, my family can make if they take to begging.'

'So you'll be ready to fire rockets in anybody's face if they pay you some money! Did you know that the airport manager would be out at that time?'

'No,' Muniyandi shook his head.

The SI continued: 'You can aim a rocket at the plane too! If it hits the plane, will it burst into flames?'

'I don't know . . .'

'Did someone tell you to do this?'

Anger and sorrow began to rise up inside Muniyandi. He asked: 'Saare, does anyone carry out an airport attack with skyrockets?'

The rage was rushing into the SI's face. Blows would rain soon.

'What's your problem, fellow?'

'Nothing.'

'Who got you this job?'

'Someone called Mani Annan . . .'

'Which Mani Annan?'

'I met him in the market. In a wholesale firecracker shop.'

'Oho, so you have some link with the explosives business!'

'That I've had since childhood. I used to work in the firecracker sheds at Sivakasi. Then I was a cleaner in a company lorry. Mani Annan came there to get the skyrockets for the airport. He asked me. He too was a bird-hitter.

'A *what*?'

'He's in our line of work . . . scaring off birds.'

'Now that you are the leader, you must be the middleman for getting the firecrackers from Sivakasi?'

Muniyandi was silent.

'Buy cheap, then submit bills with market prices on them. Big corruption, uh!'

Without pausing for Muniyandi's reply, the SI continued: 'Does the Sivakasi firecracker units supply explosives to terrorists?'

'I don't know anything about that, Saar . . .'

'Why, man, why?'

'Will they talk about such things to a boy who used to be a packing worker there?'

'Then what do you actually know?'

'Nothing. Not even if my next meal will be in the jail or outside. If you set your mind on it, Saar, you can stretch it to a life sentence, or even beyond life itself. An airport attack—no minor business!'

'That the bird-shooer fellow should have thought of, before getting fresh with the airport manager! Didn't you argue with him when you went to his room with the petition for higher wages? If he made a strongly-worded complaint, that'd have been enough—the CISF, CBI, whatnot . . . and what you said will happen!'

'Oh, the truth is, Saare, I'd be much happier to stay inside now! You get fed regularly! You don't have to forage! Any other animal can forage for food, only human beings have to make money to find food. Saar, do you know? Most of the food served in the planes is thrown away. There was a cleaner boy in the catering company's lorry which takes away the waste. He used to pick out the unopened food boxes, tie them up in a sack, and throw it on the side of the Airport Road. His friend would collect it from there. A minor enterprise. You had to pay a very small price. I too have paid and tasted it. Food that was to be buried! But one day they caught him. He was beaten to a pulp and thrown on the side of the very same road. It's in your station limits. Did you hear of it, Saar? No case was filed . . .'

'So, you feel like attacking that vehicle, eh?' the SI asked.

Muniyandi did not speak.

'Are you a Naxalite, you?'

He replied: 'Saare, this is the trouble. We can't speak nowadays about poverty. Even our women won't hear of it.'

'So, you were hungry!'

'When?'

'When you fired that skyrocket . . .'

'Yes, I was.'

'Hunger for what?'

'The ordinary hunger that Saar and I feel, to eat something. My blood pressure is always low. If I am really hungry, my hand shakes. And it's worsening as I grow older. But please don't tell them this, Saar. It's enough for me to lose my job.'

'That's anyway a goner!'

'No, don't say that, Saare . . .'

'Oh, really? Why is it so important to work inside the airport? Are you a spy? For what other reason did you learn English?'

'Am I not staying put for most of the time in the sun, Saare? Just put together the alphabets, started reading bit by bit . . .'

'You know all the details of the traffic at this airport.'

'I know the times when there's no plane on the runaway. That's when we have to shoo off the birds.'

'You don't know anything else?'

'Nothing else, Saare.'

'Why're you worried about losing your job? You skipped that question!'

Muniyandi did not reply.

'Do you know, even a mason's helper gets paid more?'

'I know, Saare, but . . .'

'What "but"? Can't bother to work harder, uh?'

'No, Saare, I have a son. He's boasted to his friends that his dad works at the airport . . .'

'Don't take me for a sucker, my dear chap.'

'And not just that, Saare. I am really in awe of the aeroplane. I come from Tirunelveli. Remember, long time back, we used to fasten our knickers with a pin, tightly, when its buttons fell off? But when you saw an aeroplane up there, you can't help lifting your whole body up to see it! My knickers would fall off my waist again, then, but I'd hold them up and chase the plane. Even now, I get that same kick when I see the plane come down and fly up. And there's even more—this work is so much part of our minds, part of what keeps our lives clean . . . If we lose this, too, I'll feel—messed up . . .'

The SI raised his hand.

'OK, leave that there. Have you sent an anonymous letter to the Human Rights Commission about the problems of bird-scarers?'

Muniyandi did not reply.

'Did the judge summon the airport manager and make him submit an explanation?'

Muniyandi stood still, head bent.

'Can't hear what you were asked?' the SI growled.

'Did you write that letter?'

'Yes . . .' Muniyandi answered.

'Had no other way. I knew that everyone would see through it . . . come to know that I wrote it. But I just thought, why leave any evidence, and so left it unsigned.'

'I am going to dig up the lies even in the mother's milk that you sucked. You thought that I'd get all soft hearing your story, you . . . rascal?'

Muniyandi shifted his gaze elsewhere.

The phone rang.

The SI lighted a cigarette, moved to a corner, finished the conversation on the phone, and returned to his seat. Then he began again, sounding calm.

'How many papers do you read every day?'

'Three or four,' replied Muniyandi, rather absently.

'Any use?'

'None.'

'Why is that?'

'If you're poor and trapped, then better to know nothing. Worse, your literacy will show when you speak—and that's a headache. The listener won't like it. Now, look at you, Saar—how many times you felt like beating me up? And the other thing is that, at home, you become kind of peaceable, tactful . . . Only serves us worse! The hopelessly poor should talk like a machete. One blow, two pieces . . .'

'Say that again,' the SI cut in sharply. 'One blow . . .?'

'Not that blow, Saare! My son, when he asks for something again and again . . . Yell as loud as you can, "Your old man is just a coolie, you fool! This is all I can provide! Study, if you are keen, only." The demands will stop right then. If, instead, you try to persuade them lovingly, the lad will start telling you of the longing, the greed that's in him. And you'll have to listen! And feel the ache . . .'

'Ohh . . . That's the thing . . .!' the SI puffed up with scorn. 'Your son—how is his aim? Good?'

Muniyandi was silent.

'It was the airport manager who called me just now. He said that you have great aim. It was your own folks that told him . . .'

He threw the cigarette on the floor and began to unbutton his shirt.

'You didn't hear me, uh?'

'Yes.'

'Then why're you taking so much time to reply?'

'I don't know about my son but I . . . Yes, my aim is good.

'So if you wanted to, you could have hit the airport manager's head . . .'

'That . . .'

'Out with it now!'

The SI drew closer to Muniyandi with slow menace, gnashing his teeth. Before Muniyandi could stand up, he kicked the chair down. Muniyandi landed on the floor, a little distance away.

'What did you think, you ass?' the SI bellowed. 'That I'll stand before you with folded hands just because you read fifty-six newspapers a day?'

Muniyandi still lay on the floor, motionless, eyeing the officer without emotion.

'What are you staring at?' the SI lunged at him. Two policemen sauntered into the room. Like they were waiting for a chance.

'You can go. This is a minor job. Will deal with it alone,' the SI told them.

When they withdrew, the SI pulled up Muniyandi by his left arm, twisted it hard, and asked him with a sneer, 'Didn't you hear what I asked you? Can you . . . the manager's head . . .?'

Grunting with pain, Muniyandi said: 'Yes . . . if I want to.'

The SI paused for a moment. Then released Muniyandi's arm. And then, he said coolly: 'Fine.'

'Pick the chair up,' he ordered him.

He picked it up.

'Sit.'

He set the chair down, sat on it. His arm was still aching.

The SI took a hard, long look at him. And then he looked out through the window, giving him some time to recover from the pain.

Then the SI got up, lifted up his chair, brought it near Muniyandi's, and settled down, crossing his leg over his thigh. That's a tricky posture. Waiting to deliver the next kick.

He broke his knuckles, and said: 'Here, pay attention now.'

Then, as though he was about to discover some immense truth, he asked: 'So, if you want, you can hit the head, right on the crown . . . of anything?'

Muniyandi said nothing.

The SI continued: 'How did you become so skillful? Where were you trained? In the LTTE camp?'

Muniyandi replied: 'By birth, Saare . . . When we played marbles as kids, I'd just close my eyes and throw! And hit the marble some twenty feet away, right on the head . . .!'

'It would hit?'

'Ninety-nine out of hundred times. I used to be amazed, myself.'

'So, you can hit the flying eagle with the skyrocket and bring it down like a flower, eh?'

'I won't do it.'

'But you *can* do it?'

'I think so.'

'How do you calculate it?'

'What calculation? All that's for the big-big scientists who send up rockets, Saare . . . These skyrockets that we light up are made in Sivakasi by boys of ten or fourteen, or mothers who are thinking all the time about their crying babies left at home. So the fuel in them won't be packed—the quantity will be a little more or less . . . But all human beings have their moments of clarity. The rockets they make in such moments will be perfect—I can recognize such skyrockets and the quality of the fuel. I can guess the speed with which they will rise, at one glance. I also know how much we need to hit a flying eagle. But we always send it leaving an inch between bird and rocket. If we don't, the rocket will burst right above the eagle and the bird will be blasted to pieces. But, Saare, we can't do that. That's possible only for big-big scientists.'

'Ah, so the scientists are busy catching eagles, aren't they?' the SI smirked.

'It's not that,' Muniyandi continued.

'Saare, I am stumped when I see rockets being sent up under many names in this country, and people going ga-ga at the accuracy of the launch! Now, why have you detained me here, Saar? It's because the rocket which should have gone up into the sky got diverted and went towards the airport, right . . .? It's just like that . . . If you make the path of the rocket sent up into the sky curve like a rainbow, then it becomes a missile! The place where it lands and explodes; all that which it flattens—does not all of it become a knot of pain? It can be any country! When I send up a skyrocket, I think, ayyo, even that eagle up there that I am taking aim at has a life. It has a nest to go back to, maybe chicks in the nest, too. We hold in ourselves that care, we do. So when we send up a rocket, we tell it, hey, you firecracker, listen—when you reach up there, get three feet ahead of the eagle and burst there. When you blow up, make sure that not even a spark grazes its feathers.'

'Uh! This qualifies for sedition charges! Stop!' the SI was clearly impatient.

'Want has no borders, Saare, and so it cannot have a country or enemies. You asked me why I was not dumping this measly job . . . this is the answer. The satisfaction that we are not hurting even a feather. I, who can't even aim at a feather, how am I to take aim at that manager's head, Saare?'

'Enough, enough . . .'

The SI said: 'OK, OK, it's taken too long—get lost after you give it in writing that the wrongly aimed rocket was an unintended mistake of the hand . . . and that you no longer have any disputes with the airport management . . .'

'I can agree to the first.'

'OK, whatever. Don't think that this is over just because it is out of my hand.'

'Yes, I know, Saar. There's more of life left to live, isn't it?' Muniyandi folded his palms.

Reformer-Man

The Malayali Reformer-Man has been an abiding obsession of my life and career.

As a young woman in the 1980s, I felt that he towered over me, claiming superior knowledge of the world and therefore the right to re-form me, a mere woman. The Reformer-Man guides the woman along the path of modern self-fulfilment, promising a day in which she would become the perfect (womanly) individual—but the path seems to extend infinitely and so also his guidance. Everywhere I went, I found men of all kinds—young, old, wise, foolish, strong, weak— either assuming or aspiring to the throne of Reformer-Man. Women, no matter how old or wise or bright or accomplished they might be, were expected to pay obeisance to him.

I dug up the historical antecedents of Reformer-Man and found that the twentieth-century story of women's emancipation from feudalism in Kerala was told almost entirely by him. In this story, women were hapless damsels waiting for or rescued by the gallant Reformer-Man; women were the 'burdens' that these men were duty-bound (a bit like the 'white man's burden') to carry. I burned with shame. Like many of my peers from the late 1980s and '90s, I vowed to never submit to the Reformer-Man.

These are the twilight days of the Reformer-Man, but he is around still, and wears a progressive garb, as Santhosh Aechikkanam's superb story 'Rules for Drivers' shows. The heyday of social reform is over. Educated Malayali women of the 1990s and after are likely to resist the non-reciprocal power of re-forming, and Akhila in this story is a perfect instance: she seeks mobility, escape from traditional culinary styles, and refuses to be shamed for preferring popular culture. Aechikkanam's story puts its finger on the inner crises of the late twentieth century. No longer commanding the authority he once did, Reformer-Man plunges into insecurity and loneliness. Conjugality in Malayali society, once widely hailed as the way out of oppressive tradition and familial and community institutions, turns out to be a power- and strategy-game among partners. And the Reformer-Man lives inside his little ego box.

The folly of the steadily waning Reformer-Man is revealed to Ravichandran by another man who, however, can imagine a loving relationship beyond power, even as life makes it impossible for him to carve one for himself. He gazes at his sleeping wife—and is able to imagine her outside the ruthless and never-

ending cycle of work and material survival—and the sight moves him to tears.

Aechikkanam's story also makes us wonder about alcohol and the Malayali male. Shut up in little ego boxes of their own making, many Malayali men cannot, often, do without it. Drinking together eases ego boundaries, makes it possible for the good—as well as the bad—to pass through. Ravichandran and Ramakrishnan exchange the burdens of their hearts as the vodka unclasps their egos. Kerala is now infamous for the huge quantities of alcohol consumed in the state (though, apparently, consumption is currently falling, albeit slowly). Perhaps that is the price we pay for Malayali masculinity—with its waning dreams of Reformer-Manhood and pathetic ego boxes.

Rules for Drivers

'Roadil Paalikkenda Niyamangal'

Santhosh Aechikkanam

Once he had filed a divorce petition at the Family Court, and having secured leave from work for two months, Ravichandran confined himself to his home library for a few days. He stepped out only when he was hungry.

He read up one after the other all the books that he had bought on several different occasions, before he got married, but eating out regularly made a mess of his digestion. Will I pass away one day as a mighty gurgle astride the toilet pot, like Sukumaran in Paul Zacharia's *Hridayatharakam*—he even feared. Thinking that some broken-rice gruel for supper would do him good, he went to the kitchen. There a strange silence lay entwined with the dark. Each of the utensils brooded, head down, lips pressed on their washed-clean-and-bright loneliness.

It was then that Akhila's absence of many days pressed hard on Ravichandran's mind. Searching for quite some time among the pots and pans for a pot of the right size to cook rice for just one person, he found a small pressure cooker. When he tried to remove its lid, he got a sense of the intense sort of protest these things are capable of. A minor tug-of-war ensued on the marble countertop between the pressure cooker and Ravichandran. In the end, he admitted defeat, leaning on the wall and panting hard. Drops of sweat slipped down his legs and fell on the floor.

All the pots that he picked up clung to the granite slab and collectively sabotaged his effort to cook some rice. Taps, when opened, let out mocking whistles.

That the pots and pans had joined together in a collective force now arrayed against him through a quick series of glances thrown at each other riled Ravi *maash* (he was a college teacher; maash is short for 'master') to no end. He tore his hair and screamed: 'I am famished!'

'Stop yelling, man,' the mixie scolded him. 'You go get that girl back. Then we'll see.'

'Ah, go find some other sucker for that job,' Ravichandran hit back. 'This is our family matter. Keep out of it.'

'Back off it, Saare,' the pressure cooker cut in. 'I am someone who's cooked you a lot of rice!' The cooker was female.

'That's all fine—but how long can I carry on with a woman who's hooked to the TV all the time, who's obsessed with eating and visiting the Margin Free shops and cutting out recipes from magazines for her fancy cooking—how to live for long with someone who thinks that this is life?'

The large bronze wok, the *uruli*, remembered the war of words that had broken out between Akhila and Ravichandran in the library of this house.

'Look, Akhila,' Ravichandran invited his wife into his library. 'See, this room is full of books. Why can't you browse through some of these instead of eating popcorn and watching TV all day? That would make you a little more serious about life.'

'Uh-uh . . . this level of seriousness will do!'

Akhila threw him a look as she changed the channel to watch *Vaalkkannaadi*.

'You are not just "Akhila" any more.'

'Really? Then who am I?' she turned to him with surprise.

'You are the wife of Ravichandran. A philosophy teacher, a writer.'

'But I am Akhila.'

'*Edi*,' Ravichandran's Malayalam moved to the disrespectful mode of address; his voice grew stern.

'When you are in the shade of a five-figure salary, you'll think that life is tasty and smooth like a continental dish. That's a general delusion shared by middle-class. In this world, there are people other than those who feast on continental food—people who struggle with immense challenges, many immense challenges. It'll help if you remember them sometime, feel bad for them. Your mind might improve.'

'Two drinks, and he's super tipsy!' Akhila teased gleefully.

Ravichandran snatched the remote from her and switched off the TV.

'Edi,' he continued. 'Open that window. Look. You will see real life going on out there.'

'Real life, my foot!' she exclaimed. 'You can see Major Saar who lives next door.'

'Edi . . . I'll punch . . .' Ravi maash raised his hand.

'Try lifting your hand and we'll see,' Akhila stepped two feet forward. 'You've been making a fine drama here for some time . . . writing . . . reading . . . society . . . commitment . . . I know nothing of all that, I admit. But lemme ask—can you drive a car? Change a bulb? Reserve a ticket through the mobile phone?'

Ravichandran froze. His tipsy mood evaporated like water spilt on a red-hot floor. He did not say anything; just rubbed the tip of his nose.

'Don't talk big,' said Akhila, taking the car keys and stepping into the porch. The Alto car went out the gate crushing Ravichandran's silence as if it were just a *musumbi* fruit, mercilessly.

'Goodbye,' he turned towards the kitchenware with a contemptuous smirk. 'I know that all of you are on her side.'

'Of course she's seduced you all—touching, caressing, washing clean, even dropping on the floor to make you laugh! You dishes are exactly like women. *Ordinary* women! All you need is some titillation. Touch, tickle! You don't have deep thoughts, or the sensibility refined enough to appreciate love. If you had, you wouldn't be talking like this.'

'What was wrong with Akhila's question? Can you drive?' the washing machine that stood in a corner of the pantry piped up.

'You better shut up and be quiet,' Ravichandran clenched his fists menacingly. That shook up the washing machine somewhat, but it still continued: 'Hey, at least show yourself to be tolerant of another's opinion, mister! You are the one who made things so awful! You read, you write. She does not read or write. But she can drive a car; and above everything, she is a superb cook. People have their own skills and weaknesses, you know?'

Ravichandran lost his cool. 'Don't you dare equate creativity and driving!' he shouted. 'You probably know, the world-famous movie director Akira Kurosawa could hardly hold a telephone receiver properly . . . was Vaikom Mohammed Basheer a driver? Leave that, take all the eminent writers in Malayalam—how many of them can ride a motorbike? When you evaluate genius, these are hardly the criteria!'

'Stop the blather,' the casserole was heating up a bit. 'You need a bit of skill to drive a car. And some pluck too. People like you who live in a dream world have neither. Akhila *kochu* often tells us this when she makes chapatis.'

'Oho, so she's been talking,' Ravichandran murmured to himself. 'Edi . . . I used to feel a sort of pride when you were in the driver's seat and I sat next to you . . . But this was what you were thinking, uh? Mocking, uh? I realized it just now!'

'Oh, just go away, maashe,' the pressure cooker entered the fray.

'Isn't it true—that in the way you used to sit beside her in the car, with that paperback open on your lap, as though you weren't anywhere in this world . . . actually, covering up your insecurity . . . Wasn't there a nicely hidden lie in it? A lie hard to notice?'

Ravichandran was sore and itchy by now. He yanked open the pressure cooker's lid and threw lid and bottom into the kitchen sink along with the dirty dishes.

'Stay right there, you wayward creature! Just two— just two months—and you'll see—Ravichandran's car will glide in through the gate!'

'Stop the boast, maashe. Let's see!' the kitchenware issued a collective challenge.

'Yes, we'll see!' he accepted the challenge.

He stuffed his neck into a t-shirt and set out. In the autorickshaw on the way to Patturaikkal Mother Driving School, his thoughts were these: 'To me, learning to drive is not an escapade that exacerbates the privatization of travel or aestheticizes it. Rather, it is meant to shake off the metropolitan consciousness characteristic of shallow people like Akhila.'

'I have seen you earlier, Saar,' said the driving teacher Ramakrishna in Paatturaikkal Mother Driving School. A slight man, bearded, about fifty. Eyes grown light with constant smoking; they shone with the firmness of mind of a man who saw everything lightly. Though Ravichandran was a new student, he wasn't offering any excessive politeness.

'I saw you in Hotel Hero in front of the Sahitya Akademi . . . I looked up hearing a glass fall and shatter. You were standing there! There's that Meera Jasmine movie . . . Ah, I forget . . . *enthootta* tha name . . . *Paadham Onnu Oru Nelooli* . . . You grabbed the neck of the guy who said that the movie was no good and pushed him hard! Asokan had to rush out of the counter and pull you back . . . you let go only then. Not . . . like . . . ornery folk like us . . . you *buddhijeeviyal* . . . you intellectchual people . . . if you lose it . . . then hard to calm you down.'

Ravichandran felt foolish. He kept his eyes on the floor.

'Driving is a skill, Saare,' Ramakrishnan said. 'But I must say. Please don't get me wrong . . .'

He prepared to speak, wiping the grease off his fingers. 'I am talking from the experience of some twenty-twenty five years . . . there are only two kinds of people who can't be taught to drive . . . the first is people who are mentally disabled . . . and the other, intellectchuals.'

Ramakrishnan's discovery jolted Ravichandran.

'The first group do not know anything—so, no confusion. The other group can't set aside their doubts even for a second. In effect, both are the same. They bump the car somewhere, inevitably. That's it.'

Ravichandran paid Ramakrishnan the advance.

When the blue Ambassador car with the board 'Mother Driving School' honked at his gate early next morning, Ravichandran was on the portico fastening the straps of his sandals. 'Good morning,' said Ramakrishnan, as he invited Ravi maash to the driver's seat.

When he held the steering wheel and took a turn, his gaze reaching out through the windshield towards the extreme end of the road that receded on two sides, Ravichandran felt that the driver's world was utterly different from that of the passenger. It was difficult and dark. These two worlds maintain a unique mutual distance, moving in parallel line like day and night.

The driver is not fated to enjoy carefree pleasures of the ride, the indulgences of sight—they are the passenger's. He cannot shift his legs as he pleased; nor could he daydream or yawn while descending a steep incline. He could not let his mind fly off with a gentle breeze. He had to get past dangers that sped by unchecked . . . and move ahead with the lives entrusted to him.

Ramakrishnan lifted his leg off the clutch and shifted to the first gear. He said: 'First, get the steering wheel ready. This way . . . slowly . . . to the left side . . . now you must watch . . . keep moving the steering as the vehicle moves.'

Helping Ravichandran with his right hand, Ramakrishnan continued: 'Pay attention here, Saar.

When the vehicle's moving . . . our eye should be fifty feet ahead. Only then will you be able to know the car's direction . . .'

By then the car had moved to the wrong side of the midline by two feet; a tempo van that came at full-speed towards the car missed it by a hair-breadth and zoomed off in a second.

The screech of its wheels on the wet sand sent a shiver down Ravichandran's spine.

'Oh, that was scary, wasn't it, Saar? You've only begun . . . these guys will whoosh off like that . . . we have to be careful . . . Saar, don't think all of this road . . . is ours . . .'

Ravichandran launched into a discussion of the terrible condition of Kerala's roads and the exponential increase in traffic.

'No use saying this . . . it's not going to get us driving . . . There'll be a hundred or a thousand vehicles, but God has laid out a path for us. If we drive peacefully on it, we'll reach where we want to . . . We may be a bit late, that's OK. If we hurry and go hit something then it's going to be trouble—injury, police case. And will you reach on time? No way! Only tension remains. They say that it's the pill to ease the tension that's selling the most in this world! Is that true, Saare? Narendran Saar who got his driver's licence last week told me. He's a medical rep.'

'Might be true,' Ravichandran laughed.

'*Haai, pinne enthoottu kaaryam* . . . what's the use?' Ramakrishnan gave it a moment's thought and declared: 'Yes, that is right. The more the land progresses, the more the tension will be!'

He lighted a bidi with Ravichandran's permission.

'Saare, this road has taught me a few things. That life is a long road an' such stuff . . . what yuh folks say in lit'rary style . . .? I didn't learn any of it from a book . . . it was from driving the car . . . twenty-five long years . . .'

That night Ravi maash stood under the shower, palms out, more confident than he ever was. He'd taken a quick U-turn and got on the highway. The moving wiper cleared his view. Ravichandran's car zipped through the sheets of rain that fell from the shower. Glancing at Akhila who sat on the passenger's seat, he bragged: 'Edi, just look at the speedometer. Not your miserable forty, I am flying on ninety! Oh, the girl's scared . . . just hold on tight! Do you understand now? Don't measure writers with your ignorance . . .'

But a voice sounded from the kitchen quickly. It was a bowl speaking: 'Don't get too smart, maashe, you've just started!'

The next day, Ramakrishnan stopped his car at the gate of a multi-storey apartment complex and honked a few times. The window curtain of a second-floor apartment was drawn open, and a woman extended her rather puffy neck out.

'Please wait. I'll come,' she said.

'That's Latha Madam. Teaches English at the Kerala Varma College,' Ramakrishnan said. Five minutes passed.

'Tell her to make it fast. What's there to dress up so much?' Ravichandran looked at his watch and made haste.

'You don't know the psychology of these lady teachers, Saar . . . that's why,' Ramakrishnan smiled. 'They can scold everyone. But no one should scold them!'

When she came down, Ramakrishnan introduced her to Ravichandran. It was two months since she passed the Learners' Test, but she was still making major mistakes. Seeing Ramakrishnan correct her with infinite patience, he marvelled. Here was one who'd seen the bottom-most *nelli* wood plank that lay in the depths of the well of patience—in other words, the rock bottom of patience.

Getting off near the newspaper office, the English professor showed Ramakrishnan a photo.

'We are going to celebrate our twenty-fifth anniversary,' she said in English. Then, switching to Malayalam, she continued: 'We are putting it in the papers! Let all these young things around know!'

When she left, Ravichandran spat out: 'Shameless! Professor, indeed!'

'My dear Saare, it's not a small thing that a man and woman managed to live together for twenty-five years! Try getting married, and you'd know!'

Without replying, Ravichandran shifted to the driver's seat.

'A car and a woman aren't so very different. If you have some patience, pay some attention, then you can go without getting knocked off the road or knocking someone else . . . Then the twenty-fifth anniversary . . . that's all a show. Because they themselves can't believe it? Ah . . . signal to the right . . . turn fully . . . you've got to bend that steering more, OK? . . . Steady now . . .'

'Saare, these men and women, they will never get along. Then, you can have maybe a picture pasted of them side by side with mutual agreement. Below it, you gave a big name—*daambathyam*—conjugal life! That's all to it . . .'

Ravichandran looked wonderingly at him.

'I know the *guttance* of that look, Saare . . . you're thinking, ooh, what's going on! Now drivers are beg'nning to spout lit'rature? Am I not right? Saare, in the very seat you're sitting now, so many famous buddies have sat before . . . I am like the stone on which diff'rent sorts of pollen has fallen . . . when we chat . . . it brushed off me . . . the law, cinema, hist'ry . . . Uh, just think o' me as someone who can pull out an ace in any o' these! The truth is that all these cult'ral leaders and lit'rary people you see on TV . . . they are good to admire from far . . . If you sit next to them and talk with them for a littl' while, you'll know . . . they don't have the sense of life that even we have. Not talking 'bout you, Saar, *ittaa*?'

For a second, Akhila stepped into Ravichandran's mind. She pulled up the blanket to her neck, turned, and lay facing him. Her mouth smelled of toothpaste.

'Hai! Where is your mind, Saare?' Ramakrishnan pulled him back into the present with a reminder. 'Let me tell you, if you get distracted like this at the wheel, that's end of the car, OK?'

'Now, let's shift to the side, Saar. We'll start with the clutch and gears tomorrow.'

Ravichandran got out and went towards the house.

In a way, the intellectuals these days, including writers, are as safe as snails in their shells. More than any ordinary person perhaps, it is they who hanker after pleasure and luxury and fame. From the safety of these shells, they stick out their antennae. Ravichandran's thoughts ended up in these reflections as he pondered on Ramakrishnan's observations.

The water in his fridge was cooling. The sunflowers that bloomed on his bed sheet at the touch of the embroidery needle invited him to sink into an orange-coloured slumber. Two ATM cards that made him say 'What more to be bothered about?' in a Kottayam-drawl were in his wallet. Since these were his thoughts, since he could not really claim a personality superior to Akhila's, what authority did he have to edit Akhila's habits, or accuse her of childishness?

He switched off the lights and lay down to sleep. But sleep evaded him. Time slipped away like algae on a lake on the display of the mobile phone that lighted up in between. Ravi maash got up many times and visited the bathroom, went towards the earthen jug filled with cumin-scented water. Noticing his unease, the jug said, '. . . My dear maashe, the things that you are turning over and over in your head right now are precisely those which the washing machine tried to tell you the other day! You were so furious then. If this is how things are going to be, then you'll end up with just more unease!'

'Saar . . . the car is a body,' said Ramakrishnan the next day, trying to make it easier for someone who knew nothing about motor vehicles. 'The heart is the engine. The oil tubes are the arteries.' Ravichandran found this comparison useful. The moment his feet released the clutch, the car's vertebrae trembled and the wheels got ready to fly light as feathers. Ramakrishnan continued: 'Now when you ride it, the car speaks . . .'

'Speak?' Ravi maash asked.

'Uh, yes . . . pay attenshun, Saare . . .' They began to climb and incline and the car's sound changed.

'Are you list'ning, Saar? The car's started to talk.' Ramakrishnan patted him lightly.

'Yes, it is complaining.'

'. . . Nth-ttta, maashe, . . . what's this! I can't climb this incline on this gear! Move to the second gear!' Ramakrishnan smiled. 'You heard it say that?'

'OK . . . then let's shift the gear . . .'

Suddenly a Maruti Alto car came dashing from ahead of them at breakneck speed. Ravi maash swerved sharply to the left, but his leg went to the accelerator instead of the brakes. The car veered off the road, hit a telephone post, the door flung open, and it slipped into the paddy field—and then he regained control.

'What have you done, maashe?' Ravichandran could only press his forehead to the steering wheel and control his panting, unable to face Ramakrishnan's accusing tone.

When he returned after taking the car to the automobile workshop, he felt that he could unwind a bit only if he told Ramakrishnan why he had lost his grip that morning. They went to Peninsula Hotel; and over half a bottle of Smirnoff, Ramakrishnan got to know all about Ravichandran's matrimonial troubles. He did not seem the least surprised, though. Only two drinkers can do it: break through the bubbles of privacy at a certain point in the shared euphoria.

'So . . . Your wife was the driver of that Alto?' Ramakrishnan asked.

Ravichandran chewed some grains of saunf brought along with the bill absent-mindedly.

'Saare, there's no point in insisting that one person should necessarily live like another person. Haven't I told you . . . God's already measured and assign'd each of us our unique road? Isn't it enough to just drive on it?'

Ramakrishnan drank up the last bit of vodka in his glass along with the ice.

'D'you know, Saar? In a factory they make thousands of cars. If you look at the quality, they're all the same. But one among these will be different . . . defying the engineer's calculation. Its mileage, pulling . . . our eyes'll pop, so extraordinary it'll be! The one who finds it, he's the lucky one. Marriage is a bit like that, a lott'ry! But then married people are like, in the saying, a cat worth two rupees drank up milk worth five rupees! Frustration! Listen, Saare, I turned fifty-five this November, and my wife is just four-and-a-half years younger to me . . . If I reverse into the twenty-two-year-long marriage, there is no fragrance of memory or an'thing; it's the smell of grease, the kind that won't go however you scrub your body . . . That smell follows you everywhere . . . in the rice you eat, the mat you sleep on, the words you say . . . And it's all over after forty-five, Saare, your body is already in the seconds . . . Sex happens for Onam or Vishu . . . tepid annual affair, it becomes. Then what you need is understanding, for life to be smooth . . . In my case even that won't work, Saare. My day starts at six and I am back covered with dust and grime late at night! Where's the time for understanding after that! When I am rubbing the medicinal oils, she'll call out from the kitchen-side, "The water's boiled and ready . . ." I'll take a bath. When I comb my hair, she announces: "Supper is ready!" I read in a weekly magazine once that your marriage'll be firm and smooth if you chat about something nice and light with your wife before bedtime. Oh, I have really wanted it—but what a pity, Saare, I lie down and fall asleep at once! The whole day through, I am working non-stop, it's so exhausting . . .'

'Uh huh! I know perfectly well that if I leave her this very moment, just like that, it won't make a jot of difference to her. But . . . that's something I can't do . . . Saare.'

'When I wake up in the middle of the night, I see her asleep, lying on the edge of the mat. I stand there quietly for a long time, just looking at her face.'

Ramakrishnan remembered the nights he had spent like someone sitting quietly on the bank of a still, deeply lonely lake and looking intently at it.

'Then . . .' his voice faltered. 'I feel that all the sorrows of this world are flowing into her face, like the gushing waters from the mountains . . . and then my heart . . . it jus' breaks!'

Unexpectedly, Ramakrishnan squatted on the road and began to sob loudly. It felt awkward, but Ravichandran tried to pat him on the back and console him.

'*Ilya*, Saare! No! If you've looked even once at the face of your wife when she's asleep, you can't leave her!'

Ramakrishnan continued to sob and wail with a sincerity that came to him naturally. People began to notice. Ravichandran helped him up and sent him home in an autorickshaw.

The driving test happened after two weeks. When Ravichandran successfully made an 'H' and got out of the car, Ramakrishnan squeezed his hand and expressed his delight.

'Nothing to fear now! The forward's easy . . . Phillip Saar is my own man . . .!'

Ramakrishnan called that evening. He said that he'll bring the licence to Ravi maash's house in three days.

'No, I'll get it when I step out into town as usual,' said Ravichandran. Three or four days later, when Ramakrishnan returned from his day's work covered in sweat and grime as usual, his wife told him: 'That Ravi maash's license, I gave it to him.'

'When did Saar come?' Ramakrishnan asked.

'Not Saar. A girl came and got it. I was too busy, didn't ask her who she was.'

Ramakrishnan's eyes widened in happy astonishment. He took off his shirt, hung it up on the nail. Then his wife called from the kitchen, '. . . The water's boiled and ready . . .'

Migration and Melancholy

There is a strange melancholy that hangs over the semi-urbanized places that dot the rapidly urbanizing Kerala of the present. Many of us with lush memories of a verdant countryside alive with the rhythms of agriculture feel it acutely. It has become increasingly difficult to return to one's native village which looks quite desolate. Too many old houses locked, or inhabited by a single senior person or an aged couple, the fallow, weed-infested fields, the untended, undernourished coconut palms; old village ponds overgrown with weeds and choked with waste.

The flip side of this melancholy consists of the visible signs of wealth in the rural areas—massive mansions, fancy cars, supermarkets and other sites of globalized consumption. The painful transition from a primarily agrarian society into a mass of high-consumption individuals, and the desolation of the aged left in the lurch is very real. All the more so because these rich folk are very often settled in the prosperous regions of the globe, pursuing futures there and they or their descendents may never return to settle here. Kerala at present has a large, thriving population of migrants in the Gulf countries and beyond and many of them plan futures in Europe or the Anglo-American world.

Migration has been a feature of Malayali society since long. Large numbers of Malayalis migrated to different parts of the British Empire in the nineteenth and twentieth centuries, especially to South East Asia. Post-World War II, Malayalis migrated to Europe especially as nurses and careworkers, and in the 1970s, another large wave of migration to the Persian Gulf countries began which has continued well into the present; since the 1970s, the Gulf migration has also contributed to Malayali migration to the Anglo-American world.

Migrant wealth also widened social and economic inequalities enormously. At the bottom of the social pyramid today are female-headed households—led by women who engage in low-skill, low-status, precarious jobs with poor remuneration. Kerala reduced its birth rates significantly by the 1970s; now poor households too have aged adults to care for.

This gem of a story by the Canada-based Malayali fiction writer Nirmala brings all of this together in the short space of some two thousand words. The ghost-like presence of an agrarian past and active social bonding envelops the story in a light veil of melancholy. Sujatha's job is averse to building emotionally stable, fulfilling relationships, imbued as it is with the logic of the market. This logic imposes an inner void on all the characters in distinctly different ways—the hollow, high-consuming migrant elite, their desolate mother, and the home nurse who struggles to support a bed-ridden mother herself, offering her labour to older people who can pay.

If you drive through the Kerala countryside, you may be impressed by the wealth on show, especially in the form of dwellings. But these houses are as much about lonely ageing and isolation as they are about the achievements of the owners. And, as Nirmala reminds us, they also are sites of carework denuded of its capacity to build loving relationships. Under the canopy of wealth, the social body incapable of putting out new roots is dying slowly.

Sujatha's Houses

'Sujaathayute Veedukal'

Nirmala

Yes, the car was approaching that very house—that astonishingly large mansion which could be seen from very far. The walls around it were newly painted, adorned with fancy iron grille work—and bore the usual warning against pasting advertisements on it. The dog's spacious kennel was next to the gate. Just one look, and Sujatha knew that it was bigger than her one-room house.

The car had barely reached the house when the dog in the kennel began to bark loudly. Sujatha looked at it fearfully. The reddish face with a black scar was scary. But in the place of its tail, it had just a stump. It wiggled a bit. Sujatha felt very sorry for the dog that did not possess a curled tail—which, as the old saying went, would not be straightened ever.

Crossing the front yard covered with soft sand and lined with potted plants, Sujatha reached the porch. She removed her sandals.

Many heads appeared in the doors and the inner courtyard. She heard the sound of muffled talk.

—Already here?

—She's here, did you hear?

—Get the coffee now?

—No, after we ask.

They went past children playing caroms and watching TV at the same time and reached Sujatha's new room. Ammachi lay on a cot, her face to the wall.

—Ammachi, here, look—see who's come . . .!

Swallowing the pain of the prospect of staring at the walls with dull eyes for the rest of her life, Ammachi lay on her side, not moving.

The playful words hit somewhere outside Ammachi's ears and broke. They scattered on the fancy mosaic floor.

In her mind, Valsa and Molly ran around playing with their friends, having a whale of a time. Thampi and Sunny fought to sit on her lap. She knew how they smelled when she kissed them. Now they smell of Allure and Chanel and other French words she can't pronounce.

Thampi and Sunny sit in the chairs laid at a distance from her cot. No one wants to snuggle up close to her before they leave the country after their vacations get over. Valsa and Molly are so busy, they have no time to smile, even.

There was a time when Ammachi gave off the comforting smell of the Asanamanjishtaadi oil. Now her children sighed inwardly, even though they did not mention it to each other, that her room was filled with a faint hospital-like smell, of cleaning lotion.

I was never anyone's companion, Sujatha noted. Others see the harbinger of death in me. I am the end of the journey from illness to hospital, then from hospital to the restrictions of one's own bed—the home nurse. The fear—that the next step led to death—glinted in everybody's eyes. Half of them complained to God for denying them release without this hurdle.

It was to this house, where Ammachi had bustled about without anyone's help, barely a month back, that Sujatha had arrived, like a bad omen. She had been busy getting a feast ready for her children who were arriving from the cold of Chicago, the heat of Doha, the rush and tumult of Mumbai and the dust of Kolkata. She slipped on the kitchen floor tiles—she blames herself for the careless hurry.

Sujatha was the very first nurse in this house. As if she couldn't forgive her for that, Ammachi lay face turned towards the windowsill, looking out through it, refusing to even smile at her.

She knew perfectly well that after two weeks, her children would fly back from wherever they came. And it wasn't that she was unaware of the fact that after her children's departure, this Sujatha—or some other Sujatha—alone would keep her company. But somehow, the smile of friendship lay dead on her lips.

Looking through the window, she could see the huge pots and pans that Ammachi had hauled on the stove with much effort. They now lay under the tap outside, awaiting a good scrubbing and cleaning. They have been lying out too long, she grumbled. The crows will spoil them. Radha, who was going to wash the dishes, was sent off to the tailor to get a sari blouse stitched by the younger daughter-in-law. Ammachi, you know well, the cruel truth is that there isn't a single tailor in the whole of North America who can stitch a decent sari blouse.

—You have to manage for the next three or four years with the saris and blouses you got on this visit home.

The daughter-in-law unburdened herself. Pots and pans will surely wait under the tap without complaint. But if the blouse does not reach the tailor on time, Daughter-in-law's fashion world is going to go topsy-turvy.

Ammachi's mind reaches out again through the window and complains again, with effort. A banana flower was almost done blooming on the banana tree down in the garden. It should have been plucked and chopped fine, for a *thoran* with lentils.

A clothesline of blue plastic thread was drawn and tied across the empty cowshed. Clothes hung to dry on it made faces at the rain which fell fitfully and flapped mischievously.

It was Ammachi herself who had removed the bell that had hung on the cow Omanakkutty's neck and put it on the roof of the cowshed. Her mother who used to shake her horns menacingly was called Bhadrakaali! Sunny's doing, that name—Ammachi smiled to herself. There will never be an Omana, the darling of a calf to live in that cowshed again, she thought.

Seeing the nutmeg ripen and fall off the trees, their skins breaking, Ammachi's heart sank.

There's no one around to pick them and lay them out in the sun to dry!

All Ammachis have the same voice, Sujatha felt. The broken-up, scattered voice of desolation.

This was her eighth house in three years. Her agency would not let her grow roots anywhere. Three months in one place; then a few off-days at half pay. Then a new house. To be with someone who was left all alone when the children became busy.

All the houses looked alike, she thought. Well-kept exteriors. Inside, the floors gleamed with expensive tiles and mosaic. Showcases and walls bright with curios from all over the world. In between them, family photos of children, like Horlicks ads.

Only in Sujatha's room, an old cot and an aged body on the foreign-made coverlet. A life that loved the world intensely, and yet yearned to leave it. When she held the thin, twig-like arms, Sujatha felt that the muscles, loose and hanging, were as soft as clouds. Each pair of eyes had a whole Ramayana to tell, she knew. Restless eyeballs upon which cataracts had thrown veils tell her often about an Urmila who was neglected, a Seetha who could not escape the fires of humiliation into the outstretched arms of mothers, and a Rama who was torn between dharma and adharma.

Only one among these houses stood out in Sujatha's memory. That house did not have cavernous rooms that threatened to shrink and suffocate its inhabitants one day. It was an old and traditional house with an inner *ara*-room and a row of rooms, the *nira*, and more modern concrete extensions with a terrace that embraced the whole structure. The monsoon drew vague sketches on its outer walls bleached by the sun. There were no pretty objects that came from abroad in there; Sujatha felt a coolness there that seemed to flow from the love that blossomed in the house.

The mornings in that house smelled of cow dung and elanjhi flowers. The calves in the cowshed would call out impatiently to a grandfather—Appachan— who simply could not be convinced to take it easy even after crossing seventy.

A grandmother who lay curled up, worn with fever, upon an old woven cot. She had to be fed, bathed and dressed.

When the cook left after finishing her work, Appachan called to her.

'Kutti, child, bring some salted rice water please?'

Sujatha did not tell him that this was not part of her job since it was not for the patient. Appachan took it from her, drank it, and taking off the thortu-towel from his shoulder, fanned himself with it. 'It's terribly hot,' he said. Sujatha stretched out her hand to switch on the fan, but he stopped her.

—Acchamma finds the fan's breeze very irritating.

Acchamma Ammachi, trying to sit up all by herself, when the fever had barely abated. When she was almost able to bathe herself if helped into the bathroom, the old couple said in one voice that they didn't need a nurse anymore.

—From now, I'll help Acchamma up.

—Just help me to get to the bathroom.

The wheezing sounds in Ammachi's phlegm-filled chest subsided a bit. That was the only house where Sujatha did not stay for the three-month maximum period of employment.

Usually, once her work is done, she meets a plump hand holding out fresh currency notes—a token of gratitude outside the monthly wages. This Appachan plucked her a whole basket of rose apples.

—Kutti, you like them, don't you? Who's going to eat so many, here?

—Did you pick some pomelo fruit for the girl?

Ammachi's fever and fatigue had flown off. When she took leave of them, taking the parcels of fresh fruit, Appachan reminded her.

—Kutti, do consult the healer Varghese *vaidyar* about your mother's illness. Everyone was so sure that Acchamma would never get up. It was vaidyar who got her out of the sickbed.

She nodded in agreement; he continued:

—If you need any herbs or leaves to make the medicinal oil, there's plenty in this yard. The stuff that you find in the bazaar is mostly bad. We have the great five *moolams* in this compound! There, in the corner of the front yard, *neelayamari*. Near the cowshed there's *amukkuram, adalodakam* and *kacholam*.

Surprised, she asked—do we have a healer who knows vaidyam in this house?

—Our son left home to study Ayurveda . . .

That half sentence remained unfinished. Sujatha did not ask about what had happened to the son who had left to study Ayurveda. When she turned back to look at the parents who had preserved the pancha-moolams for a son who was now just a photo hanging on the wall of the inner room, a huge root slid down her throat and got stuck there.

When she went out through the cool shade of the koovalam tree, she made a wish that did not help her professionally: may this Appachan and Ammachi never be bed-ridden, she prayed.

Sujatha knew very well that after some days of protest, this Ammachi, too, would hold her hand out to her for help. There will be no other hand in this house to help her up. Her trembling arm cannot reach Chicago or Doha or Mumbai or Kolkata. Still, Sujatha was hurt when she refused to even show her face to her.

Ammachi gave up eating supper when she had to chew the low-salt-oil-free thoran of cabbage, lightly cooked to preserve nutrition. She must have remembered the taste of thoran made of lentils and minced banana flower.

Supper done, Ammachi had gone to sleep lying down face to the wall. Sujatha lay down on the mattress on the floor and tried to summon sleep.

As usual, even though she had forbidden herself to remember it, a house completely unlike this one, got tangled up in Sujatha's heart and yanked it hard. In the single room of this house, on a decrepit old cot lay an aged mother. She asked:

—Did Suja's money come yet?

—No, Amme. It is only the second of the month now. It will come only on the fifth.

A brief involuntary moan escapes Amma when she tried to press down and bury the accounts of worsening pain and medicines that get over too soon. Shobha *chechi*, still unmarried at thirty-eight, tries to ease it with hot compresses—unsuccessfully.

Sujatha pulled up the nursing teacher's advice to regard every moan, whimper, sob, as part of the job, covered her chest with it, and summoned sleep once again.

Empowered Wife,
Envious Husband

In present-day Kerala, no one knows the pulse of the local better than the lower middle-class woman leader of self-help groups. If you were to visit a panchayat, you'd see it teem with women—as elected members, leaders of women's self-help groups which distribute welfare resources, members and leaders of the Standing Committees of the local body, and so on.

I have spent a large part of my life as a researcher in Kerala among women newly empowered by the reservation of seats for women in local bodies in the 1990s and after. In the mid-1950s, working class women formed the backbone of the massive working class protests for public welfare here, but these women rarely enjoyed power. In the 1990s, however, a small share of political power, in the panchayats and urban bodies, was offered to women. The self-help groups of poor women—called the Kudumbashree groups—

worked closely with the elected local bodies, and soon, women in this network came to be much sought after as candidates for local elections.

The life story of such women, we found, was remarkably similar: the local woman leader was usually a woman in her thirties or forties, with higher secondary or matriculation-level education, rarely working and more likely to be a mother and housewife with one or two children, and of largely lower-middle-class origins. Making her way up through the network of self-help groups, this woman's ambitions were usually about becoming an elected member of her local panchayat and an indispensable element at the local level in the Party of her choice. By no means did this mean an immediate challenge to local patriarchy: quite to the contrary, this meant even tighter adherence to conservative gender and moral codes and the willingness to accept limits to women's ambition and aspiration. But it also meant changing family life to a limited degree at least. No wonder, the husband of such a woman is worried.

Dhanya Raj's masterful portrait of a woman raising herself up and growing beyond the status of a housewife and watched with silent envy by her mediocre husband captures the complexities of this challenge well. Slander is perhaps the most potent weapon to break a woman down especially because she pitches herself almost exclusively at the local level. We learned of husbands who were 'supportive' on the surface, but raged with insecurity, suspicion and envy—men who tracked their wives' mobile phones, and indeed, did not flinch from loose talk about them in both men-only spaces as well as family and community circles. But equally important is the fact that elections unleash competition between empowered women which hurt women's collective interests.

Dhanya's 'Green Room' was extraordinarily prescient in the way in which it uncovers all of this, including the dirty tricks that competing women can unleash on the other. Published first in 2010, it pointed to a crisis that was only still growing. In the present, the empowered woman in Kerala faces a backlash of unprecedented proportions. Women seeking power is no longer news here, but breaking the limits set by patriarchy now calls forth much harsher punishment. Working one's way up through 'merit' is no longer the path to power for women. The power of literature is that it is able to predict the future, perhaps much better than social science. If only we listened better to our storytellers; if only we took them seriously.

Green Room

'Green Room'

Dhanya Raj

The saying that there is a woman behind every successful man is absolutely true, if you consider my life. I don't like to think even, where it would have ended up without my wife Syamini. But if you ask what great victory I have won with her help . . . there's not much I can point to. But carrying on in life despite minor scrapes and falls is itself an achievement, is it not?

Our life, which was very ordinary, definitely uneventful, which moved in a straight line, began to change in the past three or four years. Until then, Syamini was the mistress of this house. In other words, the monarch of this tiny empire. Think about her transmogrification from being the cook to cleaning lady, and from the cleaning lady to the mistress of the house, and then back to being the cook—you'd be amazed! What a shape-shifter! This house has witnessed her take up so many roles, all of which she performed like a gifted actor! So many of life's moments Syamini made unforgettable! Also, one must credit her with the extraordinary ability to take crucial decisions whenever necessary. Should we educate our daughter in an English-medium school? Which brand of refrigerator should we get for the house? What premium should we pay for the insurance policy? She decides all this and my role is simply to execute efficiently and accurately. When I do that, I describe myself not as the 'head of the household', but as 'a responsible member of the family'. The two are not too far from each other, are they?

Back then, Syamini stepped out of the house rarely—just to the fish market or to the tailor's. Except for these necessary outings, neither she nor I felt any need to go out and interact with people. But I remember that when the local Kudumbashree unit was set up she had been very keen, excited about a women's collective, etc., etc. I must admit that I was a little surprised when I heard her use with marvellous ease tough words like 'women's empowerment', 'self-reliance', 'financial upward mobility', and so on. Those days, women in the Kudumbashree were mostly into making such eatables as acchappam and neyyappam and banana chips and rice murukku, and selling them around here. I was pretty confused, not able to see how these were connected to the abstruse words that she flaunted. When I saw how eagerly she dressed up to go to the Kudumbashree meetings every Sunday, I did not ask her anything about it. I believed that women's getting together like this was quite harmless; until such a meeting was held in our own house one day.

Even though this happened a few years back, this has stayed in my memory. On the evening that day—it must have been 6.30 or so—I was returning home after hanging about town for a bit. When I reached the outer veranda, the sounds of terrible altercations reached me. I had borrowed a considerable sum of money from some people around here to open a grocery shop; I feared that they had come seeking me. I felt that it was better that I disappeared. Syamini has this ability to smoothen out any crisis. I ran back the way I came and hid behind a tamarind tree at the boundary of our yard. The moments passed; it seemed that even the branches of the tree were listening, still and alert. The evening light was beginning to withdraw. Even the wind, which blew on that path somewhat reluctantly, had a touch of mystery. When things seemed to have calmed down, I went to the house.

'What was the issue here?' I asked her, very worried.

'What issue?' Syamini looked straight-faced.

'It was our Kudumbashree meeting,' she said, coolly.

'You see, it's about money. In things to do with money, calculations may go wrong.' I turned to her, astonished. Syamini was the Treasurer of the Kudumbashree unit, I learned later.

That was also the time when she started doing minor sorts of Party work. Nothing big, that is. Say, making a speech as women's representative in the

Party meetings organized around here now and then. Or ushering regional-level leaders to the dais. In other meetings, simply ensuring women's presence, even if she did not speak or greet leaders—Syamini's political activism was limited to these.

And we do have some political activists in my family—so I don't oppose her activism. The customers who patronize the little grocery shop which I opened not far from our house are usually people with political connections. So I have not put up a board saying 'Do Not Discuss Politics Here' in front of my shop. Politics, art, cinema—all of these can be discussed under some broad limits. But gossip cannot be encouraged at all. That's my policy.

Let me come back to Syamini. In those days, making a public speech at a Party meeting was a huge challenge for her. I used to be so amused, seeing her memorize the speeches? A six or seven-page speech written for her by some local leader—like a schoolkid on the day before the exam! But all this preparation would go to naught when she actually appeared before the mic! She would become nervous and recall only the beginning and the end of the speech. The speech planned for ten minutes would wind up in barely one minute. After the programme, she would come to me, the powder on her face smudged, hair in disarray.

'Why do they insist that you must learn the speech by heart?' I asked her once, seeing her so helpless. 'Do ministers read out a prepared speech on the stage?'

'Hey, that won't do,' Syamini said, sounding like an experienced public speaker.

'Only words that come from within are sincere and honest. Only those can produce some echo among the masses.'

I was amused by this, again. But Syamini refused to accept defeat and continued to be active as a speaker in Party meetings. Gradually, things changed. She gained the confidence to speak for three or four minutes before an audience. I am talking about things that happened some months back.

Anyway, to cut things short, it was when Syamini won the lottery—to become the candidate for the panchayat elections in the Poomaruthikkunnu ward of our Aanangottukara panhayat—that I was truly flabbergasted. Her rival was P.V. Leelamani, of the Kunnuvila Charuvinkal house. Aanangottukara panchayat has fifteen wards. My friend and avid Party worker Krishnamohan, however, was utterly shattered when the Poomaruthikkunnu ward was declared a women's reservation ward. So sure he had been of becoming the candidate, we had all thought that his candidature was firmly locked down! This friend, who's also our neighbour, was not to be seen outside his house for quite a few days after this. I had apprehensions about Syamini's ability to live up to the busy life of an elected people's representative. When the Party members who came to congratulate her with sweets had left, I told her about my fears.

'What's impossible if one tries hard enough?' she asked. 'These are all valuable experiences in life, are

they not?' In a few days, it became evident that my
fears were misplaced.

Syamini dived into the election campaign with
unprecedented enthusiasm. It appeared that Syamini
the Housewife had now vanished from my life. Not
able to adjust with this unfamiliar, new Syamini, I was
utterly perplexed.

In the morning, I lay in bed mulling over things
for a long time even though I had woken up quite late.
No sign of cooking in the kitchen! Syamini must have
packed our daughter's lunchboxes with the shop-made
chapathis and chicken curry that we bought last night.
She must have left for the campaign straight after seeing
her off to the school van. I found out that the cooking
gas cylinder was empty when I tried to light the stove.
There was a new, full cylinder there, but I don't know
how to fit it—not confident, actually.

Disappointed, I switched the TV on. A kind of void
seemed to appear on the screen. Then I remembered
that I had received a notice the other day that our cable
connection will be cut if the three-month arrears were
not paid. I think it's around a month since the last
date for paying the telephone bill elapsed. This was all
because Syamini had not reminded me of the last date
for payment! I gnashed my teeth in sheer frustration.
I changed my shirt, deciding to go out, and stood
before the mirror. Grey, creeping around my hair and
moustache! It was Syamini who always mixed the
hair dye—only she knew how to do it! Customers at
my shop would never have encountered me, ageing,
greying, my charming looks lost. I paced the room in

utter confusion. The house seemed to be challenging me, like a battlefield. The inferiority and sadness of a soldier who did not know how to handle a single weapon engulfed me. The loneliness of the rooms filled with the whitish light of emptiness suffocated me. Syamini . . . Syamini . . . a silent whimper crumpled and died in my throat.

I remembered with a jolt something that the local Party leader had said the day before. The President's position in the Aanangottukara panchayat was also reserved for women. The trend here favoured the Party too. So, Syamini, who seemed poised to win as Ward Member might well become the Panchayat President! Already, she was so busy, I hardly saw her, I remembered uneasily. What if she became the Panchayat President? The masses of Aanangottukara will surely arrive here like a whole *jatha*, along with their unending problems and issues. Whatever peace left in life will soon evaporate. There's no panchayat anywhere in the world with so many troubles as our Aanagottukara, for sure! The more I thought, the more I felt that I was losing my mind. Holding my head in both hands, I sat there motionless for a long time. Then, slowly, some thoughts rose in my mind like the silvery fish-like flashes in unrelenting darkness. My decision is right, I made up my mind. I sat up, feeling somewhat relieved.

Past noon, I met Ananthan and Lukose who are regulars at my shop and close friends of mine. You look tense after Syamini became the candidate,

Sudeva—Ananthan quipped. I did not reply; just stayed silent, my face clouding over. They looked puzzled; I described to them my sorry state. My throat failed me when I finished. For some time, no one said anything.

'. . . But, Sudeva . . . we work for Syamini's defeat? . . . How can that be . . .? Lukose asked, sounding utterly dazed. 'It's our Party, remember!'

'What in the blazes—Party!' Anger and sadness flowed together in me.

'If she gets into a public career, she's going to become wilful. The end of my family life!'

Ananthan and Lukose looked at each other in confusion.

'Then, there's this—a Member's position is a lucrative one. Who deserves it more? Leelamani for sure! She's from such a poor family!' I put on the garb of a lover of humanity. I managed to convince them both after long arguments. Syamini had a slight edge over her rivals by now, so we had to move cleverly. We made some plans.

'My wife Thresiamma will get this done beautifully,' said Lukose. 'She is very well connected with the women in this ward.' Lukose had great faith in his wife's abilities. I already knew that Thresiamma wouldn't waste a single chance to put down Syamini. She was the Secretary of the Kudumbashree unit. How many allegations she had made against the Treasurer, Syamini? I paused for a moment, worried, thinking of the kind of rumours that she may unleash against Syamini. But then it was all for the good, I tried to console myself. 'Let us give this a thought,' said Ananthan, as if to calm me down. 'We should be able to do something.'

'We know all the voters, after all?'

'Of course . . . if you build a bridge, it should be of use to people on either side.'

Lukose said that hesitantly, avoiding my face. In a little while, we reached an agreement by which the two-month arrears both of them had at my grocery shop were annulled. I had cheered up and looked bright when I reached home. Syamini was already back.

'How did the campaigning go?' I asked her with a loaded smile.

'We have covered all houses two times over,' she said.

'Hmmm,' I said, thoughtfully.

The next day, when some woman called on our land phone asking for Syamini, I told her: 'She's not at home . . . she's gone to the beauty parlour.'

'Uh! What for?' the woman sounded anxious now.

'For a facial, bleach, threading, waxing, pedicure, manicure . . .' I recited these words that I remembered reading in a women's magazine. The phone went dead with a hiss of disbelief. Syamini's complexion was clear and golden, unaffected by the heat of the cooking stove or the sun, I remembered. When a male voice inquired after her on the phone some time later, I told this somewhat differently: 'Syamini has gone to the dry cleaner's to get her silk saris dry-washed.' No request for clarification arose from the other side. That was a relief.

After a few days, I was seated in my shop one afternoon. The election campaign was reaching a crescendo. Syamini's posters were everywhere—all around the bus stand and on its boundary walls, and even on the tarred roads. Hearing that she was speaking at the junction nearby, I went over. She was making promises to people, quite generously. I will get the panchayat to agree to the plan for the new road, she proclaimed. Will approach the KSRTC for more bus services; will have a waiting shed built; make sure that all deserving families receive below-poverty-line ration cards; will stand with the people through thick and thin . . .

Such confidence in her words, so eloquent her body language—Syamini's form left me awed. She wore a sandalwood-coloured cotton sari and ear studs of white pearls. Her shoulder-length hair was neatly combed back and clipped into a ponytail. In general, Syamini looked like Sonia Gandhi's caricature come alive! I staggered at the sight of her high-heeled sandals—I had never seen her in anything other than worn leather slippers. Will she twist an ankle walking around in these? I was worried. But then she'd better be careful, alert—for her own good.

The days went by and I too became very busy. Once Syamini left for her campaigning, I too would leave the house in about one-and-a-half hours. I found a boy to take care of things at the shop. I paid no attention when he asked me, 'Sudevan *chetta*, why do you look so flustered?' This boy seems to have a special talent to seek out what was uprooted and what finally sprouted. I visited the homes of many acquaintances on the pretext of seeking votes for my wife. I realized only then that this Poomaruthikkunnu where I was born and raised had so many tiny paths and wild patches.

I found wells that lay with mouths open in the middle of overgrown plots of land like crafty animals lying in wait for prey; slithering creatures' secret lives under the weeds as tall as a grown man; some hosts whose deadpan faces refused to change . . . the way may be hard, but what matters is our goal, right? I know that what is fated alone will happen. But that does not mean we should do nothing? Despite my migraine, I continued undeterred in the blazing noon sun. I went to people who knew us well and dropped sly remarks, nicely packaged, about Syamini's loose ways, her selfishness . . . I did not forget to indicate that her interest in public life was directly linked to her pecuniary predilections. I noted with satisfaction that at the end of the conversation, inevitably, the expression on their faces would be 'Oh . . . so Syamini is such a . . . lowlife . . .?'

I kept meeting Lukose and Ananthan regularly. They confirmed that things were moving as planned and P.V. Leelamani would win hands down in the Poomaruthikkunnu ward. They also vowed to keep hushed all our moves hitherto. Like it is said, the right hand should not know what the left hand does.

A whole month passed by. Just thinking of it overwhelms me. Didn't the things that we had not

seen even in our dreams happen? But anyway, do the
distinctions between dream, truth, illusion and so on
have any meaning? In the moss-covered bylanes of
the mind . . . OK, no need to go round and round . . .
Syamini is sitting beside me right now. Tomorrow is
the polling day. The exhaustion from such intense
campaigning has cast a shadow on her face; it is also
filled with anxiety about the poll results. She raises her
eyes and sends me a tired look. To tell you the truth, it
filled me with great sadness. I placed my hand on her
shoulder and in a tenderly affectionate voice, told her:
'Syamini, please do not worry, on any count. God will
never forsake those who persevere with all their heart.'

Globalized Bigotry

If Malayalis has been saved (up to now, at least) in large measure from intense and violent religious bigotry, the credit for this goes in large measure to the lingering legacy of the great seer Sree Narayana, widely accepted in Kerala as 'the Guru'. Born in what was an untouchable community those days, the Ezhava, the Guru nevertheless became a remarkable scholar in Sanskrit, Tamil and Malayalam. He provided a vision of the individual and society that rejected the order of caste from its roots. It advocated a culture of anukampa *which went beyond its usual translation in English, 'compassion', and demanded* anu-kampanam, *or 'resonance'. This implied equal respect to all faiths, as existing in a relation of resonance between different* mathams, *which, as the Guru liked to remind, are in the last analysis, 'opinions'—*matham *in Malayalam, too, means 'opinion'.*

However, the Guru's thinking as life practice has steadily waned since, and not just due to its ossification in the community movements that claimed it. The burgeoning upward mobility aspirations among the followers of the Dharmam became evident in the late twentieth century. The abandonment of the spiritually oriented life practice also meant the embracing of elite Hindu rituals and worship, now suitably refurbished to take on the function of conspicuous individual consumption. The aspiration for material upward mobility and visibility within the majoritarian imagination of the nation also facilitated a tendency to lean towards religious faith endorsed by the powerful. This meant the breakdown of the Guru's dream of religious faiths co-existing in mutual resonance.

The highly educated, prosperous NRI Malayali Hindu who embraces every global elite habit and taste, and who does not intend to return to Kerala is also very often bigoted of faith and harbouring ill-will, if not hate, towards alleged religious enemies. They can also be incredibly superstitious, even mobilizing the language of science to justify them, especially when it has to do with 'tradition' and 'custom'. I will never forget, for example, a US citizen, an NRI Malayali, cardiologist by profession, who made a video in which she claimed that the 'energy' in Hindu temples is inimical to the 'energies' of menstruating women and that this could have catastrophic effects. When this video attracted criticism, and possibly from her colleagues in the modern medical profession, it was removed.

K.R. Meera's 'Sanghiannan' is a masterful portrait of such an NRI. 'Annan' is an affectionate reference to one's older brother; the word 'Sanghi' once had a very different connotation, too. This story is set in a Kerala where fascism is no longer untouchable and religious bigotry is common, especially among the consumerist elites. The narrator is a practitioner of Sree Narayana Dharmam and through his eyes, we see the transformation of a whole culture, from the gentle, peaceable, generous, resonant practice of the Hindu faith to a more aggressive, belligerent, bigoted, involute form of Hindu belief. The story is also a celebration of Sree Narayana Guru's thought, filled with splendid allusions to his writings, speeches, poetry, and his associations with other great reformers of his times, like Sahodaran K. Ayyappan. Meera points to the canker, but through the eyes of the healer.

Sanghiannan

'Sanghiannan'

K.R. Meera

I was waiting for Sanghi *annan* at the airport, and
there was he, rushing in the opposite direction with his
trolley, not bothering to even look for me. If it were the
good old days I would have hollered after him, 'Sanghi
annaa, he . . . eeyyy'! And would have rushed to hug
him saying, 'Been waiting here so long!' Dropping bag
and basket, we would have looked laughingly at each
other for the next few minutes. He would have joked,
'What the heck, Anikkutta, going all grey so soon?'
and I would have retorted, 'If you're going to colour
your hair like this, bro, next time I'll have to call you
little brother.' 'Here, take this, for you,' he would have
said, pressing a bar of milk chocolate into my palm,
and I would have said the same, pressing into his palm
a packet of Nasrin's delectable *unnakkaya*. This time I

didn't bring the unnakkaya; not because I forgot. The occasion isn't right, and Sanghi annan's tastes have changed too. I have no clue what he likes these days. Whatever. Let him eat what he likes. Be it to marry, be it to gorge on banana chips, if your mind repels, how can the body accept?

Not that I failed to yell out to him this time. Just that my voice did not come out. First, the anxiety of having to tell him. Secondly, the suffocation afflicted by the knowledge that this wasn't the old Sanghi annan you could holler out to. Most importantly, how would people hanging about outside the airport respond if I shouted 'Sanghi anna'? True, our father had given us names for special reasons. Recalling the Guru's advice to seek strength in the Sangha—in the coming together of humans beyond all divisions in a collectivity—he bestowed the name Sanghamitran on him; me, he named Vidyasagar, so that we would be reminded of the Guru's call to Become Enlightened through Knowledge. But wasn't sure if we'd have the time to explain all that. These are terrible times indeed!

Luckily, Sanghi annan turned around and spotted me. I went up to him like always but my enthusiasm dimmed when we came face to face. Not like old times, for sure. Looked like he's downed a whole barrel of bitter castor oil on that flight, from his grimace and handshake. He's spent all his time in the past twenty or twenty-five years in air-conditioned spaces, and so he looks all fair and rosy. On top of that, the clean-shaved cheeks and the dark glasses. It was clear to the onlookers that he was not pleased that I failed to suitably recognize and acknowledge the tremendous sacrifice, all this castor oil drinking— done, apparently, for my sake. And bloody Kerala, so terribly hot! Right in the middle of that full-sleeved shirt as unsullied as a slab of fresh white butter, a black hole of sweat opened wide. The golden cufflinks and the ring set with nine auspicious gems glittered in the bright sun. I too got the feeling that all this is because I conspired in some way.

Besides, my car is a modest Alto. Not suited to his form, bearing, pride. He kept the suitcase, handbag and the laptop bag in the back seat and squeezed the six feet of his body and the respectably small paunch into the front seat verily like the rich man entering heaven. I didn't take any of this hard. We adore God, not His idol, don't we? All this, while actually the worry writhing painfully inside me was about when to begin, where to begin, how to begin. I even started, saying, 'I came here to get you because you said you'll come for *acchan*'s *bali* rites, anna, or I'd have called yesterday.' But Padma *chechi* called just then from Dubai to ask if he had landed safe, and my talking broke. They kept on till we reached Shanghumukham. And then when we were waiting in the blocked traffic near the Chaakka traffic lights, from the nearby school, as if by God's own will, the '*Jana Gana Mana*' floated by, and I heard him cry, 'National anthem, national anthem', and barely in a blink, our man had slipped out of the car and was standing at attention by the road!

The traffic eased quickly but how could I start the car without his attention returning to standing-at-ease? The vehicles behind us were blasting us with their horns. A moment in which I prayed like in the old times, reciting the Guru's prayer, 'God, be our shield; forsake us not, forever'. Gingerly, I pulled up into the side of the road. Will tell him after he pulls out of the attention mode, I decided. But where was the time? No sooner had the long bell rung in the school, than annan ran back, opened the car door and started scolding, 'What's the matter, you? Can't you spare a couple of minutes to stand up for the national anthem? What stops you, a rotten sore in your bum or what? Patriotism—that's what you need, fella, patriotism!'

That felt like a blow. But silence was the best response in that moment. But can one correct the Inescapable, what the Guru speaks of, the '*vidhi varacchathu maarivaraan pani pratividhikkumakattarutaathathu?*' So it just dropped out of my mouth—'Oh really, national anthem and patriotism in the middle of the road! These days I am not so patriotic!' And all hell broke loose. You fucking son of a bastard born of a murderer, I'll pull your tongue out if you utter another such depravity! What the hell did you say? That patriotism isn't needed? *Eda*, you are a nobody without this country. What did you think of me? You'll betray this country on the strength of a rotten government job? Get lost if you are not a patriot, go to Pakistan . . .!

Remember, this is a person who never even once uttered words like 'bastard' and 'murderer' until four or five years back. More importantly, this is someone who didn't give the slightest sign that he would change so drastically and so soon. And even worse, this is a patriot who went abroad to reap the riches, though a product of public-funded education, who then secured a government job. My blood boiled. I froze in my seat and stopped the car. He leapt out and paced up and down the road. Why not get out and tell him all to his face, I thought. But how to hit someone deliberately on what one already knew was the weakest point in his body? Just when I thought why Father couldn't find another name for this fellow . . . Many of my friends frown at his name. The threads on his wrists, the rings on his fingers, the chains on his neck—my friends often expressed their suspicions when they noticed those. And speaking with him, they said, he's *that* sort alright, nothing to be left to doubt. Really painful, but not just him, even our Father became suspect in their eyes. Father, who till his dying day, woke from rest each morning imploring, along with the Guru, that treacherous darkness be alleviated by the radiance of the Blessed Word—*Arul*. I grew tired of explaining to them that we were an inter-caste family since long, and that Father was a close ally of the great anti-caste reformer, Sahodaran Ayyappan. My grandfather married my grandmother whose caste name had a long tail. My father got himself registered in the Society for Inter-Caste Marriage and married my mother whose caste had a short tail. The two of us were born to them. Because he firmly believed that caste and religion are the two scourges the nation had to be rescued from, he raised us without either of these.

I am trying to say, Sanghi annan wasn't like this always. In school he was a meek fellow. Top student, came first in every class, scored a perfect hundred in maths and physics, went to school from home and from school back home. Used to play cricket with me in our yard with coconut palm frond stems, but never ever saw a playground. As for the local fair, it fell during exam time and so was an absolute no-no. Onam exam-Christmas exam-Year-end exam—that was his calendar. School-tuition-home—that was his clock. He didn't bid for even the class monitor's post. Leave alone avoiding political processions, till he turned seventeen or so, he never even dared to utter the name of a Party. I still remember all this and that is why I am able to forgive all his foolishness. Right now, when he got a bit sweaty standing out there, he forgot his anger. He came back and got in. That's the thing. Never mind his going ballistic now; sooner or later, he'll come right back and get into our car. He'll beg for some water and let us take him wherever we pleased without even asking us about the destination. He's the first-born, the family simpleton. Like the Guru said, human beings are not born with the power of discretion. They have to strive for it, read, gather life experience. And we must have the compassion—anukamba—to persist with men as fruitless and short-lived as water in the desert, like the Guru described them.

But easy to say, hard to do, this anukamba. To be convinced of that, try being with him, like now. He's ashamed of his tantrum and all those expletives and so, to hide it, moves to smooth talk and friendly surgical strikes. 'Whatever, you must get rid of this attitude of yours, Anikkutta. Only when we live in a foreign country do we realise the worth of such things as the national anthem and the national flag. This is the time we should be standing together. You won't know how the ground beneath our feet slips away otherwise. You know well, right now, who owns all our land? If we are not united, they'll take over this place and make us all snipdicks down there. You'll see your daughter walk around in that blasted black covering.'

God alone knows, I couldn't make out who was the 'we' he was referring to. I smiled, remembering Nasrin and Isha. He caught it, and said, 'Oh I know why you're smiling.' Why, I asked. No response, but he shot out the question soon: 'What's Isha's religion?' Aha, am I any less canny? I pretended to be thirsty and drank some water from the bottle. Then asked an innocent question, 'But, Sanghi anna, this "we" and "us"—aren't all these people of India?' But the times have changed for sure; annan does not like innocence. He gets angry. Also doesn't answer to the point. Ask him, how many measures of lentils, and he will answer, horsegram won't soak.

'Stop getting too big for your boots, OK? Oh, the flawless angel! I am just a fascist, of course! Just wait, if you won't learn by seeing, you will when it hits you. Whatever you say, things are going to change. Wait for a year. Till now the problem was that we did not have a majority. *Now* you'll see what the business of ruling is. And so, Anikkutta, don't play so cool. You'd better make a decision about Isha soon. Make sure she is one of us. If not, she won't have a future.'

What is Vidya for? Surely not to argue and win? Surely to receive and give knowledge? So I turned even more innocent. Isn't it better to have no religion in childhood, I asked. So that it becomes easy to join those who come to power in the future? I recited to him the Guru's verses that Father had taught us when the headmaster sent home a form to get the caste column filled. That verse said that the name, place and occupation are good enough to identify a person; no need to answer the question who you are—for the body itself reveals the truth about you, a human beyond caste and creed.

But before I could finish, he burst out. 'Chhii! Stop, you bastard! How dare you make fun of me! I'll knock your teeth down!' What a relief. He gnashed his teeth and contorted his cheeks virtually to the *kapalabhathi* pranayama for the next five minutes. After having completed it satisfactorily, he turned to me again, 'Oh, big secularist. It is because of people like you that the country is like this. Yeah, at this rate, they may rule the country after all, yeah, right, they may be the majority,' he lamented. I couldn't help asking, 'Why don't you and Padma chechi . . . make a determined effort towards stopping that?' My mistake, for Sanghi annan exploded again, 'What a question to ask! Not one a younger brother should ask his older brother in *Bharateeya* culture!'

The truth is, I was exhausted by now. What a simpleton! He's going to make me cry, surely. Thinking of a way to change the topic and to finally break it to him, I started again about how I didn't call yesterday because I knew he'd be coming today, but a dog jumped in front. Now the topic shifted again. 'So, the stray dog menace isn't over yet? What's the stupid government doing? The dogs are tearing people up and the government's crossed its arms and watching! If this were somewhere in north India, what a furore it would have been! How they would have all moaned in the social media!'

Yeah, in the north it is after all human beings who tear up other human beings—I was about to say that, but he wouldn't let me. 'You won't like the facts, but try to be a bit objective? Why do we suffer from stray dogs only here? Because of all the waste. Because of the slaughtering! When they tried to ban slaughtering, all of you were up in arms! Why did the government ban it? Because this menace will end only if beef is banned in Kerala, don't you see?'

In response I should have just whispered to myself the Guru's question about knowledge being not singular, but how we need to know where each of it comes from. But being obsessed with thinking how to tell him, I mistook this for an opportunity to come to the point. 'But Sanghi anna,' I began. 'How could that be? Aren't there many people who love that food?' That provoked another blast. 'Oh really, in that case why insist on people wearing helmets? So many people prefer to drive without helmets! The government has the responsibility to ban harmful stuff! Eating beef is like swallowing a bomb. Tell your government to finish off all Malayalis with fifty-one slashes of the knife, like they did in their last murder! That's way better! Just google it, at least? Beef is full of saturated fat, the chief reason why Malayalis are dying of heart attacks, you know? It has something called new 5 GC which causes cancer of the colon. It creates blocks in the heart . . . and what about diabetes and obesity, what causes those? And even if you leave all that . . . go and find out how they raise cattle for slaughter—by pumping it with hormones, how else! Our kids have autism and Down's Syndrome because they are eating it!'

Not that I forgot Father humming the Guru's line that warned of how sorrow flows out of a heart devoid of love. But I had to prolong the conversation till we reached the point. So I asked, 'But what about pork?' That made him go red in the face, but I continued all the more innocently, 'I have been a vegetarian since I was a kid and so don't know what the taste of beef is, but there was someone in our home who used to carry beef fry in glass jars, in quantities large enough to last two whole weeks in his hostel!' I said that to myself.

But he was clearly embarrassed. 'Oh, that . . . that was in the old time,' he said, and I quickly reminded him: there are such people in these times, too. The truth is, I fervently wished to hold him close, give him a kiss, and tell him, 'Sanghi anna, you don't know how much I love you!' But I didn't do it, and said, out of sheer compassion, anukamba, 'You are right; there is no diabetes or obesity or colon cancer, or autism or Down's Syndrome in Gujarat and Haryana!' That hit the bull's eye. Nothing like sarcasm to make him go wild. Till the Medical College Junction, the Alto ceased to be a car; it became a Chariot of Victory, shining bright with Sanghi annan's radiance! The very *'Jaitra Radham, Tejasaal Samujjwalitam'* that's so much sung about these days!

'Stop saying rubbish, OK? In any case, the dogs don't like anything good. Only in Kerala you find them barking and biting. Just because you have four-five seats in the Parliament! Just go to the north. Do these fellows who are big down here have enough numbers to fill a cargo-ferrying autorickshaw? Whatever you say, tell me, what is it that our nation needs now? Good leadership! You'll say, it is not democratic. I'll say, this much democracy is OK for me.'

Good luck, his phone rang then. I escaped. But, good God, what a trial this is! Two people born of the same mother, raised by the same father—he is one of them! More anukamba, more anukamba, I begged myself! Am I not the only one who knows what a simple fellow he is? Forever worrying about what's in it for him. Forever scared of what he may lose. Right now, he's talking of what difference it will make to the dollar and the rupee if the dirham falls by half per cent. He's talking of each penny. This would rattle the rest of us, but that's all there is to poor Sanghi annan. He used to be a Leftie of sorts when he moved to the hostel of the engineering college at Calicut after clearing the entrance exams. Used to be crazy about beef biriyani and unnakkaya. When he completed his studies, the Right was in power. It was Father's Gandhian friend who recommended him for a government job. At that time, he shook his head and agreed that the Right was better, all said and done. Our man's fabled love affair followed on the heels of this. 'No bride for mixed types' was the slogan of the blue-blooded battalion from Changanashery certified by the hair in their ears which reached our home in Valakam to do battle. The Left was in power then, and one of Sanghi annan's friends was an MLA. He flipped now and said, 'Whatever, only the Left helps you in a crisis.' And then he went abroad, became rich, had a son, named him Sriram, bought flats in many cities, and became the Sanghi annan of today. I, in the meanwhile, became a government officer, met Nasrin and we married without converting or demanding conversion, had Isha, borrowed money towards the end of the month, and had a fine time generally on other days. Not clear why, but some ten years before, he added a caste tail to Sriram's name. The next step was to add it to his own name. That was a huge blow to Father who had believed that his sons had broken out of the stifling narrow vessel of caste and climbed over the wall of religion. But I teased him then, asking whether caste was even relevant at all these days. I said that it was now just a surname and as neutral as 'arthropoda' and 'phylum cordata'. Even joked that it would be fun if we added a caste tail to Isha's name.

It was when we—he, I, Padma chechi and Isha— were returning from Guruvayur after performing a *tulabharam* in Sriram's name at the temple, that he first asked me, 'Hey, have you ever been to Gujarat?' He described how two of his colleagues had travelled there and returned impressed with all the growth. But it was only after Sri cleared the entrance exams and they came down to join the medical college here that annan told us that he had given up beef for good. The very same day, he asked what Isha's official name was, and that she could have been given a more culturally appropriate name. I didn't get it even then. 'Culture' meant Bharateeya samskriti, five thousand years, Sanskrit, Sanatana Dharma, Ayurveda . . . he rolled round and round. In the next visit, he wore the red thread on his wrist. 'What's this?' I frowned. 'Oh, so you don't know?' growled he. Nasrin tried to convince me—it's like wearing the burqa, and anyway it is tied on his wrist, not heart . . . and she reminded me that Mother had tied a red thread from the temple on Isha's wrist when she fell ill. But she didn't see it. The thread that Mother tied was of faith, not of branding. This is Sanghi annan. He never held aloft any flag in his life.

Never raised a fist in solidarity with any cause ever.
Never stood up to question. Never took any risks. If
such a person now tied a thread on his wrist, that is out
of sheer fear. Fear of who? Of what? I threw a glance
at his face. Though speaking on the phone to his friend
about some mutual fund, his eyes were on the road. He
was turning around to take a good look at every new
apartment complex. At each signboard advertising
land for sale, he was sighing that land was becoming
too expensive. Peering at the name board of a house
we passed by as he ended the call, he snarled—'oho, so
these fellows are taking over this area, too!'

He tried to restart the conversation asking, 'Would
Sri's classes be over by now?' A tongue of fire seared
my guts but I stayed silent. We were trying to sneak
into the long queue of vehicles in front of the medical
college. I stole a look at his face again. How long it
must have been since he had a hearty laugh? I pulled
into the parking lot and led him to the canteen. Ignoring
his suggestion that he wasn't hungry, that we could
just pick up Sri and then either eat at home or go to a
non-veg restaurant he liked, I ordered two coffees and
a masala dosa and made him eat. What if he wouldn't
eat anything after?

'Sanghi anna,' I asked, 'do you remember our
childhood home back in Valakam?' I swear, there was
a hint of a smile in his eyes as he said, 'Yes, of course.'
That was a tiled house. The table in the corner of the
low veranda in front was our study area. Though sceptic
about caste and religion, our father insisted on God

and prayer. 'Do you remember how I used to tickle you when we sat on the ground before the lit lamp to recite the evening prayers?' 'Ah, don't I?' He said, 'Didn't I get scolded by Father all because of you? You'd start when he went in, and the prayers would all come out wrong because I giggled. And acchan would call out, "Sanghi . . .!"' He now laughed wholeheartedly.

'You want some unnakkaya?' I asked. 'Now you can get it here too, not just in Calicut.'

His eyes went briefly to the food on display, but because his face fell back to the usual half snarl, my mouth stayed shut. But when we paid the bill and stepped out, I felt utterly drained. So as we came past the security and walked on, I asked him, 'Do you remember the hymns we used to sing back then?' And I recited the Guru's line exhorting us to know that there is One who could swallow both the body and the soul. 'Uh-uh,' said he, and I sighed that I grasped what that meant only now. My voice did falter, you know. But only when we reached the ICU and Nasrin and Isha hurried to us with eyes red and swollen with weeping did Sanghi annan wake to it.

He suddenly looked feeble. 'Wh . . . what's up? What's wrong?'

'Sri was also involved . . . in the beef festival . . .' I struggled to say, 'No serious injuries . . . except to the head . . .'

If it were the older days, I would have wailed louder than him. But not now—am I not the only one who can and should hold him up? Didn't I tell you, in the end Sanghi annan will fall upon our breasts once again? To stay patient, you need anukamba, more and more anukamba . . .

The Othering Machine

Like elsewhere in India, the Othering Machine works full time in Kerala too now. 'Othering' refers to the processes by which some people, or groups, or castes, faiths, genders, ideas . . . whatever, are labelled as not fitting in a social group. It is actually another, less explicit name for hate—a whole bunch of negative characteristics are attributed to the othered person/ group/idea/quality; they are found responsible for all the ills that plague the community in general, and sometimes punished. Cruelty towards the other can get dangerously normalized, as we see evermore frequently in this country and elsewhere. The Othering Machine has always been, but nowadays it is all over the world, and works to nearly full capacity, churning evermore objects for us to hate.

In the past years, we have witnessed the number of Others multiply—women who assert their bodily existence, Dalits who refuse the state's welfare doles and wear black-coloured t-shirts with Ambedkar's

*face boldly embossed on them as a political statement,
the ubiquitous worker from eastern India (Othered
as the 'Bengali'), teenagers who evade parental and
school authorities, girls in sleeveless clothes, single
women who live alone . . . Almost inevitably, each of
these groups is accused of breaking/polluting Malayali
society to differing degrees. Each of these has been
violently ejected or attacked by both state and civil
society, again with differing intensities.*

*But the full force of the Othering Maching seems
to be slowly falling on Malayali Muslims nowadays. It
is not easy to other the Malayali Muslim. Islam's entry
and spread in the Malayalam-speaking regions dates
back to its earliest days, and was not violent. Islam and
other Semitic faiths were welcomed by Hindu rulers
and given a place in the caste order—their followers
filled the place of the Vaishya varna and served the
Kshatriya/Samantha rulers. The role of the valiant
Mappila seafarers in bringing great prosperity to the
Hindu kingdoms of Malabar, as well as their struggles
against the Portuguese, and for the Hindu rulers, is the
stuff of both history and legend.*

*However, the strident anti-Muslim atmosphere,
the changing global exposure of the Malayali Muslims
and their recent prosperity seems to have sped up
the Othering Machine. The Muslim community has
benefited from their migration to the Persian Gulf
countries since the 1970s; their wealth is visible
everywhere; Muslim students are a substantial presence
in higher education; and their styles of dress are now*

both national and global, drawing from Islamic styles from northern India, the Arab countries, Indonesia, Malaysia, the Maghreb, and so on.

Shihabuddin Poithumkadavu's 'K.P. Ummer' is about the Othering Machine. Funny and terrifying at the same time, it revolves around one of Malayalam cinema's most beloved senior actors, (the late) K.P. Ummer. In his career as a movie star, the astonishingly handsome Ummer played the villain, but was beloved as an absolutely non-violent person who once remarked that in his cine-avatar, he had lent his body to the self-destruction of all villainy. But even he cannot escape the Othering Machine.

K.P. Ummer

'K.P. Ummer'

Shihabuddin Poithumkadavu

I once worked for some time as the sub-editor of a children's magazine in Kozhikode.

A not-very-comfortable office, dusty newspapers and magazines stuffed inside, the horde of mosquitoes that arrived to bite you the whole night and feed on your blood, sometimes just for the fun of it, the haphazardly arranged furniture, and in the middle of all this, my wake-and-sleep-and-work.

It was in a moment in the middle of the most damning work-related panic that I received a phone call.

'Hello, I am K.P. Ummer.'

'Who?'

'K.P. Ummer who works in cinema.'

I laughed: 'Hey, Kadar, stop mimicking and making a fool of me in the middle of this crazy-busy time . . . let's meet in the evening.'

I cut the call and got back to work. Then it rang again.

'Hello, isn't this the office of the *Thalolam* children's magazine?'

Ah, K.P. Ummer again.

I remembered his famous movie dialogues: 'Sarade, I am such a sentimental creature . . .'

K.P. Ummer was speaking from the other side: 'You have misunderstood me . . . this is indeed K.P. Ummer speaking.'

Stupefied, I thought: K.P. Ummer—who has never met me, calling me?

Ummukka then said, 'The cartoon that you publish, "Pankru and Chankru", I just love it! Had to go to the US and missed two issues . . . Can you please get them for me? I'll send someone to pick them up.'

I panicked out of sheer astonishment.

K.P. Ummer, one of my favourite cine-stars, the unforgettable, handsome, perpetual villain of Malayalam cinema? He, a fan of Pankru-Chankru? It was about Pankru, who was always the target of conspiracies and attacks—but each time, the innocent Pankru escaped unscathed. Yes, it was popular, but to think that someone like K.P. Ummer was a regular reader? Am I dreaming?

I said, 'Ummukka, I'll bring both issues myself, right now.' The joy and astonishment made my voice break.

So many movies!

The thatch-roofed Rupa Talkies at Poothapppara—so many black-and-white shows in that C-class theatre—the dialogues, the fights with Prem Nazir, the policemen who rushed there in the end clad in their khaki half-trousers and pointed police hats . . . My own Ummukka who would inevitably be either arrested, or die from Prem Nazir's bullets begging forgiveness and soaked in black-and-white blood! When colour film arrived at last, he arrived in the air-conditioned theatres in the city as a powerful patriarch.

Standing in front of the door of the air-conditioned special room in Hotel Maharani, I checked the room number again with a beating heart. Praying that this not be yet another of Kadar's voice pranks, I knocked slowly.

The door opened and there was he, the astonishingly handsome, golden-skinned K.P. Ummer! Age had definitely not withered his charm for sure. The large red-and-yellow towel on his shoulder made him glow like the morning sun. How radiant, his eyes!

When I told him that I was from the *Thalolam* magazine, he curled his lips in that quintessential style and said, 'Welcome', the word perfectly formed.

He pointed to the chair and continued, 'I am very fond of Pankru and Chankru, and always make sure I get a copy of the latest issue of your magazine, no matter how busy my shooting schedule is! Did you know, your magazine is available at the Madras railway station!'

'It is a great relief to see that each time, the evil one gets defeated!' he added.

Yes, that is how we celebrated the Ummukka of the black-and-white times, I thought in my mind.

He chatted on, mixing compassion and knowledge. He had read many literary classics. He stored them in his heart; the non-literary books stayed safe in bookshelves.

In between I also reminded him of some short stories he had written.

'There is no hero or villain in the stories that I write. I am a writer of limited talent. It must be because so many villainous characters have passed through me in movies, the desire to be a villain in real life could not come true.'

'Ummukka, didn't the constant blows and bullets from the hero frustrate you?'

He laughed heartily.

'Maybe because it was all delivered by the gentle and mild Nazir, it never hurt . . .' he said and kept smiling like a child as though he'd recollected something. But soon his face clouded. 'No greater spiritual merit to be earned than making every single villain self-destruct inside oneself! Actors who specialize in villainous characters render more social service than those who play the hero!'

The moment I heard this, I remembered K.P. Ummer of Badiyadukka in a flash. By some quirk of fate, he, who was originally a Gopalakrishnan, came to be known as K.P. Ummer. Even the people of Badiyadukka forgot his original name.

The family of K.P. Ummer of Badiyadukka was a very large one.

He had seven siblings; of these just one was a sister. The oldest was a high court judge. The second brother was a prominent engineer. The others were in Delhi or settled in the US. K.P. Ummer was the fourth. The youngest wandered about here and there and ended up as a poet; his name was Sasikumar. He had not crossed high school but was a gifted writer. I met him many years back when I was hanging about Kasaragod. Prabhakaran introduced me to Sasikumar who was writing then under the pen name *Nishedhi*, or the Rebel.

It was past sunset. Darkness which had stolen inside that ancient *tharavad* house at the height of noon, greeted me.

Outside the rusted gate of that two-storey house built of granite, there was a sign which said, 'Araikkaatt House'. It must have been years since the front yard was cleared of the weeds and grass. But in the distance, the pond lay smiling in the first flush of its youth. The decaying walls with the lime paste peeling off, and the solid rosewood doors faced each other and were in conversation. When we climbed the stairs, at each step the aged plank sniffled. When Sasikumar stepped into the cobweb-covered room and opened the narrow windows, many bats flew in all directions, raising clouds of dust.

Sasikumar smiled a crooked smile through his cross eyes which rarely rested on my face.

'I know that you aren't someone to be brought into such a house,' he said. I put my hand on his shoulder: 'My house was much worse than this.'

'It's been many years since I came to Badiyadukka. I'll clean up all this dust right now. Please stay overnight! I really adore your writing. And besides, tonight is a full moon. There is a small room on the third floor. The ceiling there has glass tiles; we could sit there and see the moonlight. I know that you love the moonlight.'

The little windows which he was opening parted giving out suppressed sobs.

The expansive and solitary silence of the house left me astonished.

I asked, 'Are you all alone in this old house, Sasikumar?'

'No,' he said, 'my older sister—Edathy—lives in two rooms below. She is unmarried. Then I have a brother—Gopalakrishnettan. Our other siblings are all educated and employed in high places; they have flown away and built their nests far away. This dust and cobwebs have been left to us!'

No one seemed to be around, though.

'Gopalakrishnettan is a strange man. He goes to bed only at four at dawn. Edathy has got used to his routine waiting for him.'

'Very strange. No wonder you are such a wanderer!'

His smile was filled with pain. 'For me, this soil is hot; it sears my feet. That is why I console myself by going away.'

We lay on our backs, looking at the glass tiles, and then the moonlight appeared. As we gazed at it, we slowly drifted into sleep.

I started awake some time at night rudely, hearing the deafening sound of a blast from the lower storey.

'Don't be afraid,' said Sasikumar. 'That's Gopalakrishnettan, below. Don't worry, there'll be some more noise, and then he'll go to bed. He is not well. It's been many years now, and I am used to it.'

Like Sasikumar said, soon, there was a commotion below: 'Eda, K.P. Ummare! Did you think that I am an idiot? You rascal! I know that you appear on moonlit nights at my window to see if I am dead yet! Eda, Ummare, tell me, you need some good news to share with that woman when you two are cuddling up together! And that is the news of my death! C'mon, if you are a man! No use just claiming manhood! Stop creeping and stealing around—face me if you dare! This time too you had a narrow escape. But I still have bullets . . .'

I sat up.

'What's all this,' I asked Sasi. 'What's this thing about K.P. Ummer . . .?'

'Yes, it is the cine-actor.'

'The only foe my brother has on the face of this earth is K.P. Ummer . . . he firmly believes and argues that this country will have no progress at all unless K.P. Ummer is exiled. He has written a whole treatise of a thousand and five pages on this, titled *Why K.P. Ummer?* One of the chapters is titled "Why Does the Price of Rice

Rise Unrelentingly?" He establishes theoretically and empirically how and why this is caused by K.P. Ummer. He is a great collector and reader of books.'

Sasikumar sat up on his bed and stretched his limbs. The overwrought moonlight stared at us through the glass tiles.

'When land value rises when it is acquired for the national highway at Badiyadukka, when the trains get too congested, when your favourite candidate loses the election, when population increases, when unemployment soars, when factories close, when there is tension and explosions on the national borders, when someone sets off a bomb in a crowd . . . my brother says, "it can only be the handiwork of that K.P. Ummer."'

'In fact, there is a whole chapter titled "Seventeen Reasons Why K.P. Ummer Should be Expelled from the Nation".'

'In the chapter on "Cinema, Black Money and Swiss Bank Deposits", the connections between K.P. Ummer and Dawood Ibrahim are described at great length. Also, there is a small chapter—an appendix on K.P. Ummer's links with Chhotta Rajan. People here now call my brother K.P. Ummer. They have even forgotten his name, Gopalakrishnan.'

The glass tiles dimmed as large clouds dragged the darkness over them. The full moon was actually cornered and covered now. Sasikumar took out a beedi from under his pillow, lit it, drew a lungful of smoke, breathed it out, and said, 'Gopalakrishnan was the most brilliant one among us.'

He was admitted to Oxford, but he said: cinema is my calling. That is how he joined the Adyar Film Institute. He was so like the Prem Nazir of the old days, so handsome! In those days, the house was a thriving place, with much farming going on. Money wasn't scarce. He was always dressed to kill.

Though many beauties were in hot pursuit of him, he fell for just one—a Malayali woman settled in Bangalore who had come down to study acting, named Mercy. She was a great beauty; but her interest in him was actually quite minor.

One day, when they were chatting casually, Mercy remarked to my brother: 'I like Ummer, not Prem Nazir. The truth is that Ummer ought to have been the superstar, not Nazir.'

It wounded him somewhere. What began as a mild argument ended in a massive quarrel.

And Mercy would deliberately heap praises on Ummer whenever she could, just to provoke my brother. On top, he felt that she was slowly distancing herself. There was some truth in it, actually.

Once, when he was arguing against K.P. Ummer, my brother declared: '. . . Anyway, no matter how high a woman may reach, she cannot be but a teeny bit challenged as far as intelligence is concerned.'

Mercy lost her cool and yelled, 'Shut your mouth!' That was the very last conversation they had.

The stench of patriarchy that my brother had inherited put her off completely.

My brother did not complete his course.

His routine, his speech—all of it began to come unhinged. But nobody really noticed it first, not even Thomas, who used to be with him at the institute, who was from these parts. It apparently happened during a practical session, when they were shooting. They were looking at the scene through the camera's viewfinder.

Someone stood there, someone whose presence was completely unnecessary. It was K.P. Ummer!

'Mr K.P. Ummer, do move out of the field!'

My brother said that Ummer apologized at once but left the field only after bestowing a grim look that promised revenge.

But when he switched the camera on again, K.P. Ummer was dominating the viewfinder.

'Keep to yourself your pride at being a big star,' he lashed out. 'Keep your fame away from my workplace!'

That's when things began to sour at the institute. My brother began to send a series of complaints about K.P. Ummer to the authorities. First to the principal, then to the head of administration. He even wrote to the president about how K.P. Ummer was conspiring to destroy the institute. Some Naxalite-sympathizers among the students were hand-in-glove with him in this nefarious plan—the country must pay heed immediately, he wrote to the authorities—and on the fourth day, a central investigation team laid siege to Adayar and things went terribly awry. Reading the principal's telegram, our eldest brother was utterly shocked.

My brother quarrelled with anyone who tried to defend K.P. Ummer. He had, by then, amassed a whole array of facts and arguments to that end. First, it sounded like a bunch of spiced-up lies, but he soon convinced himself of their truth through sheer repetition. Revenge, lying, convincing, convincing the self—these sprung up around him like the flowering buses of madness. If only K.P. Ummer wasn't around, this world would have been paradise—he got himself to believe. The lies that he crafted lived in the house of madness; they went in and out of it.

In the morning, Sasi and I went downstairs.

There, in the easy chair, he sat, clad in a khaddar jubba starched stiff and ironed perfectly. He sat so erect that the ironing folds of the jubba were quite intact. He had thick eyeglasses on and was reading newspapers. Four newspapers including the *Times of India* were stacked beside him, and the way they were kept there seemed to announce that they were not to be touched by anyone else. His forehead was smeared haphazardly with the sacred ash and in the middle of it was a dark red vermilion mark. His wrists were covered with several sacred wristlets and threads.

Sasi introduced me: 'Gopalakrishnetta, this is Bahis. He is a writer.' Gopalakrishnettan stood up, folded his hands in salutation, and greeted me with a gracious expression on his face and a namaskaram.

He spoke much. There was nothing that he did not have some knowledge of. He had conquered all of it and stored it in that storage bin inside his head. The knowledge was in thrall to him; it waited on him. Jack of all trades, master of none—I whispered to myself almost involuntarily.

Then their sister appeared from inside the house with some black tea, as though from the interior of some ancient cave. The vulnerability of affection rested in her eyes like a becalmed sea.

Sasi touched his brother's feet before he set out again.

He blessed him, touching his head and whispering something.

When we were past the gate, Sasikumar smiled and told me: 'That feet touching is meant to avoid a misunderstanding.'

I looked at him puzzled, and he suppressed a laugh and said, 'If I don't do it, he'll decide that I am off to see K.P. Ummer!'

In Hotel Maharani, Ummukka was talking on and on about world affairs. In the middle, he went in and got a plateful of banana chips. 'These are Kozhikodan chips,' he said, 'fried in pure coconut oil!'

'Do try some,' he urged. Calling the reception and ordering us two cups of tea, he came up and sat next to me, saying, 'now it is all mixed up—you can no longer make out the good from the bad.'

I then put the question to him, very, very reluctantly: 'Ummukka, have you ever heard of a certain Gopalakrishnan from Badiyadukka?'

Many different emotions flashed across his face in a moment. Then, after a brief silence, he said: 'Haven't ever seen him. But I do know! Earlier, he would write at least twice a week. Some Mercy apparently left him because of me; he wanted me to help him patch up with her. This was the very first letter. Later his letters were full of threats and obscenities. I have never even visited the Adayar Film Institute. I learned my acting on the streets. The temple festival grounds and the Party conferences. From the very many plays that we presented in these places.'

'Did you feel annoyed at him?'

'What for? Fame is like a rose. It inevitably has some thorns, too.'

When the banana chips touched my tongue, the divine scent of coconut oil spread all over the room. It made me come alive, suddenly. It was none other than the waking up of hope in life. It crumbled between my teeth with a crispy *kiru-kiru* sound. It is true that the chips did linger for a tiny moment between my teeth, refusing to give way. But then they fell with uncommon delicacy upon my tongue, leading my taste buds on to an extraordinary celebration of life. The tiny crumbly bits of the chips were escorted towards the saliva like a sweetheart led to her lover. In a single second, the pleasure of taste of many years swam by. My eyes closed in ecstasy. Who would disrupt such experience of taste that would have let one live in such joy . . . that question stopped my mind in its path.

When I bid him goodbye, Ummukka asked me, after a moment's thought: 'Do you know Gopalakrishnan of Badiyadukka?'

'His brother is my friend. He writes poetry under the pen name "Rebel"—Nishedhi.'

'I have seen that name.'

Then he again thought for a moment, went inside, and came out with a packet of chips wrapped.

'Can you please give this to Gopalakrishnan?'

'Sure,' I said, 'I will have it delivered.'

'If possible, please deliver it yourself. Banana chips are very good to alleviate Other-hating. When the teeth crush them, our ideas about borders also crumble and scatter. Also, he will soon start becoming aware of the scent of our local coconut oil.' He briefly wiped his eyes with the red-and-yellow towel.

Several moons passed, me seeing some, some seeing me. A postcard would arrive now and then from Badiyadukka. It was Sasikumar. 'Come, let us look at the moonlight again through the tiles of glass. You tell me stories, I will recite poetry for you. Let us be alive for a little while.'

That is how I went back to the Araikkattu family's old mansion after many years. The slippery moss and thriving weeds and grass had not changed much. The gate looked even more human-like and was more rusted than ever. Only the pond seemed ever-youthful, turning to smile at us as she tightened the green-coloured blouse on herself. As we gazed at the full moon through the crystal tiles, I asked, 'Sasi, you weren't around for a long time, right? Where were you?'

'I keep shifting and shuffling my feet when the ground gets too hot . . .' he said. 'That turns into a journey without me even noticing . . . my sister died. A relative now comes over every morning to sweep and clean the house. She brings the meals, home-cooked, for him. She has to eat first; only then will he taste even a morsel. Apparently, there are eyewitnesses to K.P. Ummer going around Badiyadukka in a car with windows fitted with sunshades. And apparently he almost reached this house, in the form of some banana chips. An attempt at poisoning!'

'No end to vengeance, eh?' I asked.

'Gopalakrishnettan has modernized the vengeance a bit; now there is a WhatsApp group named "Anti-K.P. Ummer Committee" or something like that.'

'There are people who'll be part of it?'

'You bet! The overseas president is one Advocate Kunhabdullah based in Dubai! Most of his admirers are based there, actually.'

'Shall I try talking?'

'Are you nuts or something?'

When we came down the wooden staircase the next morning, there he was in the easy chair, in the same perfectly starched spotless jubba.

When we were about to leave, Sasi touched his brother's feet reverentially, like before. He closed his eyes, uttered some mantras and words of blessing.

'I have visited earlier,' I said to him.

'I remember,' he replied. 'I have written down all that we discussed that day in a notebook. It is inside . . . hmm, do you have a WhatsApp number?'

'Yes,' I said, and told him the number.

He added it carefully to his phone.

'We have a WhatsApp group. Now there are more than five hundred members in it. We use some special software also. It is called the Anti-K.P. Ummer Committee. Please add it?'

I nodded.

'Don't let that cad escape, that K.P. Ummer! Please stand with us!'

I asked him: 'Gopalakrishnetta, isn't it many years now since K.P. Ummer died?'

In a split second, I saw a menacing trident lunge out through his eyeballs: 'Isn't it all just him play-acting . . .?'

From behind us, Sasi kept pleading piteously: 'Please, please, don't argue, don't argue . . .'

The Spiritual Entrepreneur

Non-Malayalis tend to think that Kerala is the land of secularism, but nothing could be farther from the truth. Malayalis have always been implicated in religious communities and faiths and their greatest contests that marked periods of intense social change have inevitably been around religious faith.

The early twentieth-century social churning in Malayalam-speaking areas was a time when upper-caste interpretations of the Hindu faith faced severe challenges from lower-caste intellectual, social and political assertions. These were powerful thrusts, but they did not annihilate traditional caste power in the Hindu faith; instead, it merely retreated into the temples and remained largely confined within their walls for a few decades. But by the end of the twentieth century, this power began to rear its head again. The Hindu faith began to expand in unexpected and unforeseen ways. New centres of faith around teachers of Vedanta or living gods, grew apace. Upper-caste nostalgia

about rituals and customs began to climb—and indeed,
reached a crescendo in 2018, when the Supreme Court
allowed women of menstruating ages to undertake
the pilgrimage to the forest shrine of Sabarimala.
Upper-caste sentiment exploded perceiving a breach of
aachaaram—*customary ritual.*

The 1990s and after saw the rise of 'spiritual
entrepreneurship' in Malayali society. Upper-caste
family homesteads often have small temples or sacred
groves dedicated to ancestors or minor deities. Till
the 1990s at least, these were not prominent places of
worship; the plaint was about their neglect and decay.
However, since the 1990s, many sudra *family shrines*
(in the Malayali caste order, sudras are privileged) as
well as some shrines of Ezhavas and some lower castes,
have entered into a new phase of life. They have even
been converted into temples for major Hindu deities.
Some of these have gained much popularity, expanding
the range of rituals and attracting worshippers through
aggressive advertising. The executive committees of
these temples protect and build the 'images' of the
temples, and also build connections between temples.
The erstwhile shrines of ancestor worship recently
converted into Bhagavathy temples, for instance,
add such mass worship rituals such as the ponkaala
(women cooking sweet offerings to the Goddess in
open hearths).

Not surprisingly, the growth of Hindu spiritual
entrepreneurship is deeply intertwined with the rise of

a new Hindu sentiment in the state that is stridently upper-caste, sexually conservative, and often violent.

Unni's superb story takes a close look at this transformation with wry humour and pathos. The politics of the shift is hard to miss: Chandran and Parameswaran, in their youth, were aspiring secular intellectuals. The travails of finding a livelihood lead them into spiritual entrepreneurship—and they try to apply their secular, liberal legacy to it. The result is a strange faith inspired by Vatsyayana, the author of Kamasutra—*which is inclusive, laid-back and sexually liberating. However, this success is woefully short-lived. Capitalism promises us free enterprise; Hinduism claims plurality and even the tolerance of sexual freedoms and non-conformity. But sadly, those are just promises, claims, as the two friends learn.*

The Temple of Vatsyayanan

'Vatsyayanan'

Unni R.

The deity of this temple is an avatar of Bhagawan Krishna. Worshippers have testified again and again to how they have gained offspring, domestic peace, wealth, prosperity and physical well-being through the devotion to the Lord Krishna Vatsyayana. Since over a hundred years now, it is the Brahmin tantris of the Vadakke Illam who have performed the pujas and rituals at this temple that belongs to the Pidikayil family. The main offering is of sweet food, mainly unniappams. The details of the other offerings are as follows:

Kadum Payasam: Rs 50
Koottu Payasam: Rs 50
Trimadhuram: Rs 15

There will be special pujas every Wednesday.
(From the notice printed and distributed by Suresh,
president of the committee of the temple of Krishna-
Vatsyayana, owned by the Pidikayil family.)

When Chandran's mother passed away, the family's
last source of income was extinguished. How was
Chandran to live now? This single thought had caught
hold of Parameswaran over the whole of the past
week and it held him relentlessly now. Chandran did
not have many needs, was not greedy. His body could
easily be fitted on a rice-pounder, that slim it was. But
that wasn't it. There was the bank loan to repay. With
interest. If it was not repaid, he wouldn't even have a
roof above his head. To think that he may have to spend
the rest of his life on some shop veranda or a destitutes'
home? The very thought made Parameswaran utterly
uneasy. Without even telling his wife, he set out early
that morning to meet Chandran.

Chandran was not at home. Parameswaran sat
waiting for him in the veranda. A few hens, a mongoose
and its cub, a cow with its rope loose, and other such
creatures familiar with the house and the premises
came and went through the front yard. When the hens
began to scratch out the *maaran* yam planted at the
spot where Chandran's mother had been cremated,
Parameswaran got up and shooed them away. They
cleared disliked it—Parameswaran could guess from
their gestures and noises. He walked around the yard

for some time. Then came back to the veranda, sat down first, and then, stretched out on the floor. The coolness of the veranda, which knew Parameswaran very well from his childhood, hugged him close.

Chandran's father the accountant Krishnan who had died when Chandran was just twelve, the dog named Tampuran—Lord of the Realm—which opened its mouth only to eat, the native variety mango tree on which Chandran and Parameswaran had clambered up and played on the swing (which was chopped down when there was a cash crunch), the cycle tyre they had taken turns to drive—all these came into the yard and stood there, looking at the sleeping Parameswaran.

'All gone grey—hair and beard,' observed Chandran's father.

'Ah, it's been fifty years, Krishnan *cheta*—will it stay black forever?' asked the cycle tyre.

They did not try to enter Parameswaran's dream and create a nostalgic stir—and give the day a romantic hue. All of them, who had lived their lives as perfect realists, just wanted to catch a glimpse of the boy of the old days—that was all. They just gazed at the sleeping Parameswaran. They disappeared when they heard Chandran's steps.

Chandran and Parameswaran were silent for a few minutes. Parameswaran thought that he was about to speak about how she had raised him alone after his father's death, how the relatives had all scoffed at his mother who was a peon in the local government school, how she would stay awake at night waiting for him, no matter how late he returned, how she had left him all alone, leaving in her sleep . . . about all the pain . . . But Chandran's mind was not going anywere there. Instead, he said: 'Paramu, there isn't a single photo of her here . . . I was at the old headmaster's house to ask if they had one.'

'And what did he say?'

'That they'll find out and let me know.'

'Chandra, did you eat anything? *Ennakilum?*'

He nodded yes but Parameswaran did not believe him.

He took Chandran with him to the town. To the Indian Coffee House, the upper storey. They sat on either side of the table just next to the window that opened towards the market below.

The smell of dried fish bobbed up from within the nets woven of the sounds of the marketplace and peeped at them.

'*Athe*, yes, now what is your plan? *Enna ninte paripaadi?*' Parameswaran asked.

Not looking up from the masala dosa, Chandran replied, 'Not decided yet.'

'Don't you have to make some decision, ennayenkilum?'

Still chewing his food, Chandran nodded.

'Is it going to be book publishing again?'

He raised his head suddenly. The word 'book' brought radiance to his face that quite overpowered the fleeting comfort from eating the masala dosa.

'Shall we publish a short version of the Hobson-Jobson?'

'And who's going to buy those? The printed stuff is still in the corner of the house?'

'My Paramu, we should have published it first! That would have brought us readers! That's where our strategy went wrong!'

'So the rest of our strategy was perfect, uh?'

Chandran tried to smile.

It was a small publisher who used to come to the local Lipi Press who instilled in them the idea that publishing was a noble art. They were just second year BA students then; all the money that they had saved up till then and loans raised with their mothers' gold jewellery were invested in printing five hundred copies of the famous novel that was making waves in high literary circles—*Khasakinte Ithihasam*. The art thus bloomed. However, at the very first sale, they learned that publishing without copyrights was a crime. The small publisher had not warned them of this danger that lay concealed in the art. Thomachan who ran the Lipi Press reassured them that the trouble from four or five copies sold could be remedied by approaching the lawyer Rex Vakeel of Kalvathy, Fort Kochi. That is how they came to meet Rex Vakeel. A short man who wore his hair and beard long. Nothing to fear, he comforted them, and they took courage. Thus baptized by Rex Vakeel, the two friends began to see another face of the world. They did not write the third year BA exam. Visits to home became infrequent. They travelled all over

Kerala. They worked as proofreaders, became editors of journals that died after the second or third issue. Even then Rex Vakeel's advice reverberated in their ears: never mind that you publish just a single book, but it must be a landmark. *Hobson-Jobson: A Glossary of Colloquial Anglo-Indian Words and Phrases and of Kindred Terms, Etymological, Historical, Geographical, and Discoveries*, published in 1886, was that landmark book. Vakeel's marketing research indicated that all the IAS officers in India would buy a copy of it and so it would rake in profits. A translator who the Vakeel himself had hired started working on it. In the middle of this, one day, when he was arguing in court, Rex Vakeel's heart stopped. By the time Chandran and Parameswaran ended their wanderings and returned home, much time had elapsed.

One day, Parameswaran's father Raman Nambutiri said, 'Paramu, you will turn forty tomorrow. You can marry and settle down now if you wish. Or spend the rest of your life gadding about like a dog.'

When Parameswaran remained silent, his mother added: 'There's this girl at Tiruvalla. The man who married her first left. There's a child he fathered. If you agree, we'll approach them. There's still time to become human.'

This was around the time when the first volume of the book with the long title was at the printing press. They had divided the book into three volumes and wanted to dedicate the first one to the memory of Rex Vakeel. That was a time when they had new financial obligations.

Parameswaran spoke with Chandran—remembering the history of the great Malayali Brahmin reformers—of the reformist organization Yogakshema Sabha—like M.R. Bhattatirippad, V.T. Bhattathirippad, and others who married helpless widows from the Brahmin community, he said, let that great history continue in this way at least. And so Parameswaran got married.

'Paramu, I don't mind you and your family staying in this house,' said his father. 'But you must support them yourself.' That single statement felled Parameswaran's claim to be a publisher. That smug claim which he wore like a mundu tucked up on his waist jauntily had to be pulled down humbly.

And so Parameswaran got off books and began to accompany his father to do pujas. Chandran, however, published the remaining two volumes of Hobson-Jobson. It was these volumes that caused the transfer of the ten cents of land that he owned to hands of the America-returned Kunhumon. Even though the interest accumulating on the loan that he had taken to publish these books appeared every month with a precision that rivalled the sun rising every morning, Chandran still gathered courage from Rex Vakeel's claim about the relevance of this book.

'Yes, it isn't about a book,' said Parameswaran.

'Then what?'

'I am going to tell you, and you will just do it.'

'*Ennaa kaaryam*? What are you going to tell me?

After he gulped down two glasses of water, Parameswaran said, 'You must open a temple.'

'A temple?'

'Think of it as a start-up. You won't need to invest a lot. Just do as I say.'

Chandran looked blank.

'Isn't there a temple in the yard in front of your house?'

Nodding in agreement, Chandran said, 'Yes, but not much of a temple. A small room, a hut of sorts, barely big enough for one.'

'That's big enough! What deity did you worship there?'

'Well, not very clear, really. Some stone—half sunk in the soil. Some elder, a *karanavar*, maybe, set it there. Amma used to light a lamp there sometimes.'

'That'll do,' Parameswaran said after a moment's thought. 'We'll turn it into an exclusive temple.'

'Exclusive temple?' That left Chandran baffled. He was hearing about such a thing for the very first time.

'Yes, we will make it the temple of Vatsyayana.'

'Paramu, what are you saying!'

'Just listen to me first! Just put out an ad—Pray in the temple of Vatsyayana and cure yourself of sexual impotence; increase your sexual prowess! And hey, it is sure to click!'

'Kind of gross, isn't it?'

'Yeah, sure, super-gross! But who's going to pay off your bank loan? The neighbours? You hung on till now because of your Amma's pension. What will you do now? Will your rich relatives give you a paisa even? Did any of the members of the Pidikayil family show up to look you up when she died? Chandran Pidikayil, you call yourself! What's the use of that family name? Aren't you ashamed of dangling it so?'

As Parameswaran's voice rose, looks from diners at other tables around them flowed towards them rapidly.

Even when he was sipping the last of the second cup of coffee, Chandran could not step into the temple that Parameswaran was pointing him to.

'Chandra, you have to decide now. If you can't, leave it right now.'

'No, Paramu, it isn't that . . . you know perfectly well that I don't really care for temples and faith . . .'

'Ah! Am I doing the puja business because I believe in it fervently? I go two days a week to a temple in Thiruvanchoor. I shut the door of the sanctum and sit there. Last week, I finished the whole of Mammen Mappilai's autobiography sitting inside there! In the middle, I just ring the bells a couple of times.'

'Alright, so what do you want me to do?'

'Now, tell me, what inauspicious things have happened there?'

'You know—Amma died.'

'What else?'

'The cat fell inside a well; a crow got roasted on the electricity line; and a *kanjiram* tree in the yard fell.'

'Ha! More than enough to commission a divination! An *Asthamangalya Prasnam*! I'll do it and announce a remedial ritual!'

Chandran just nodded. Ordering a double omelette, Parameswaran continued, 'We must clear the bushes around the temple and give it a new coat of paint. There's an old granite sculpture I brought back from Bastar . . . lying somewhere in the loft. Let's just brush the dust and grime off it, and it will do very well . . . we'll consecrate it.'

Chandran nodded again but said nothing.

'I'll give you the money to get this done. Once your amma's *sanjayanam* and the fortieth-day feast and the period of pollution to be observed after the death are done, we can begin.'

Chandran wasn't unwilling but still felt a tiny niggling doubt. 'But won't we have to hire someone to conduct the puja there? Pay a salary?'

'For what? You are good enough a pujari! Just shut the doors of the sanctum, read a favourite book! That's the secular idea of worship for you!'

Chandran had always been fond of secularism, and so his face now bloomed and did justice to his name. 'Chandran' means the 'moon'. His face now looked radiant, like the full moon.

They searched the loft of Parameswaran's house and found the sculpture from Bastar after a lot of effort. A statuette of a laughing man with a penis so long that reached right up to his knees and lower.

'Who's this?' asked Chandran.

'From today he is Vatsyayanan,' replied Parameswaran. 'Remember, I got him from Bastar. Apparently, there used to be someone there who used to go around the place laughing all the time and dangling a really long tool like this one! This was a carving of him.

I thought it interesting and so got it. Couldn't really keep it in the open, so stored it away inside the loft.'

Chandran liked this new entrant. The kind of fellow you'd take a liking to.

'My wife's brother runs a cable TV channel back in their place. Let's advertise in it—"The only temple in the whole country dedicated to Lord Vatsyayanan is re-opening soon!" And we can add stuff like—"The *darshan* here is eminently recommended for the fulfillment of your sexual desires" and "Special remedial pujas and rituals available!"'

'Do we need to go . . . that far?' Chandran sounded reluctant.

'It's not to murder someone, is it? Just to fulfill sexual desire?'

'But things like . . . seduction . . .?'

'You don't have to do anything unethical. Just do what you think is right. From the *dakshina* that you will earn, you can feed yourself! And if you're lucky, you can pay off your bank loan, too.'

'But if people approach us for remedial rituals, we have to tell them something?' Chandran was still doubtful but Parameswaran had an answer to that too. In the house in the isolated corner next to Chandran's yard lived Sumathi Amma; she was at one time the woman who most men in that locality dreamed about. In those days, the entire male population there bowed low before her, paying obeisance to that magnificent area that lay below her waist. Now she's old and retired. Besides, she stopped going out after her husband Damodaran lost his eyesight. She was so much in love with him, and he, with her.

'Just tell her everything, frankly. Ask her if she can help from her vast experience in case some *bhakths* had doubts and needed some practical advice. You must also promise her a share of the dakshina.'

Chandran liked the idea very much indeed.

After his mother died, Chandran's meals were all at Sumathi chechi's house. When they sat down to supper that day, he told her everything. He had expected a mighty cussword, but it was actually a big laugh that followed. He was relieved.

When he handed over the money to get the premises of the temple cleared and to give it a new coat of paint, Parameswaran also gave Chandran a cellphone with WhatsApp installed in it. Chandran consecrated Vatsyayana in concrete all by himself. He cleared the bushes, too.

Three days after the advertisement went on air, a certain Mathews called from Vaduthala. He was reluctant to come during the daytime. Is it OK to come after dark, he asked. When told that darshan was allowed throughout day and night, he sounded thankful. The day after, when it was past ten at night, Mathews paid them a visit. A middle-aged man. Was into prawn harvesting, did a bit of usury, and was also an actor by the side. He followed their directions perfectly and left his car on the other side of the yard. The lights of the vehicle beamed bright as though filled with the bewilderment at having reached a totally unfamiliar place; they stared on steadily for some time. After they were switched off, the thin stream of light from Chandran's torch approached the car.

'Come on, please,' Chandran invited Mathews formally.

Mathews stepped out of the car in response, as though he was about to do something forbidden. He walked alongside Chandran. When they neared the temple, Chandran switched off the torch.

'Here, this is the shrine,' said Chandran, opening its doors.

Seeing Vatsyayana with his big smile and big dick in full display amidst the splendour of many lit lamps, Mathews could not help smiling for a bit.

Seeing the smile spread on Mathews' face, Chandran too felt elated.

'What *aachaarams* must we perform here?' Absolutely respectful towards the deep silence of late night, Mathews whispered.

'There's no such ritual. You can just worship in a way you are comfortable with.'

Mathews did not get it.

'If you want to fold your hands in prayer, then that way. Or cross yourself and pray; or even lift up your mundu . . .'

That was not something he expected. Then, after a few moments of silence, he asked, 'OK, then shall I cross myself and pray?'

Maybe because he had bothered to drive all the way, Mathews decided to pray. He crossed himself and kneeled in front of the shrine and prayed for a full fifteen minutes.

He expected some blessed food—prasadam—since it was the practice in temples to give it to devotees. But instead, surprising him, Chandran asked, 'Did you have any supper?'

He wanted to lie first, but then desisted.

'Come,' Chandran called him.

He followed Chandran. As they went, Mathews' voice caught up with Chandran in an utterly unhurried way. 'I have something to talk.'

'I know,' replied Chandran 'We are going there.' When he said that, Chandran's voice took on the tone of someone who possessed the powers of divination, of seeing the mind of another, without him knowing.

Making their way through the dense foliage that covered the yard more than the darkness of the night itself, Chandran, Mathews, and the torchlight reached Sumathi Amma's house.

She was sitting on the open veranda when they reached. Chandran introduced Mathews. She went inside to get him some supper.

'Who is this?' Mathews asked.

'The temple oracle,' said Chandran. That was what came to his mind at that moment.

Mathews nodded.

After he finished supper, Mathews revealed the reasons behind his visit, rather hesitantly. Sumathi chechi listened to all of it patiently, and then told him how to deal with it.

Getting ready to leave, Mathews held out some cash to her. She merely pointed to Chandran and with a single word, 'There', she stepped back in and shut the door.

Mathews tried his best to persuade Chandran to accept the money, but he refused.

'Let everything become alright,' he said, 'and we will see.'

Next morning, Chandran told Parameswaran in detail about how the very first bhakth from Vaduthala had visited them and about his troubles, too. When he had sex with his wife, his dick would suddenly shrink and collapse as though paralysed. But it was always fine when he fucked other women. This was growing into a complex problem between wife and husband. The wife felt that some awful disease, like the root wilt that felled tall coconut palms, had afflicted her husband's member. He knew, of course, what it actually was. He had come here to find a way to avoid this wilting.

'And what did Sumathi chechi say?' Parameswaran was eager to know.

'Sumathi told him flat to his face—you just don't like your woman, that's it. Just that—there's nothing wrong with your goods. Your thingie stands right up when it sees other women? If you start liking your woman then this will be cured, fully. The root will stay strong—nothing will wilt it. Love is the axis—if it doesn't exist, not just your dick, but you yourself will fall flat.'

'Chandra, our Sumathi chechi is a wise woman, uh? *Bhayankara* philosophy!'

'Yes, I was thrown too! That guy was melting, nearly, hearing all that. But it was OK because I'd told him that she is the oracle and all that.'

'And then?'

'Then what? He just sat there and yowled and yelped like a puppy! She comforted him first, and then I did.'

'Did you get any dakshina?'

'Paramu, how to take any money from this sort of person? Just seeing him yowl like that made me feel so sad! I didn't take any money.'

'My dear Chandra, why couldn't you take what he offered? I've set this up so that I can see you prosper a bit! Not to get random passers-by to come here and moan and groan . . .!'

'That isn't it, Paramu . . . we'll take the money . . . let him get a little better . . .'

'Oh, you are NEVER going to learn,' said Parameswaran, adding a few select expletives. Declaring that he didn't want to see him anymore, he told Chandran to leave.

After Mathews, many people began to make discreet phone calls. Some of them came over and prayed too, in secret. Some came when dawn was barely breaking; others, late at night. Except for one or two women, all devotees were men. That a few children came became a cause of worry for Chandran. Because he still held fast to the idea that all deserved equal respect in a democracy and because he did not believe in censorship, he did not prevent them from coming. Many of these phone calls directly sought practical advice. Sumathi chechi gave them excellent counsel. Paramewaran knew that there was nothing foolish or impractical in Chandran's hesitation about taking dakshina. But strangely, as though they felt the same as Parameswaran, many devotees just left some dakshina somewhere, on the door of the temple after worship or under the betel box on the veranda of Sumathi chechi's house after the visit to the oracle. Sumathi chechi certainly was not greedy for cash. She wouldn't take what Chandran offered her, even. When people insisted on paying him, Chandran would request them to bring rice or provisions next time, or better still, tapioca or mangoes or something that they could pluck from their own yards at home. Or a sapling, or a seed, would suffice too as dakshina. When these things began to arrive in large quantities soon, he gave them away first to the neighbours, and then to places that needed them, like destitute homes. Many would send money after they returned home with grateful thanks to Sumathi chechi and Vatsyayanan.

Chandran had many occasions to watch, his mouth hanging open with awe, Sumathi chechi offer advice on a whole range of problems, from troubles with anal sex to violence in sex with utmost ease, as though she were merely removing a thorn or barb.

But even on such occasions, there was one nagging issue that kept circling him incessantly. She had a way of spitting the whole damn thing out, in very rustic Malayalam, with no care at all about who her listeners were or where they came from. When this happened, Chandran's usual response was to just look down and stay still. Once he spoke with Parameswaran about making an effort to clean up her talk. But Parameswaran was insistent that trying to take apart Sumathi chechi's turn of phrase that was so uniquely organic would be to Sanskritize it, something totally unjustified. All that Chandran demanded was that Sumathi chechi should use some of the words that Parameswaran had employed—for example, 'organic'. He would have much preferred that she use a little more lightly words like 'cum', 'blowjob', 'ass', 'pussy', 'cock', and so on—and opt for more serious ones. Parameswaran, however, disagreed completely and so Chandran too withdrew from that attempt to Sanskritize.

The realization that not a single devotee had been disappointed, evident from their later phone calls, drove away the seemingly perennial fatigue that had taken over Chandran's body. The flow of money orders over six months made it possible to rehaul the house and the roof, give the house a new coat of paint, buy a new almirah for the books, clean Sumathi chechi's well, and get a new water pump too. At this rate, in two years, all of Chandran's debts would be paid back—Parameswaran felt really relieved.

Sitting in a bar in town, he asked, 'Chandra, what do you think now?'

Chandran smiled mildly and replied: 'What you said about the chance to read many books was true indeed! The other day, someone from Kothamangalam

had come. They came early, at four-thirty in the
morning. I told them to pray and got inside the room
and shut myself in. I'd kept a copy of Puthuppally
Raghavan's autobiography ready. I started reading it,
and quite forgot the time! One hour later, I suddenly
became aware of the time. I rang the bell inside a
couple of times and opened the door. That chap was
still there, lost in prayer, hands folded! I forgot the
time, so did he!'

'My dear Chandra, that isn't what I meant—hasn't
your life climbed back somewhat now? Don't you feel
somewhat peaceful now? Tell me!'

Chandran took up a handful of the spicy mixture
that seemed to have gathered together all the sorrows
of the world into its sharp chilli taste—a savoury mix
of fried things the fate of which, it seems, is to lie
in plates on the tables of bar, free of all controlling
centres. He said, 'You know what is at the bottom of
all these troubles? The lack of love! Just that!'

Parameswaran saw his eyes well up—why, he
didn't know—maybe it was the chilli of the mixture,
or maybe it was the high tide of emotion induced by
the two pegs of liquor . . .

'My dear Paramu, though her tongue is foul, this
Sumathi chechi is quite someone! Be sure to love in
and out of bed; be respectful of each other; trust each
other—if you can manage these three things, she says,
you can, in her words, bang marvellously well even if
you are on your deathbed.

'Really?' Parameswaran found that hard to believe.

'Yes, that's her cure-all!'

'Will someone turn her into a living god, Chandra?' There was a tinge of worry in Parameswaran's voice.

'Hey, no! She isn't that cheap!'

Jubilant at the gradual success of their attempt to start a business of faith that was beyond religious and caste divides and free of bogus rituals and prayers and offerings of all sorts, the two friends celebrated with a couple of extra pegs. When they stepped out of the bar, Chandran told Parameswaran, 'Look, Paramu, I have a little something to tell you—please don't get angry!'

'Oh, just shoot—anything, Parameswaran was swaying in ecstasy, filled with love and compassion.

'When I am done repaying my debt, I want to get the biography of someone written, and publish it.'

That was unexpected. Parameswaran grabbed the wall next to him to steady himself and asked, 'Whose?'

'I'll tell you when it is time.'

Though he was quite certain that not even a single copy of that book would be sold, Parameswaran still lifted his arms and saluted the publisher who had not fully exited Chandran's inner self.

When they were going to climb into an autorickshaw and go home, the waiter brought them the parcel of beef fry that Chandran had bought for Sumathi chechi and her husband—he had forgotten it in the bar.

Chandran held him close, wrested some control over his slurring tongue, and said, 'God resides in this bar, in you, in this beef fry, and this *chetan* who will drive us in his auto.'

When the auto reached the turn of the road towards home, Chandran said that he would get down there.

Parameswaran offered to drop him at home, but he refused. It was dark there; the only light was inside Chandran—from his total familiarity with the place. Chandran walked slowly. Suddenly, a few young men stepped up from the dark. Chandran did not recognize them first.

'Cheta,' one of them said to him, 'I am Suresh—Pidikayil Suresh.'

He was Chandran's father's younger brother's younger son.

'What's up, Eda?' Chandran asked him.

'Where are you coming from?' It was another guy in the group who asked. He did not look familiar. Chandran did not reply.

'Didn't you hear the question?' It was as though the questions too were forming a circular snare around him, like the men.

'I was at the town,' Chandran said to them.

'What a reek!'

Chandran did not respond.

'Yes, we've been noticing this for some time . . . was just waiting to see how far this would go. Well, you'd better shut shop soonest.' That was Suresh.

'I don't get you?' Chandran said.

'That's our family temple, too. Hard to tolerate your monkey business in there, Cheta! You go in there without bathing or washing yourself after a dump . . . and we as a family have to suffer the evil from it! That's no good!'

Chandran was silent for a few moments. Then, in his usual low-key style, he said, 'This temple is in my property. As far as I can remember, none of these family members that you talk of have ever come there to worship or light a lamp. My mother too could recall nothing of that sort. So then how can you say such things, Suresh? This is my business, mine alone.'

'Hey fucking *mayire* . . . crotchfur . . .! Let me just throw it at you—you'd better stop messing around inside the temple! If you won't, we too won't bother about blood and kin connection and all that!' Suresh's face was just next to Chandran's when he muttered these words angrily.

'Let him go . . .' One of the men pulled Suresh aside and stepping up towards Chandran, said: 'Edo, you won't get it now. We'll tell you when you are sober. Go for now. If we have to tell you later, it won't be like this!'

For some time, Chandran could not even walk as he felt a sudden cold weight grow on his legs.

Seeing him sit on the veranda quietly staring at the dark without eating his supper, Sumathi chechi asked him what the matter was. But he didn't tell her anything; he just went home.

He lay sleepless in bed. Then he got up, went over to his mother's bed, and sat there for some time. Then went out and sat on the veranda's half-wall. After some time, he returned to his room and lay down again. And drifted into sleep at some moment.

He woke up when the phone rang early at daybreak. It was Chacko, that chap from Kaippuzha. He wanted directions to reach the temple. From what he said, Chacko was barely ten minutes away. Chandran brushed quickly. He knew that the memories from last night would not go away soon but took a long bath. He made himself coffee. Closed his eyes tight when the sour taste from last night's happenings became unbearable. Chandran found it insufferable. How they had abused him! Were ready to beat him up! Called his parents such names! The more he thought of it, the closer he was to tears. In the end, he opened his eyes and waited for Chacko.

Chacko was getting rather late. Chandran called him as the time dragged on. He called him several times, but he did not pick up. He had been so near—what might have happened? Chandran felt the tug of an unnecessary fear. Setting aside the fear, he stepped out to open the temple. As he went closer, he spied some vague figures lingering in the dark. Gripped by fear, Chandran asked 'Who?' There was no reply. Again, he asked, 'Who is it?' There was no answer, but they opened the darkness and came towards him. They were all people he knew. But the mask of unfamiliarity covered their faces. Chandran tried to talk with them. They did not respond. That silence between them soon grew stale.

All the brinjal plants and the greens lovingly gifted by the devotees were now trampled underfoot. Two people pulled off and threw aside the bitter gourd vine and its trellis as though it were a mere cobweb. The mangosteen sapling that Mathews had brought was pulled up with its roots intact; the man who did it now gazed intently at it with a botanist's curiosty. Suddenly some of them began to clamber up on the old varikka jackfruit tree that stood next to the temple, a tree that had been either planted by some elder in the dim past of this family or grown from a seed dropped there by some bird; a tree which had grown past many decades now. Their machetes slashed its branches that held out shade and coolness all around. In the end, felled by the repeated blows on its trunks, that venerable tree-body crashed down helplessly on the earth. In that yard that was earlier filled with gentle green weeds and small trees, the heat arrived in new battle formations, a whole *akshauhini* of warriors and beasts and chariots, like in the Mahabharata, ready for war.

'Chandraa,' Parameswaran called.

Chandran looked at him. Parameswaran racked his brains. He still didn't know how to begin.

The Predator and the Prey

At the beginning of the last century, vast areas of what was to become present-day Kerala were heavily forested. Far from the familiar crude caricatures of forest-dwellers, the adivasis possessed the necessary skills for survival in the formidable rainforests of the Sahya mountains. The twentieth century saw their tragic marginalization and exploitation: the white colonial authority, and then the non-forest-dwelling elite—used these skills and knowledge extensively to gain control over it. Adivasis were increasingly stripped of the claim to humanity. Modernity for them was 'bureaucratic modernity'—singularly oppressive.

Towards the end of the twentieth century, with neoliberalism opening up resources and spaces, predatory entrepreneurs made their appearance on the forest fringes. Tourist resorts that violated the law, and extractive industries like granite quarries, began to pose new threats to forest- and forest-fringe-dwellers.

But the adivasis of Kerala asserted themselves more forcefully in the 1990s for land and rights—even though it was evident by now that all forces in organized politics were against them and with land-grabbers. In 2003, when the police 'evicted' the members of the Adivasi Gotra Sabha who had occupied the Muthanga forests stung by the government's false promises of land, eighteen rounds were fired, five protestors were killed. Kerala's celebrated history of 'public action'— democratic pressure for resources and well-being on the state—rang hollow. When adivasis mounted public action, they received bullets and lathis. The magic of the 'Kerala Model' snapped.

P.V. Shajikumar's story brought back painful memories of 19 February 2003, the day of the police firing at Muthanga. Stunned, if only because our own faith in the Kerala imagined by the lovers of democracy of the past century was shaken, some of us went to the usual site of protests in the city—the road in front of the Kerala State Secretariat—expecting crowds of indignant people. But no. There were exactly seven of us.

Varadan's terrible loneliness and the precarity of his existence, the casual cruelty of the political class engrossed in its games of power and pleasure—these are realities we would like to shut our eyes to. Yes, the adivasis of Kerala probably suffer worse than their Indian counterparts. But it is not just about their small numbers. It is also not just about access to education— indigenous people in Kerala today perform better than their counterparts elsewhere, for instance, in literacy. But marginality is not just about just material deprivation. Remember, here we are also talking of feeling, inner experience, in this instance, of suffering. Varadan's inner world is filled with memories of struggle for rights, dignity and justice; with the perception of tremendous injustice and cruelty unfolding all around; with the acute perception of how his skills, knowledge and feeling are devalued. It throbs with constant hurt.

As Shajikumar's story tells us with subtlety and compassion, the Malayali indigenous person probably suffers oppression with greater intensity. This is because of a tragic betrayal. When, finally, they fought for and gained entry into the theatre of democracy as empowered citizens, the adivasis of Kerala found it empty and meaningless, vandalized by predatory capital and unscrupulous power-mongers.

Null and Void

'Asaadhu'

P.V. Shajikumar

As he got out of the bus and began running up the road that lay curled uphill like a python after swallowing its prey, three fancy cars and a larger vehicle—a Tempo Traveller—went past Varadan. They were headed for the resort, Swargam. They had to get past fifteen steep hairpin bends on the road to get there. Varadan was undeterred by neither the steep climb nor the transient but by the cloudy hills of dust that the vehicles left behind. Ramanandan, who was in the last of the cars, saw him and was immediately captivated. This guy might even outrun the car—the thought did strike him. Then there was a call on WhatsApp, and he put it on speaker, and forgot Varadan. 'Yes . . . we are almost here,' he said.

Varadan was just past the sixth bend on the road. A girl who was coming downhill with a load of forest vines on her head flashed a smile at him. He used to see her here sometimes. He returned the smile. The wild plants and trees, animals and birds, looked intently at him running.

Varadan had started running the day he learned to walk. He *had* to run—even if it was only a little. 'This fellow couldn't bear to be lying down; he was running in there too . . .' Pointing to her belly that hung down decisively like a bell, Boli used to complain to all the women who came to see the baby.

When he reached the tenth bend, Varadan called Matangi. He knew that it was hard to reach her, but he felt like calling. There was never adequate network—at home or at work. You were lucky if you found two bars on BSNL on top of the hill at Chaligadda! And if there was wind and rain, then that too will vanish. The usual thing to do was to add your guesses into the broken conversations, complete them on either side.

They used to talk in the evenings. He was freer then. Her worries would have calmed by then. Five-thirty: that was the time he set. By the time she wrapped up things and came uphill, it would be dark. The dark made him afraid; she did not fear it, though. He would try to end the call without letting her speak much. She would try to speak much and not end the call.

Bringing the broken display screen closer, Varadan tried to find out what the time was. It was past nine. Work started at nine. Today, the manager, Tom Thomas, was going to fill his belly with choicest cusswords—he was certain. Varadan was returning from home. Every Friday, after work, he would leave for his native place, his home. According to the shift, Saturday was the holiday. It was a month now since he started working here.

He had set off from his *kudi* at three at dawn. Without eating anything. There was nothing to eat. Cross two hills, and by four, you can catch the bus that goes to town. He'd started running at three, and it ended at the bus stop; then again, he was running from the bus stop. The two bowls of cold water that he had drunk when he stepped out of the kudi seemed to be leaping up and down. Water in the belly was beginning to give him a stomach ache. Varadan pressed down on the left side of his stomach and did not let the ache affect his run.

When he reached the reception, the rain ran after him and tried to hold him. Wrapping both its arms around him from behind.

There was no one there. He could hear Tom Thomas's words and so realized that a workers' meeting was on in the hall on the left side. He slipped into the dormitory, pulled out the sweepers' uniform from the wall closet and wore it. Opening the door to the hall soundlessly, he heard Tom Thomas speak. He was concluding his speech. Abhishek, who was also a sweeper, gestured a hi to him with his eyes. He tried to smile back.

'Everyone is ready, I suppose?'

Tom Thomas was asking his audience. Heads shook together. Though he could make nothing of it, Varadan also shook his head—what if they did pay the salary!

The meeting ended. A buzzing rose from the hall like someone had hit a beehive with a stone.

'Hey . . . If you have to call someone now, do it immediately . . . you may not be able to call later.'

Abhishek told Varadan as he dialled his girlfriend's number. Seeing his stumped expression, he explained.

'We have all been asked to surrender our cellphones to the reception in half an hour.'

'Surrender . . . what's that?' Varadan asked.

'Oh, they want to keep our phones. No idea when they will return them.'

Varadan started.

'What for?!!'

'Don't know . . . something big is happ'ning . . .'

Abhishek lowered his voice.

'We are not to go out without that asshole Tom Thomas's permission . . . so . . . need to go back in the evening . . . they won't let me?' Varadan became very uneasy.

'*Alla*, how can that be?'

'I don't know. Now, call if you want . . .' Abhishek went after his girlfriend. Varadan was left alone. Everyone was on the phone, speaking with different shades of emotion on their faces. He took out his phone from his pocket to call Matangi. He had no one else to call. The woman inside told him that Matangi could not be reached. Nowadays he heard that response more frequently. He used to rib her about that—was she making the woman say that? She responded with a few familiar oaths.

Tom Thomas passed by Varadan's side busy with a phone call and talking into a headset's mouthpiece pulled close to his mouth. Varadan lowered his arms and looked at him humbly. Chances of Thomas noticing a dog over Varadan were higher. Fixing his eyes on the breaking news on TV, he pressed the elevator button to the sixth floor. Ramanandan was in room number 603, sipping on Jack Daniels and checking his mobile phone. Thomas stood before him with utmost reverence.

'Is everything OK?' he asked, not taking his eyes off the phone screen.

'Yes, saar, we are going to collect and stow away the mobile phones of all employees. Have given strict orders that no one is to step out until things get sorted out.'

'Good. There are sixteen persons. They should be taken care of in every way. You have to be here constantly to make sure. Understand?'

'Sure, Saar.'

'And you have not assigned rooms to any other guest?'

'You had left instructions that no room should be allotted to anyone else.'

'I'll be paying for all the rooms. We can't afford any change of plans; we'll lose our grip.'

'OK, Saar.'

'Saar, it's begun to appear as breaking news.'

'I saw. That was bound to come. It wasn't totally hidden or something.'

'Yes, Saar.'

When Tom Thomas turned to go, Ramanandan called him. He handed over six crisp two thousand rupee notes.

'No, thank you, Saar,' he said.

'Ah! Take it, man! With my compliments! You'll receive many more! Just keep the guard up with your very life!'

Tom Thomas nodded approvingly. Ramanandan was reminded of the feng shui laughing Buddha, bringer of good luck. The phone rang when Tom Thomas stepped out of the room, and Ramanandan picked it up and spoke in Kannada.

'Day after tomorrow is Independence Day. The Assembly will not meet for a few days. You know well, the hours that we have now are crucial. These fellows are little better than cattle. Loosen the rope, and they will escape. I'll settle the cash today itself. A decision must be taken before tomorrow evening.'

A famous Malayalam actress was on the line now. Ramanandan's face took on a shade of libidinousness that looked decidedly odd on it. He cut short the conversation in Kannada, promised to call back at night, and fell on the bed, dialling her number.

When Tom Thomas descended the steps with the money Ramanandan had given him in the back pocket of his trousers, he saw Varadan stand there, mop in hand. He frowned.

'What's it, fellow?'

Varadan broke out in cold sweat. He was terrified by people who bristled with confidence, and people who spoke too loudly. He was alarmed by the thought that the world was indeed under their feet. His words would get caught in his throat. He began to cough hard; Tom Thomas moved away from him. Varadan followed him.

'What's it?'

He suppressed the cough.

'Need to go back to my kudi today, Saar.'

Tom Thomas whirled around.

'Ah! Not bad, uh! But you just came back today?'

'Have to go, Saar, there is a probl'm.'

He bowed his head so that Tom Thomas would not see his face.

'Then why the fuck did you drag that corpse-like body of yours here?'

For my salary, Varadan wanted to say. Tom Thomas's phone rang.

'No, you can't. No matter what your problem is.' He cut the call and said with pitiless insistence.

'I must go, Saare, I must go!'

His words were hard as stone.

'You won't be allowed to, Varada, not even if the person who brought you to me came here in person and requested. That's how things are here at this moment.'

'Don't say that, Saare, it is a bad problem.' He was about to fall at his feet. Thomas jerked his foot back as though he'd trodden on a slithering thing.

'That MP who recommended you deserves a beating. Leave if you want. But don't show your face again. You won't get the tenth day wage either.'

That upset Varadan's rhythm totally. He fell silent instantly.

'*Jaathyaalullathu thoothaal povillallo* caste defective cannot be made effective.' Thomas recalled traditional wisdom. 'I never wanted to appoint a senseless idiot!'

Everyone at the reception desk could hear him. Tom Thomas's voice was loud. He did not need a mic to address a meeting. His voice reached everywhere. Beads of sweat rolled on Varadan's forehead.

'So, you won't be leaving?' he asked, seeing his strained expression. Varadan shook his head. He discovered that the droplets of dirt on the mop all reflected Tom Thomas's coke-bottle glasses.

'Edo,' Thomas called Subhash who was handling the reception. 'Haven't you removed this fellow's mobile phone?'

'Yes, Saar.'

'Uhm . . . then, go, get cracking, do your job!'

Thomas tightened his belt and went off to the restaurant to tuck in the puris and chicken mapas. Varadan drank a couple of glasses of water from the water dispenser in the corner of the reception and got into the lift. He was going to mop the hallway on the ninth floor. The Varadan in the mirror inside the elevator stared at Varadan. The Varadan in blue trousers and shirt was a stranger.

The candidate who contested the last Lok Sabha elections from Varadan's constituency was the opposition leader in the last Lok Sabha, Gokul Sahi. Till then, Varadan's family had lived in the deep forests, and they were used to the wants and lacks of that life. Varadan was one of the pawns in the moves devised by Party workers to please their leader. Varadan knew absolutely nothing about the winding trails that lay coiled inside the space of politics, but he was presented by them as a loyal worker with the Party spirit in his very blood. They painted the walls of his insecure mud hut white and drew the Party symbol and the candidate's face on it. Gokal Sahi faced the forest with a smile, his hands folded. They replaced the roof of the hut with asbestos sheets painted the colour of the Party flag. They framed pictures of Gokul Sahi's parents and grandparents and hung them on the wall inside.

'Who are all these people?'

Mathangi and Boli asked him.

'People from Hindi movies', he had told them, holding his head up, sounding like an all-knowing fellow.

'An Adivasi Family with Unending Love for Gokul Sahi,' ran the headline.

'Our family has had a close and loving relationship with Gokul Sahi's family from a very long time. That he is fighting the election from our constituency brings us such happiness!'

Varadan said such things in the reports.

When one of the Party supporters read this news out to him, his mouth fell open with surprise. A bee that had lost his way wandered in there. He had to cough quite a bit to get it out.

When the channel reporters arrived, the Party workers got him to deliver the right sentences. Some people thought that he sounded like the government ads that were translated from Hindi to Malayalam. They fed Boli with two glasses of arrack and made her break down in front of the camera. She is weeping for Gokul Sahi's murdered mother, the channels whined.

Seeing the news, Gokal Sahi took time away from his election campaign and came to visit Varadan's hut with his sister. Tapioca, chicken fry, fish curry and payasam were brought from the Taj hotel. The Party workers announced that Matangi had cooked these for her guests. Gokul Sahi and his sister shared lunch with Varadan and his family. After he left, the mandalam president took away the rest of the chicken fry for their booze party.

'Can't they just live inside the cinema? Why take so much sun?' Boli asked as she sunned her legs.

Later in the evening, Matangi got stomach cramps and vomited; the unfamiliar food had not suited her. When the vomiting grew worse, Boli knew what it was. Varadan carried her on his shoulder and crossed the hills. When the sun came down spreading the carpet of light on the veranda of the government hospital, he was the father of a boy. Three of their earlier children were lost in the womb. That this little one had arrived without much trouble was a blessing; Varadan thanked God and Gokul Sahi. In the TV set in the hospital veranda, a leader was making a rousing speech. He could not make out a single word of it, but Varadan gave his son his name: Sampath—'wealth'.

The framed pictures of Gokul Sahi's family on the wall later became useful; they were the fiends who were pointed at to scare little Sampath into eating his meal when he fussed over it. The wind and rain and sun wiped off most of his smiling face on the hut's outer wall, but spared the grin. Of the slogan 'Elect Gokul Sahi for a Starvation Death-Free India' painted below it, just 'Starvation Death' was spared. When he won, Gokul Sahi did not forget Varadan. Upon his recommendation, Swargam hired Varadan at a salary of six thousand a month.

'Varada, don't kill us,' the spiders hanging on the ceiling of the corridor opened all their arms in a plea. He lowered the mop. The ants making their way in an unbroken row just below the wall made the same entreaty. He moved to the other side and started mopping. Then Abhilash came up and swept away the spiders and ants with a single swish.

'What's this, you owl, didn't you see this?'

'Was going to mop it,' Varadan lied.

'No, no, I know you. All these creatures are your father and grandfather and so on, isn't it? I know.'

Varadan did not respond.

'If you're going to mop like this, it's useless. If I have to do all the mopping then what are you for? I'll complain to the manager that you don't do your work.'

Varadan dipped the mop in the bucket, thinking of the next lie. He could not find one. Abhilash went downstairs grumbling. Owl! That epithet did not leave Varadan's ear. He was called that because he was so silent. Words came very rarely to him. Not that he did not wish to summon them; they just didn't come. He feared that he may go wrong if he spoke. He worried that he may not say what he wanted to; that he may be mocked, abused. Varadan was a whole tent of apprehensions. But fear had him by the throat—all the more—particularly after joining Swargam. The more he tried to fight it, the more it expanded, like locusts.

Varadan tried to wipe off anger and sorrow from the floor where slippers had left their marks. In the water that Abhishek had thrown on the place where the ants had been marching in their row, a solitary ant now struggled. Another ant ran about madly, seeking a way to save it. It sought out the others who were scattered violently around from Abhishek's genocidal act and together, they locked arms and made a circle, trying to pull out the drowning ant. Varadan bent down and placed his index finger in the water. The drowning ant climbed on it, spat out death that had clambered into its mouth, and thanked Varadan. Just when he had entrusted the ant to its siblings and risen it, Ramanandan walked in.

'You are here?'

Varadan looked at him, amazed.

'I saw you run. Super!'

Varadan tried to smile.

'What is your name?'

'Owl . . . no, Varadan.'

Ramanandan laughed.

'Where are you from?'

'Chaligadda'.

It took hardly a moment for Ramanandan's face to look like a soot-soaked rag.

'Isn't there are large mountain around there? Is your place near it?'

Varadan nodded—yes.

Ramanandan grunted rather firmly.

'OK, see you.'

Ramanandan stepped into room number 904. L.A. Subramania Shenoy, MLA of Mangalapuram North was sitting there nice and tipsy and watching a video on his phone. His enormous belly which looked like a huge round vessel rose and fell at a passionate pace.

'A minute, Ramandanda, it'll be over now.'

Ramanandan sat down on the settee. He heard voices from the mobile.

A girl: 'Eda, don't show it to anyone, OK?'

A male voice panted: 'No, my darling.'

No male face in that video, Ramanandan was sure.

Women are so naïve. You just have to act like you love them, and they'll do anything for you. His own life was proof of that.

He smiled.

'Great piece, that boy is lucky.'

Subramania Shenoy stood up and re-tied his mundu which was beginning to come lose.

'There was a freedom fighter from Payyanur of the same name—Subramania Shenoy—heard of him?'

'What's to be gained from knowing?'

'I was just saying.'

The glass of booze slipped from Shenoy's hand when he picked it up, fell on the floor, and broke into bits with a loud noise.

'Ayyayyo, my peg!' he wailed involuntarily.

'Be careful,' Ramanandan said. 'The shards can pierce the skin of the foot and you wouldn't even see.'

He opened the door and peeked into the corridor. And saw Varadan who was waiting for the lift with his mop and bucket. He clapped.

He came in, picked up all the broken pieces that he could see, and wrapped them up in a piece of paper.

'I'll throw this and be back soon, Saare.'

He left with the packet.

'What's going on? Will we lose what we had and get nothing in the end?'

Shenoy opened the window and lit a cigarette.

'No, it's going to settle soon.'

'Give me back my sim, Eda, I am firm about my word. I honour it.'

Shenoy stared ruefully at his signal-less mobile.

'Not because I don' trust you, Shenoyetta . . . just that if I give it to you, the others will start asking, too. You know that they are all international frauds! Now they are standing somewhat still. But if Sivamohanan comes and offers more money, more fun—then they will return.'

'That's true. Ah, has he found out that we are here?' Shenoy asked in his north-Kerala-style Malayalam.

Varadan knocked at the door. Ramanandan opened it.

He bent down, began to wipe the place where the glass had shattered.

'No one has got the wind of this yet. And it doesn't matter now if they do find out. The deal is done, after all.'

'Just speed up things. Have so much stuff to do.'

'Everything's OK. Wait just a bit,' Ramanandan winked.

'The birdie? Available?'

'Have sent a feeler. Should be ready by evening.'

Ramanandan grinned.

'Ah, you are fated for much more, Ramananda!'

'Wherever you go, you need to get the smell of this place on your body, am I right?'

'They see local is international, don't they?'

'Uh, yes, yes,' laughed Shenoy.

Ramanandan switched the TV on. Like expected, the main news was about the crisis of government in Karnataka. Sixteen MLAs of the ruling party were untraceable. Horse-trading, P.K. Thomas was bawling aloud. It made Ramanandan giggle.

'The man will soak himself in any detergent of compromise to secure his power and image . . . that hairless head is stuffed with shrewd moves!'

Ramanandan spat out the words as though he were delivering a fancy dialogue in a Renji Panicker film— full of garrulous indignation against politicians.

'Yeah,' Shenoy mocked. 'You do have the right to be indignant!'

'But I don't preen around as respectable?'

Just then, someone from Delhi called Ramanandan. He showed Shenoy the image of Rajendran flash on the mobile phone screen. Ayyo! Shenoy hit himself on the head in frustration.

'Don't tell him that I am 'ere!'

Hearing Shenoy say that in a whisper, Ramanandan laughed and attended the call.

The laughter did not end when the call was over; it just grew deeper.

'What is it, Eda, tell me!'

'The guy closest to the High Command orders me—pull down the government by hook or crook!'

'Hey . . . what's up . . .? He's a true-blue Party man? He wouldn't say that!'

'You are so heedless! Tell me, who's in-charge of Karnataka?'

'Mammen John.'

'Correct. If the government does not fall, Mammen John's going to bask in glory. He'll slide right in—the guy's so sharp, he can see even a millipede's eye! He'll angle coolly for the CM's position!'

'Where? In Karnataka?'

'Oh, you are so thick in the head, Shenoyetta!

'That's why you got me to win! You meant Kerala?'

'Yess . . .'

'But how are you sure they are going to come back to power in Kerala? What if the others win?'

'No, they won't . . . it's like the pilgrimage to the Sabarimala temple each year . . . a religious vow we Malayalees keep . . . That bunch rules for five years, then this bunch rules for the next five . . . that won't change.'

'Ah, Alla, now we too have roots there, Ramananda, you don't forget!'

'Keep them safe in the water this year. If you keep them from the rot, we'll see next time.'

'*Alledaa*—why're you blaming the Party? You are one of us now?'

'Yes, but the truth is still the truth.'

'Ah. OK, tell me, what's that Rajendran scheming?'

'He wants to become the CM. No point aiming for the Centre for the next ten years.'

'For that?'

'Once Mammen's fate is decided, then Rajendran can score a goal at the unguarded goal post! He's in Gokul Sahi's good books, too. If so, he'll take the cup. That's good for us, too.'

'That's true. Judging from his origins he should be with us.'

He tasted the beef, poured the next drink.

After he had mopped up the shards of glass on the floor, Varadan got up, opened the door, and began to excuse himself. But his eyes got involuntarily hooked on to the image of Thomas, still bawling on TV.

'Are, bayya,' said Shenoy, mistaking Varadan for a Bengali, 'door close karo, bayya.'

'Sorry, Saar, sorry.'

As he closed the door softly and walked away, the image of the man on the TV screen carried Varadan away to the protest pavilion of memory.

Sixteen years back, a seventeen-year-old Varadan had accompanied his father Eri for a protest in front of the Kerala State Secretariat at Thiruvananthapuram. They built a protest hut right opposite the statue of the old diwan Madhavarayar and shouted slogans. It was Mathangi who led the slogan-shouting. Varadan met her for the first time there. He was impressed, seeing her shout those slogans without any awkwardness. If it were him, the words would have choked him to death right there.

Varadan went to the bar along with the non-forest folk who'd come there to join the protest and had a drink. He spent some time keeping the beat to the songs they sang, and by the time he got back to the protest shed, they were all asleep. His friends had parted and were scattered; only he returned to the shed. He happened to sit down beside Mathangi. She was awake, sitting, leaning on the wall of the Secretariat, letting her thoughts wander. When he tried to smile, a burp escaped him.

'You're drunk?'

Her brows rose up and bent in a frown, like a bow. 'A little.'

No sooner had he managed to say than rather shyly had her hand landed on his cheek, in a stinging slap. The hands that wove mats out of prickly screw-pine leaves. Blood-red-bright stars of love and pain popped up in his eyes and blinded him momentarily.

'This is not a place for drunks to park themselves afterwards . . . this is where we fight for a place to live!' she hissed. Varadan clambered up, holding on to the pavilion's pole. The pavilion shook a little. When he stepped into the street, he turned and smiled at her: thanks.

On the fourth day, the government pretended to accept the claims of the protestors. Chief Minister Thomas came out to celebrate with them. He took the *kol* that Varadan had been wielding and played the *kolkkali* with them, with a smile that never really reached his eyes.

Mathangi, Varadan and Eri returned to Chaligadda in the Malabar Express. It was festival time, and the train was overflowing with passengers. Mathangi hung around Eri and Varadan. When her eyelids drooped from sleep, Mathangi's feet stepped on Varadan's. She slipped; he caught her. He protected her head which almost banged on the door.

When the government did not do anything for months on end, the protestors went to Muthanga and began to build a life in the forest. Varadan went with them. So did Mathangi and her sister Gauri, with her four-year-old child on her hip, and a four-month-old foetus in her belly.

Varadan was familiar with people who went hunting animals with guns in the forest. But it was for the first time that he saw people coming there to hunt other people. Eri, who was kicked mercilessly by the police, lay on the ground till he died. Varadan, who tried to stop them, was dragged to a tree and the police rubbed his face hard against the rough bark. His lower teeth broke. Women and children were dragged to an old white man's bungalow, locked up, and beaten till the fury of the policemen abated. Gauri was thrown on the floor and the police boots fell on her chest. There's life growing inside me, she screamed; the life inside pleaded to be spared. The four-year-old was lifted up and smashed on the ground. Years were erased from her brain. Mathangi, who fell on her sister trying to protect her, was dragged up and banged on the wall. The blood splattered in her eyeballs; she fell unconscious. When she opened her eyes in the general ward of the government hospital, the first person she saw was Varadan. He was staring ruefully at his face distorted by the loss of two teeth in his lower jaw.

In the evening, once again, Varadan begged and pleaded with Tom Thomas to let him use his phone.

'You won't, even if all others will!'

Tom Thomas's commanding authority quivered. Varadan could feel Mathangi and Sampath in him. He went into the toilet, grabbed the lever of the flush tank, and wept.

When the sun went to its rest, the Governor declared once more that he would not waver an inch from the demand made by Ramanandan's Party, that the ruling government should prove its majority the next day itself. The ruling party went to the Supreme Court for a stay order. The Supreme Court convened at midnight to give a ruling. Two of the judges were close to Ramanandan's Party. He was quite sure, more than anyone else, that this was going to be smooth sailing.

Five trolley bags stuffed with cash reached his room that night. Wads of two-thousand-rupee notes. He laid out the wads in rows on his bed. A second mattress of cash. When the booze started working, he climbed on it, lay flat and began taking selfies in different poses. His lackeys grinned.

Varadan, who was cleaning the glass windows opposite, saw it all. He was seeing so much money together for the first time. Somehow, he felt very afraid. Though he just wanted to run away, his legs would not budge. Greed overflowed from the eyes of all the people in that room. Endless, bottomless, greed. Greed that would follow you beyond the grave. Greed . . . limitless avarice—nothing but avarice.

When each person left the room, Ramanandan made sure that the hidden camera had caught images of them receiving the bundles of cash. By then, the Governor's action was being reported on TV. Glad that everything was moving according to plan, he slid off the bed and jumped with joy a couple of times. Realizing that Ramanandan might notice him, Varadan pulled away his head.

He could not sleep. The hope that Abhishek might have his phone turned out to be futile. Abhishek too was sleepless—he had many loves and usually, sleep came to him only after he had soothed them all into slumber. He pulled out the country arrack that he had brought from home and downed it with some beef fry. Then, smoking a weed-filled beedi, he fell silent. He sat in a corner, measuring the moon that frolicked in the sky above, till the drunken haze left him.

Shall I walk back to my *ooru*? Varadan's mind thrashed about. No use at all leaving without his pay, his heart told him. When the very worries that had denied him sleep made him doze, he dreamed of Mathangi and Sampath. They had lost their way in the dark; they were calling to him. They wept, not seeing him. They stumbled towards a steep fall.

Walking towards the reception before daybreak, he ran into a girl on her way out from room number 904. She looked worn and helpless. Whole deserts of fear and sorrow lay smouldering in her eyes. She was like a chewed-up root. It was the girl who used to come down with the load of forest vines. The one who used to smile at him. Her eyes welled when she saw him. Varadan was about to ask her something when an autorickshaw driver who was waiting outside for her, barked: 'Stop dawdling and come here quick, you hussy! I have trips ahead!'

He stepped out of the autorickshaw and clapped his hands. She climbed into it, head bowed. Varadan hoped that she would look out. She didn't.

Mehaboob was alone in the reception. Varadan looked at him with beseeching eyes, folded palms.

'Varadetta, I'll lose my job if they find out. My wedding was just four weeks ago! Have got to fill the belly; please don't aim at it!'

Mehaboob folded his palms back at Varadan. He just stood there, silent, stooping, and Mehaboob felt sorry for him.

'If you want, make a call from here, right now . . . quick . . . no one should see . . .'

Mehaboo opened the shelf, searched for Varadan's mobile phone, and gave it to him. Though he knew that it was useless to call at that hour, he still dialled Mathangi's number. The woman on the side told him in her affectionate voice that she was out of coverage area. None of us are going to be inside this world ever, he felt.

'Not reachin' now. Can you please give it to me in the evening?' Varadan asked hopefully.

'Goodness, how? This place teems with people then.'

He took the phone back.

'Is there some way . . .?'

Varadan was holding on to hope.

'Please leave, Varadetta! I'll do something—keep the phone switched on. If someone calls, I'll take it and pass on the message to you—won't that do?'

He did not reply.

'That's all I can do,' said Mehaboob cheerily. 'Chill, Varadetta, chill!'

Mehaboob was trying to lighten Varadan's mood. Varadan forced a smile and went to get the cleaning things. Mehaboob felt sorry, seeing him shuffle off despondently.

Sivamohan's car arrived at Swargam at eight o'clock. He had got wind that the MLAs were here. Some fifteen Party workers were with him. Ramanandan spotted him from the balcony. He called Tom Thomas. Sivamohan was turned away without a room; he was not even allowed in.

'The people in there are my friends,' he insisted. 'Let me just have a glimpse at them.' He was polite, but no one listened to him. Tom Thomas placed himself as a barrier in the middle, arms crossed. Sivamohan's mood changed.

'You know well that we have the power to buy this whole place.'

He raised his voice. Tom Thomas knew that, but it was the command of those in power at the Centre that counted, as far as he was concerned. If he didn't choose that side, then tax raids would follow. Swargam would be undone and he, along with it. Sivamohans come and go. The raid would, however, take them all at one sweep.

Sivamohan and his group tried to enter by force but were stopped by the security guards. Varadan was passing that way with his mop and got caught in the middle. The dirt on the mop drew patterns on the white khaddar shirts of the visitors. In the pushing and shoving, someone's mobile phone fell on the floor. Varadan's hand hit it. He seized it, tried to call Matangi. As he dialled her number, hands shaking, the mobile phone received a call—the ringtone was a loud '*Vaishnavajanato*' . . . Some of the khaddar-clad fellows froze, remembering Gandhi. A burly man, two times Varadan's size, snatched the phone from his hand, thrust it into his pocket, stuck out his chest and got ready for yet another combat. When he realized that this was going to end up as a major hubbub, Sivamohan reined in his group. He called his media contacts.

Barely hours remained for the no-confidence motion to be presented in the Assembly. Sivamohan knew that something had to be done before that, or everything would be lost. He had rushed there hoping to meet the MLAs and get them to change their minds at whatever cost. He did not really know what to do now, but he and his companions squatted near the doors of Swargam.

When the TV channel reporters reached, they were raising slogans and things were hotting up there. Swargam went live on TV. A jeep-full of police rode in. In the middle of the slogan-shouting, Sivamohan spoke with his ailing daughter on a video call. A smile spread on her weary face hearing the slogans.

'You are impossible, Accha,' she said.

He laughed.

'Do something quick,' someone called him. 'The Assembly is about to start. The Governor is going to accept the resolution for the no-confidence motion.'

Sivamohan realized that nothing could be done. But he could not leave doing nothing, having come this far. He and his companions forced their way in, pushed past the security guards and ran to the rooms where the MLAs were put up. Ramanandan had locked all the rooms from the outside. An open fight broke out between the supporters of Ramanandan's and Sivamohan's parties. Mundus came loose from their waists and flew about. Screams and yelling filled the air. In the melee, the police entered, swinging their lathis. A fine show on TV; people laughed. Varadan with his mop, who had crouched in a corner out of terror seeing the police, was also beaten. The lathi left two straight lines on his thigh.

That night, Ramanandan held a party for the MLAs to celebrate their victory. Varadan and Abhishek were on duty with their mops and buckets to clear up the mess at regular intervels. Ramanandan commended Tom Thomas for making sure that nothing was lacking.

'Wherever there's money, there will be power. And the other way round, too. Money is the matter. I am really happy to have overseen this beautiful process by which democracy is nose down on the floor, my dear!' Ramanandan spoke the truth to the movie star who was on the phone with him. He was watching the national flag being raised before the main entrance of Swargam for Independence Day. The royal blood in him was boiling. His royal ancestors sat in heaven, in the world of the dead, and showered flower petals inside him.

'If you were here today, I would have laid you on a bed of cash and made love.'

'Missed it!'

'Come if you want it. This night is a long one.'

This actress had a peripheral interest in literature and so when he spoke with her, Ramanandan turned somewhat literary.

'Ooh, don't make such tempting invitations . . . I'll jump on the next flight.'

'Come . . . I'll pay for it.'

'No, darling . . . let's meet next week. Enjoy *maadu*. Independence Day wishes!'

Ramanandan ended the call, swung around in the revolving chair—then his eyes fell on Varadan. The others were amazed when he gestured to Varadan to come up close. Varadan went over to him with mop and bucket.

'Where should I mop, Saar?' he asked.

He held out the liquor-filled glass with a big smile. They were now the centre of everyone's attention.

'No, Saar . . . I don't drink.'

Varadan had turned a new leaf after Mathangi's resounding slap.

'Hey, go on, drink . . .'

Ramanandan persisted.

'No, Saar, I don' baant it . . .'

Varadan's face began to fill with a piteous expression.

'You will drink this.'

Ramanandan's tone changed into a menacing one. Varadan bent towards the mop.

'Drink it, you piece of shit!'

Ramanandan roared.

Varadan knew the roar of animals and liked it. He had heard from very near the loud roars of powerful animals—the tiger, leopard—he had seen it too—and had even smiled at the sounds. But the roars and snarls of human beings scared him.

Varadan took the glass without raising his head and downed it in a single gulp.

'Good boy!'

Ramanandan was a consummate politician. He knew to smile or cry or put the fear into people's heads; in short, do whatever the situation demanded.

'You sneaked a look when we were counting the cash, didn't you?'

Varadan started violently.

Ramanandan held out a glass to him again.

'You must have taken a casual look, but you must know that we noticed.'

Varadan emptied the glass again without a word. Now he could down any amount, anything.

'This fellow's from Chaligadda colony,' Ramanandan turned to the others. 'Don't you remember? Where the policeman was clubbed to death? Ah, the police have killed there, too.'

No one caught on.

'I was the MLA there back then. Should have won the next election like a breeze, too. But for these

fucking bitch-sons! Their agitation! I was left holding
the defeat! Isn't that true, Eda?' he barked.

Varadan said nothing.

'In the sad memory of my defeat, Varadan here will
sing his people's song. Friends, I request you to kindly
encourage him with your applause.'

Ramanandan mocked. Varadan shrank into himself
even more.

'The song of these forest people is excellent when
you are tipsy. Makes you feel a little guilty, teary. It's
comforting!'

Ramanandan's smile acquired a cruel tinge. That
made the onlookers sense that he had some other
intention.

Varadan knew that if he refused, he would get
beaten up. The songs that they sung together in the
forest at Muthanga before the police came seeking
with their guns rushed into his memory like a breeze.
He closed his eyes, began to sing. The forest whispered
in his ears: Varada, louder, louder.

'Enough, enough . . . this was my favour to you.'

Ramanandan's fingers shot out and gripped
Varadan's vocal cords, ending his crude singing.

His feet were not firm, Varadan noticed. But then,
when were the feet of such people ever on the floor?
Mine are firmly on the floor. They'll stay there even
after I die. Varadan knew that well. The others left
them and returned to their tipsy games.

'Eda . . . Varada . . . defeat is no pleasant thing for
me . . . I've always hauled myself up and stamped on the

place where I feel. And have never slept without making sure that I kicked in the gullet the chap who defeated me . . .'

Ramanandan guffawed. With the crazed energy of one who'd shed blood in battles of conquest.

'Let me tell you the truth—or, I always tell the truth. Your Chaligadda hill belongs to me. The hill at Thiruvangoor belongs to me. I own all the hills that raise their hoods above you!'

Replying to a congratulatory message that appeared on his phone, Ramanandan used a toothpick to pick up a piece of fried chicken from the tray and put it in his mouth. Varadan did not raise his head. Wild hornets buzzed in his ears.

'Not fair, uh, that you live an easy life there after making me trip up in the election? I will be burrowing deep in there till something definite happens to you!'

As he snickered, the hill of Chaligadda shook inside Varadan. Black-winged bats, harbingers of death, hovered in the sky. In the dark, the owl hooted. Varadan's low-roofed hut trembled as though fearful for its life. Sampath cried continuously.

That's how his hands rose towards Ramanandan's neck. Those who saw it were shocked. He removed those hands easily.

'What's this . . . have another drink?'

When he drank the liquor that was offered, Varadan cried out loud for some time.

'Never mind . . . cool . . .'

He patted Varadan's shoulder. But he did not stop. Two people carried him out of the room. They pushed him against the wall, kicked and clobbered him but he did not stop wailing. The thugs thought that he was wailing from the pain and were satisfied. Tom Thomas watched the show, arms folded. When the thugs left, he said: 'They let you live because I begged them on the knee!'

Varadan spat a mouthful of blood on the floor.

'You're not supposed to spit here.'

Grumbling to himself, Varadan took his mop and began to clean the floor.

'Others will take care of it. You can go. No need to come back here.'

Tom Thomas crushed with his shoe a cockroach that had lost its way.

'Since things have gone this far, you have forfeited your salary as well.'

He had expected Varadan to quickly raise his head and look at him. There was a call for him from the party hall; he walked towards the elevator. Varadan stopped mopping and raised his head.

'Saare . . . I need my salary.'

Tom Thomas put his phone back into his pocket, straightened his glasses and smiled.

'Oh, really, you need it today? Can't you take it tomorrow?'

Tom Thomas pressed the elevator button.

'Saare, I need it, Saare . . . I have no other way, that's why . . .'

'Yeah, wait for it, you sucker.'

He got into the elevator. The bear that used to lurk around the forest when he stepped out of his kudi entered Varadan suddenly. He lifted the stick of the mop and brought it hard on Tom Thomas's back. It broke in two. The unexpected blow brought him down, his back hitting the floor hard. Before he could scream, Varadan leapt on him, pressed down his mouth. His leg touched the door; the elevator was still open. The notes of Beethoven's piano sonata filled the cabin.

'Give me my salary, Saare!'

Varadan cried. His grip on Thomas's neck tightened. His breath struggled under the hollow of his throat. Thrashing about, he emptied all his pockets. Not easing his grip, Varadan picked up enough notes. He took just his salary and replaced the rest of the money in his pockets. He rose up, pressing down on the ground with the broken handle of the mop.

Tom Thomas wanted to raise an alarm but his breath returned only after he lay there panting for some time.

When he got out of the gate, Mehaboob came towards him.

'Mathangi called. But I could not attend it—the phone switched off before I could.'

A rush of coolness enveloped Varadan. He pressed the power switch but when the display lit up, it would die again. Trying to revive it by removing the battery, inserting it back again, shaking the phone in his arms, Varadan ran downhill as fast as he could.

The trees and animals and birds who had just woken up watched him sadly. The darkness revealed the body of the young girl hanging lifeless on the branch of the *anjili* tree at the end of the road. Her loved ones were gathered there, weeping. He did not stop. But till she vanished from sight, he kept turning back to look at her.

He managed a lift on the NP lorry that was carrying vegetables and dozed off. Sampath appeared in his dream. How he received him at the hospital soon after his birth; how he had tried to press his tiny foot on his father's chest and climb up then; how he called him *achhaaa* with the adorable lisp; how they went to see the forest, how he sang Eri's song and brought tears to his eyes; how he hugged his father the last time, outside their kudi, begging him to be back soon . . .

It was daybreak when he reached the hut at Chaligadda. Light rain was falling. The darkness still lingered. Bird cries filled the air.

Varadan saw people gathered inside the hut and outside. Something flared up in him. He ran into the hut. Sampath was sleeping. Mathangi's head was on his chest. Varadan went to her and sat down.

'Mathangi, what're you doing . . . move . . . lie down somewhere else . . .' he told her softly.

Seeing him, she let out a heart-rending wail.

'He's gone, Varada, our son's gone . . .'

He held her close and tried to smile at the others crowding there. They bowed their heads.

'He was much worse yesterday . . . I begged the hospital people . . . they sent us back . . . They wanted an advance . . .'

The words fell from her, shuddering.

'He asked for a long time . . . when acchan will come back . . . he cried a long time for you, Varada . . .'

She touched her son's closed eyes.

'You stop crying,' Varadan said. 'He's fine, he's just fooling us.'

He bowed his head towards Sampath.

'*Mone*, my son . . . wake up . . .' Sampath did not open his eyes.

'Get up . . .'

Varadan stroked his cheek gently.

'Come, let's go to the hospital. Look here, your father is rich!'

Varadan pulled out the two-thousand-rupee notes from his pocket. Two of them fell on the ground. He took the lit kerosene lamp from the windowsill, bent down and picked them up. As he unfolded the notes and put them one by one on Sampath's left palm, Varadan beat his breast and howled inconsolably. Around the same time, the Tempo Traveller and three luxury cars were setting out from Swargam and descending towards the people through mist-swaddled paths.

The Yoke of Caste

There was a time when progressive Malayalis would brag that caste oppression/discrimination was irrelevant to social life in Kerala. True, the worst excesses of caste oppression seemed to have been eradicated here by the mid- to- late-twentieth century. The Malayalam-speaking regions had seen the Ezhavas, a populous caste-group deemed untouchables by the traditional caste-order, break the shackles in the late-nineteenth early-twentieth century decades using the economic and educational opportunities opened up to them by colonialism, and embarking on active community-building and social reform. This was no mean achievement because traditional caste power here was perhaps the worst in India, because it enforced not just the rule of untouchabilty, but even 'unseeability' on the oppressed castes. In the mid-twentieth century, massive working class struggles struck hard at the traditional caste-order and brought it down in some measure. Dalit people made gains, but they were strictly limited. The

Dalits who were the sole possessors of accumulated knowledge necessary for wetland agriculture, crucial in these regions, were nevertheless not acknowledged as such by even the communist movement. Agricultural workers (mostly Dalits) were projected as in need of 'uplift'—though organized and empowered by the communist movement. Though the actual tillers of the land, they were not made the owners of those lands. Instead, their access to state welfare resources was expanded, and Kerala's celebrated land reforms of the early 1970s granted house plots to them. This proved disastrous. Agricultural wages were improved and fixed in the decade but Dalit communities did not gain also because agriculture fell into a precipitous decline. Despite tall claims, Dalit communities—and all communities dependent on natural resources for their livelihoods—here have always remained outside the mainstream of social development—as the social scientist John Kurien points out, they have stayed the 'outlier' of the famous 'Kerala Model' of high levels of social well-being despite poor economic growth.

As for social life in Kerala, it may seem more inclusive than elsewhere, yet it is yoked to caste hierarchies and exclusions in much more subtle ways. An important stream of writing in contemporary Malayalam literature prises out casteism from its hiding holes and exposes Malayali hypocrisy in an unprecedented way, and the upsurge of Dalit voices in Malayalam has vastly strengthened it. Prince Aymanam's Pothycchoru Offering *is a fine specimen of such writing. It is set in Kuttanad, famous in the tourist imagination of the present, but also once a setting for the most back-breaking agricultural labour, all performed by Dalit people. There is evidence of active resistance to caste oppression from Dalit communities through conversion, from the early sixteenth century at least, and this accelerated in the nineteenth century. But as this powerful and poignant story tells us, caste did not die with the conversion of the Dalits to the Christian faith; it merely shifted shape. And not surprisingly, at the heart of it is the question of sharing food.* Pothycchoru, *or rice-and-curry packed in a wilted banana leaf, bears the scent of home—but all homes are not granted the same worth, apparently.*

Pothycchoru Offering

'Pothycchoru Nerccha'

Prince Aymanam

'Have you heard, Napolean Bonaparte once said that history is just a bunch of lies everyone agrees upon?' asked Father Kunnumbarambil. His voice sounded as raspy as the wooden bell rung in the Good Friday Way-of-the-Cross procession, but he tried to make it sound deep and imposing. 'Truly,' he continued, 'why did we decide to write a history of this parish? To make the people of the parish gain confidence, showing them that they had a virtuous and proud past. To lead our people into material and spiritual growth through that memory. That is why we created a committee of the five of you and appointed Jinsy its convenor.'

Kunnumbarabil Acchan raised his head for a second to check if his words had found resonance in them, to read from the silence written on their faces.

He saw the olive branches of Hosanna on the faces of all except Jinsy. Acchan noticed the shadow fall on her face like rainclouds gathering on the sky at dusk. 'Alla,' he exclaimed, 'you tell me, Jinsy? Now this is like the whitening ointment that ruined the skin with white patches!' Though he glanced at Jinsy's face to gauge her response, her face looked dim and clouded, and she was silent.

'How're we going to feel any pride from highlighting that our church, this Chenkalathara Palli, was raised on the mud shovelled and firmed up by Karuppan *pelayan* and his people? *Ennaa abimaanam tharaana?*'

When she heard that from the priest's mouth, Jinsy felt like she had fallen into a quagmire and was now sinking.

'What's the use of digging up a useless past? Jinsy was asked to do it because of her PG and BEd in history. But how to say yes when you just write down whatever stupidity senile old people, silly *kaarnnonmaar*, who can't remember a thing, tell you?' The Acchan's words fell on her like a whiplash and she squirmed. As though a grating sensation had suddenly shot up from somewhere below the earth, as though it had passed through the layers of soil and pecked hard at her feet, Jinsy leapt up. 'This Karuppan *pelayan*, you talk of, Acchan,' she burst out, 'was my great-great-great grandfather from five generations back. The vast fields of Chenkalathara were the *brahmasvam* lands owned by the Brahmins, of the Vadakkedathu Mana house. My *velyappachan* was the head *pulaya* who controlled all the workers there;

he guarded those fields!' She gagged on the pain and her voice turned hoarse. She's on the brink of a whimper, the priest guessed. Something drummed inside him, insisting that he move towards his goal taking her along. So, to calm her down, he said, 'Ah, that is what you have written in the Preface,' and started reading aloud from it: 'It was one hundred and twenty-five years back that the lay preacher Brother Rocky moved from Varappuzha to Chenkalathara. The seemingly unending, rolling fields of Chenkalathara and some Pulaya and Paraya people were all that could be found there. The water—deeper that the height of two full-grown men—sliding down stakes driven into the mud—carved out the sediments below, loaded it into baskets which were pulled up by the chest. Brother Rocky found this amazing. The preacher watched Karuppan Pulayan and his mates doing this *katta kuthal*—extraction from the bed of the Meenachil river to build the outer bund of the Chenkalathara fields. Stakes made of coconut trunks with sharpened edges driven down into the mud, with areca palm trunks mounted horizontally on them for support, the dark bodies that mounted them kicking down the shovelled mud to the rhythm of *thei-thaka-thaka-thaka-thei*, the channels of sweat that ran down their backs . . . the preacher was awestruck. He went directly to Karuppan who was the leader. Karuppan could make nothing of the preacher's talk about virtue and sin, heaven and hell. Only the preacher's arm wrapped around his sweat-soaked body and the way he addressed him as *sahodaraa*—literally, brother, born of the same womb—fell on his ears like the first drop of rain on the parched earth. The Compassionate Christ who rose up before him through the preacher's words became the candlelight that lit the murky paths of Karuppan's life. In the end, he accepted baptism, and was renamed Pathrose—Peter . . .'

And I also say to you that you are Peter, and on this rock I will build My church, and the gates of Hades not will prevail against it.

The voice cut into Acchan's reading; all of them looked out through the window. Mad Mathambi stood there with a huge smile. Saying this, he lay down again on the veranda. Mathambi was an omnipresent being in those parts. The first person in that secluded village to go to college and get a degree. He was around sixty-nine. He was a distant cousin brother of Jinsy's father. His name was Mathew John—he himself had forgotten it. Only Jinsy called him by that name, that too, occasionally. He was in the class of BA English Literature of 1964–67 at the CMS College, Kottayam. The talk there was that he had gone crazy from too much *padutham*, study, that is. There is another story that he was injured in the head in a scuffle that broke out in a lane next to the KSRTC bus stand on the night after the inaugural screening at the Anand theatre in 1968. This left his memory in disarray. We have also heard that Mathambi and a Nair girl from Pallippurathukaavu were in love, and that the girl was going to elope with him, and that this was the handiwork of her brothers.

Anyway, Mathambi would pull out some powerful statements like this one, Revelations almost, from the pile of his jumbled up memories. They would smash the ignorance of the immoral world, falling on it like missiles. He would hand around the churchyard and its premises most of the time. Would sleep in the veranda of the church or under some tree. He would eat if anyone offered him something to eat. His flowing beard and hair, bony body, emaciated stomach and the seeker's wandering gave him a distant resemblance to Christ himself. Father Kunnumbarambil here had tried very hard to drive the crazy man out of the churchyard.

When he caught the thief Kumaran trying to force open the Virgin Mother's donation box in front of the church in the dead of night, Mathambi received the support of the parishioners against Kunnumbarambil Acchan. Actually, when he spotted a man come through the paddy fields behind the church, Mathambi had merely followed him. When he saw a man—whose body had been doused with a mixture of egg yolks and coconut oil to make it slippery, whose face was masked with just holes for the eyes and nose, and who wore nothing but a tight pair of briefs—come near the donation box and pry it open with an iron rod, he merely shouted a verse from the Bible:

Verily, verily, I say unto you, He that entereth not by the door into the sheepfold, but climbeth up some other way, the same is a thief and a robber.

Kumaran saw Mathambi in the light that fell from the top of the church tower—his flowing locks and beard and shoulders covered with a mundu to protect himself from mosquitoes. He saw Jesus in him and collapsed, unconscious. In the days that followed, Kumaran the Thief turned penitent, converted and became Pastor Kuriakose and wandered from one intersection in the road to another with his box speakers and cordless mics announcing the Word.

But of the fruit of the tree which is in the midst of the garden, God hath said, Ye shall not eat of it, neither shall ye touch it, lest ye die.

Mathambi shouted this verse on a Wednesday, and Kunnumbarambil Acchan caught a fever and took to bed for three whole days. He said this because he had seen the priest and the nun, Sister Anita who had brought him supper from the nearby convent, get ready to enter heaven together without leaving behind their human bodies. He had seen it through the ventilation outlet high in the wall when he was coming down the coconut tree near the parish house after cutting down a few tender coconuts. Anitaamma jumped up and ran off, but the serpent which had tempted Eve still swayed with its hood spread out, not finding a hole to hide in. The Acchan felt a rivulet of compassion rise up for him when he learned that the secret had not spread like fire in the haystack in the fields after harvest. This began to manifest as an occasional meal for Mathambi or ten or fifty rupees. The priest did not stop him even when he shifted his nightly haunt from the shade of the tree in the churchyard to the church veranda. He was lying there like this when, suddenly, in a flash of lightning in his brain, Christ's words came to him and he caught them.

Jinsy turned to him, looked at his face, raised her right index finger to her lips, gestured to him to be quiet, and continued: 'When the Thalappulayan accepted the Faith, most of his people followed him. That is how Karuppan Pathrose and his people hauled up the sediments and turned the uncultivated Kuzhikkandam field into garden land almost overnight. That was where the first church building, a thatched structure, was built and worship started. The keystone of this land, the *moolakkatta*, was first put in place by my great-great-great grandfather Karuppan Pathrose. Then, only after many years, in 1895, was the Chenkalathara Church built. That . . . is the truth . . . the truth that has passed on to us through the generations . . .' Her insides seared, the pain scorched her from within, her mouth was parched.

But the priest, as nimble as Satan who tried to test Jesus, continued: 'You may be right. But there's no evidence. And besides, what's the good from dragging up such history? That the church was established here in 1895 is history. The records of that are in the Bishop's Palace. It is here that we have to use our imagination. And it shouldn't be limited to just digging out the sediments. It should be linked to the accepted public history of those times. Only then it will be convincing.' Then, lowering his voice as if sharing a clever discovery, he asked, 'Did any of you try to find out what the most important events of the 1890s were? No, you haven't—you should. The most important event of that decade was the Malayali Memorial of 1891. And he went on and on and on. Members of that committee who had agreed to join it in a moment of weakness cursed that moment with heart and soul. Only Jinsy, alert to the traps and trenches in his words and gestures, heard his narration with the keen attention an angler pays to the fishing float at the end of the fishing line.

Acchan continued, sounding as authoritative as a scholar of history: 'What is the Malayali Memorial of 1891? It was mass petition against assigning higher level jobs to non-Malayali Brahmins alone, and it was put together with the Nairs leading and taking the Christians and Muslims and Ezhavas along with them. The Nairs got some small jobs from this; the others were given nothing. Sree Moolam Tirunal Rama Varma was the Maharaja of Travancore then. All this is written history?'

Leave ye all caught in the Written Word, Leave ye soon,

The Written Word belongs not to us.

Mathambi rose this time, holding on to the index finger of the great seer Poykayil Appachan, who rose from the oppressed, accepted the Faith, and then, seeing that the converted Christian was still mired in caste oppression, sought to shake off the Faith and replace it with his own. He called it the Faith of Immediate Salvation—he called away his people from the Word of the Christian Church, told them to leave it. Mathambi shouted a verse of Appachan's and sank back into the church veranda. Father Kunnumbarambil wondered for a moment, not knowing where that verse was in the Bible, and then returned to his speech: 'And so to pacify the Christians who were moving into even-more strident agitations, the King of Travancore began to grant them royal lands everywhere to build churches on. The Chenkalathara Church was founded on the land thus granted to the community.'

'This must be the truth. It has a touch of aristocracy . . . linked to the royalty and all,' said the unit secretary of the Youth Wing of the Kerala Congress and the son of Valyaparambil Mathachen, Adarsh Mathew Jacob. He was on the priest's side.

'See . . . just hearing it, you want to believe,' Acchan leaned back in his chair and said, '. . . And if we add a sentence like, say, "The sympathy that the Maharaja of Travancore, whose legacy was of Aarsha Bharatha tolerance towards all religions that reached these shores, towards the early Kerala Christians, was boundless . . ."—then who's going to oppose it?' Adarsh was sitting in the first row; Acchan slid his foot noiselessly under the table and poked his foot. 'And besides,' he continued, 'if we also add: "It is the community of believers led by Valyaparambil Kunhonachhan, the senior Karanavan of the Valyaparambil family, which belongs to the illustrious line of one of the thirty-two aristocratic Brahmin families converted to the Christian faith by the Apostle Thomas, which sowed the first seeds of spiritual growth in the parish", then the Brahmin legacy will also be ready!' Pausing and sipping the water he poured into a glass from a jug, he looked at Adarsh and asked, 'What do you think, Adarsh?'

'Well, this has to do with my family, and so I don't want to say anything. Accha, you please decide? It's not proper to set up my own forefathers in history when one gets a chance.'

The pointed tip of his reply bore deep into Jinsy's heart.

'Now, how does that become your family's business, eda? That the Apostle Thomas came to India in 52 AD and converted thirty-two Brahmin families and set up seven and a half churches is the community's belief, far firmer than history. That doesn't need evidence, does it, Jinsy?'

The words gushed out of her mouth like the waters from the eastern hills breaking through the bunds, flooding fields:

'We are not in the habit of changing fathers just because the Nambutiri Brahmin man is rich and fair-skinned, Accho! The story of St Thomas, two thousand years old, is history and tradition to you. Our memories, barely a century and a quarter old, are useless tales to you! You can make up this illegitimate history all by yourself, Accho. I will have no hand in it!' With this, she snatched the draft of history of the parish that she had written and stormed out. The caresses of her forefathers, dead, gone, forgotten, shook the leaves of

the casuarina trees in the churchyard, touched her, and
went past.

Jinsy's house was just next to the churchyard.
Earlier, there used to be broken-down fence through
which they used to get in and out of the churchyard.
Five or six years ago, they built a big wall around the
churchyard and so now she had to go out through the
gate, walk for ten minutes, and step down from the
panchayat road to the canal that led to the *vachaal*
water canals in the field. Though this was the land on
which her forefathers had lived for generations before
the church arrived there, today, everyone thought
that their house stood on the land that the church
had donated charitably to a needy family. The very
name of her house—Pallipparambu—'Church Yard'—
worked to firm up that idea, piercing deep into their
very existence.

She had set off for home riding on her memories.
How soon each place turns alien, she thought, how
helpless they were in their dissipation into nothing in
their own place of birth, even when they did not have
to flee it! Jincy's life was woven around the church.
Her day began with the church bells that rang before
the sun rose after its baptism in the stone tank of the
night. Except on Sundays, she never missed the day's
first Mass at 6.30. On Sundays, Bible School began
after the Third Mass at 8.30, so she attended it. Jinsy
has been the Sunday school teacher in the church ever
since she completed her higher secondary schooling.
She never missed any event or ritual at the church; she

was well-brought up. Her father Thomas and mother
Alice were believers who almost sprouted from the
walls of the church. They did all the menial jobs there.
They were paid far less than in any other job they did,
but they never left the church wanting in anything.

Most of the parishioners were converted Pulaya
and Paraya people, and a few Roman Catholics as
well. More than the church register, the vaults in the
cemetery revealed their power and their numbers. They
had vaults that rose up from the ground, that revealed
the names—and family names—of the souls who slept
inside on their marble plaques. They paid the church
grave rent of fifty thousand or more. If the Pulayas or
Parayas died, they would be simply buried in graves.
Once the graves filled up, another cycle would start,
with new occupants for the old graves. Because deaths
were not so frequent, members of the same family could
sleep in the same grave. Their guards were wooden
crosses fashioned clumsily out of the planks of rubber
wood, painted in black and white, sometimes broken
and fallen.

Jinsy's father Thomas used to also work as a
gravedigger besides all the other menial work he did
at the church. Her parents were hard workers. There
were no fields in or around Chenkalathara where their
sweat did not fall. They took pains to educate their
children. Jinsy was a bright student and she obtained
an MA in history and a BEd too. The younger boy
Jobichan failed his twelfth standard exam and began
to work as a house painter's apprentice. When

farming jobs began to become rare, her father became a construction worker; her mother became a *thozil-urappu* worker, getting the Mahatma Gandhi National Rural Employment Guarantee Scheme wages. After she became the Sunday school teacher, Jinsy wanted to become a teacher. Her dream of finding a job soon after she got her teaching degree wilted in the very first year after, like seeds sown on rock. Four months back, there was a teacher's vacancy in the church's lower primary school. Jinsy being the member of that parish, who was technically qualified for the job, should have got it, but she did not. Instead, it was sold for eight lakh rupees to Litty Mary Scaria, daughter of Vellikkunnel Kariachan of the Kudamaloor parish. It was a terrible blow to Jinsy. Seeing his daughter's worn and tear-streaked face, Thomas could not stand it anymore. Brimming over with disappointment and sadness, he said, 'Have to ask Acchan about this, now!' and set off, his resolve risen and spread like a serpent's hood. Jinsy went with him.

'It's been over seventy-five years since we started this LP school . . . it's the same now. Many other schools which were started later have already grown into Higher Secondary schools. Three years before the government was ready to upgrade our school to the Upper Primary level. But we need to improve the infrastructure . . . build classrooms, toilets . . . we need money for that. If we hire Kariachan's daughter, we can build two classrooms. If you have that money, give it to me. I am only happy to give this girl the job . . .'

The crafty parish priest who knew well the family's top and trunk, aimed a blow at the risen hood. Thomas prepared to return, crestfallen. 'Ah,' continued the Acchan, 'this school belongs to all of you . . . parish priests come and go . . . if the school is well-maintained, then good for you and this place . . . don't let selfish desires stand in the way of the Divine Will. That's all I have to say . . .' He delivered another blow just to make sure that the snake was really dead, and went off into the parish house. He mumbled something all the way back to comfort his daughter. She hung on and swirled around those words like a log floating on flowing waters.

Many vacancies appeared in other schools in the diocese and were filled by those who had money to pay. Because she was determined to marry only after she got a job or found a bridegroom who was both educated and employed, Jinsy was still unmarried at twenty-nine. Worry about their daughter kept splattering in the hearts of her mother and father like water boiling and falling over the rim of the pot. Thanka from Vechur who stayed in the Vattakkaad colony had once proposed a marriage alliance between Santhosh, a traffic policeman and the son of her distant cousin, and Jinsy. Because they were Hindu Pulayas, they wanted the girl to re-convert and Alice had stoutly denied it; now there wasn't a single day in which she didn't regret it. Sometimes she would see him on the traffic island at the Baker Junction in Kottyam and her mind would melt, thinking of her daughter. Jinsy too

had liked Santhosh back then. After that alliance was
aborted, she insisted stubbornly that she would marry
only after she got a job.

The family used to say that in her stubborn
and fixed ways, she was exactly like the old woman
Kunhanna. She was Jincy's father's grandmother.
She was the heroine of a story that people there still
liked to tell. Kunhanna was the cook in the house of
Jaikochan of the Maliekkal family. His beautiful wife
Clara grown nice and rounded eating all that beef
and pork, had a problem. Clara kochamma's farts
were huge and completely ill-timed. They resembled
the hiss of the water pushing into the field when the
thoombu was opened. No way could she control it.
Her fart-nerve's broken, Kunhanna used to say. The
poor woman couldn't even go to church. Kunhanna,
who was really sad for her mistress, agreed to help her.
The deal was this: if it happened in church, Kunhanna
should hurry out looking embarrassed and then return
after some time with an expression of relief at having
taken a good dump. This gradually became a regular
thing. Kunhanna even got a nickname, Break-wind
Kunhanna. Kunhanna put up with everything not just
because of her devotion to her mistress but also because
of the extra eight annas and the *edangazhi* measure of
rice each week. Some rascally kids would even make
fart-sounds and squeals when she passed by. One day,
Jinsy's father Thomas came home crying from school.
He said that Cleetus, of the Maliekkal house, had
made fun of him, calling him 'Break-wind Kunhanna's

grandson'. That was Clara's son. Kunhanna found it unbearable. When she complained to Clara kochamma, she dismissed it saying, 'He's a kid, let it go.' Kunhanna decided to act; she planned it. On Sunday, as usual, Clara kochamma's bowels began their usual hyperactivity. Kunhanna did not move. Clara tried to poke her. In the end, thoroughly irritated, she stood up, coughed and announced: 'Hear, everyone . . . like every time, Clara kochamma of the Maliekal House has farted and I am taking it for her for the price of eight annas and an edangazhi of rice every week . . .' And she strode out. After that she never went back to that house; Clara never went to Sunday Mass ever. Jinsy's baptismal name was her great-grandmother's. After that spat with the parish priest over the history of the parish, she never went back there. For most of the time, she lay in bed. Would eat only when she was utterly famished. If up, she would go see Mathambi and listen to his singing and stories.

'The soul of some old man, some *karnnor*, has got into her when she was digging up the past,' Alice was really worried. 'My girl has ended up this way because of the black magic and *koodothram* your old folk did,' she complained.

'This is truly the devil,' she said. 'Or how could anyone cut down Kunnumbarambil Acchan?' Thomas felt that she was right. 'He is a really good man. How hopeless this parish was before he came?'

Before he arrived three years back, the parish was totally unpromising. Very few people attended church on Sundays or special days of worship. This was one of the parishes to which priests who were on the brink of being sent off to the old age home for priests, or a punishment appointment for erring priests. When he arrived here from a prosperous urban parish with numerous parishioners, in the early days, Kunnumbaramil felt that he was in living hell. He had been sent away from the other parish because he had taken an interest in a choir girl, Rosemary—in not just her voice but also her body.

Not past forty-five, still strong, the priest sighed that his good health and new ideas would wilt away unapplied. But Kunnumparambil who was adept at turning hurdles into possibilities did not give up. In the next days, he stayed glued to the parish register. The total number of families, the number of members, male and female; he made separate lists and tables of their age, education, employment and income. He moved around the length and breadth of the parish every morning and evening with that list. It changed the very fate of Chenkalathara. If Christ made fishermen the fishers of men, Acchan used fishing techniques to bait human beings. He set the right trap and bait for each and waited.

The kids who played cricket with coconut frond stems in the fields after harvest were the first group which took his bait. The bait was this: proper cricket gear and the permission to create a pitch on the paddy field near the church. Children who first went there to just enjoy a game soon began to attend prayers. The change in their self-indulgent offspring was the bait that their parents took. In the middle of this, some of the prayers of those who the priest had blessed by placing his hand on their heads or by administering the holy water came true by some stroke of luck. With this, his popularity grew like the grains of sand on the seaside or stars in the infinite night skies above. As for those whose prayers remained unanswered, he quoted Bible verses to exhort them to grow firmer in the faith. He lined up the poorer members of the parish in front of their rickety huts which announced their poverty loudly, snapped their pictures, went abroad, showed them to white people and brought back refined flour, rava and milk powder. Thus, soon, the church which had struggled to throw off the stigma of being a pela-ppalli—pelaya-palli, or the church of the Pulaya caste worshippers—began to attract some upper-caste Christians on special days. The novena and renewal meditation ending today were the culmination of his multi-pronged efforts. Jinsy who was suppressing a smile and pretending to be asleep when her parents were discussing the possibility of the devil possessing her, got up when she heard her mother call.

'My child, today you must come to church . . . it's the last day of the novena . . . the last days, oh, so many blessings and miracles!'

'Yes . . . miracles,' she murmured.

'Yes, miracles, why do you think so many people gather here? For nothing?'

'Really, do we have so many people here in our parish?' Jinsy picked and picked.

'But it isn't just people from our parish, is it? All the Christians from Kudamaloor and Olessa and Aykkarachera are here. They are all inside the church. Our people are outside. Anyway, come today, girl! I want the Acchan to put his hand on your head and pray.'

'Really—I am not coming!'

'Don't be so full of yourself, child,' Thomas tried to correct her. 'The Lord won't forgive . . . it was so crowded all these eight days; the food offerings weren't enough to feed all! On each day, a certain bakery-made food was the *nercha*-offering—achappam, kuzhalappam, vattayappam, unniyappam, avalose balls, bread, biscuit, cupcake . . . like that for eight days. Whatever you take there will be put into a basket in front of the altar. Then Acchan sprinkles the holy water on it and makes it pure . . . Then it all gets served to the faithful as offerings. No matter how many times the basket gets filled, it all gets over—such a crowd! On the eighth day, the offering is the packed rice lunch we bring from our homes . . . cooked in our own homes. Acchan has especially told us not to pack fish or meat as we are keeping a vow . . .'

But Jinsy did not go to the church that day despite her parents' persistent pleas. The prayer songs and chants emerged from the south-facing loudspeaker, fell on her ears, melted and flowed out. She tossed and turned in bed till Thomas and Alice came back after the novena. When she felt that they planned to spend the whole night marvelling at the miracles performed and cures effected, she turned over and slipped into sleep.

In the morning when the sacristan Vareeth chetan came over to say that they needed two people to clean up the mess after the last day of the novena, Jinsy's father had already gone to his construction site. So Jinsy had to go along with her mother to help her. When they reached the church, the leftover food packets from last evening were dumped in a big hole dug near the cemetery, and stray dogs and cats were having their fill of the food. Rice scattered around from broken packets was being pecked at by the crows and hens. The churchyard and premises lay completely dishevelled. The packed food which had already begun to rot was reciting and humming something to the wind. The thought that no matter how well you cover it up, some things just burst out was heaping itself up inside Jinsy.

'Get the hoe and the broom from the lean-to over there,' said Alice. 'Let's sweep everything into this hole and burn it all.' Jinsy went to the lean-to near the parish house to get the implements. When she reached, she saw Mathambi sit in the veranda of the parish house, near the window. She was about to hail to him, but he silenced her putting his finger on his lips like she'd done last time—and bade her to listen. He made her sit down beside him affectionately. Someone was talking in Acchan's room.

'But then I was really wondering—how did we get such an excess of food packets?' Jinsy knew the owner of the voice—it was Adarsh.

'Don't make me say bad things—it was an offering for a vow but you people just didn't take the food packets brought from the houses of Paraya and Pulaya,' Acchan washed his hands off the matter.

'Accha . . . but when you put it all into a single basket . . . how to know . . . where they came from? And even if we take it home, how to eat what these low people make in their homes? That's why we went back without taking even our own packets . . .' Adarsh opened up about his dilemma.

'Who told you to eat? Could you not have taken it back home and thrown it into the dustbin?' Acchan was riled.

'Ah, that's true . . .'

'On all eight days, there weren't enough of bakery things as offerings. The huge waste on the ninth day . . . just on the day of the pothycchoru offering . . . they will surely smell a rat . . . That's why I said all that in the final blessing . . .'

The words in the final closing prayer from yesterday gushed up in Jinsy's mind: 'The hands of the Lord who turned water to wine at the wedding feast at Cana . . . Oh Lord who fed five thousand with just five loaves of bread . . . Lord who sent us the sign of your Compassion this night, here . . . Praise the Lord! Lord, after the shortfall of offerings on all eight days in the past, you fed us sumptuously . . . Thank the

Lord who made our food basket overflow tonight . . . Depart in Peace!'

A scream that nearly tore her heart out got stuck in her throat. Sobbing loudly, she rushed to the grave where her family members, including Grandfather Karuppan, were buried. Hearing her approach, a black dog which lay on the grave shot out of the cemetery. The rice and curry that it had dragged there lay open on the banana leaf as though the souls of her dead forefathers were suddenly hungry. She fell on her knees in front of the grave and wept aloud.

Witnessing her daughter's transformation, Alice beat her breast and cried aloud, 'Has the devil got into my girl again, Karthaave . . .!' She managed to sweep and burn the rubbish and somehow get her daughter back home.

Oh My Grandfathers, please receive the fruits of these rites . . .

Mathambi's song that wafted there from somewhere in the churchyard went home with them.

Jinsy fell into bed as soon as they reached and slept off. She woke up with a start, dreaming that someone had shaken the legs of her cot. It lasted a few seconds, barely. But before she could make out if it was a dream or not, the sound of something huge collapsing on the churchyard was heard. Her Chaachan, Ammachi and Jobichan stepped out to look, and so did she. It was barely daybreak. The non-stop ringing of the church bells brought the entire village to the churchyard. Mathambi was hanging on to the bell rope and sounding an alarm with all his might; he summoned people again. There was Father Kunnamparambil, sitting in the corner that Mathambi usually occupied, drenched in sweat and shivering uncontrollably in absolute terror. The century-old Chenkalathara Church had fully collapsed and lay in a heap before them, face down.

People argued among themselves about the reasons for the collapse. Some said that the mild tremors early that morning had brought the church down. They cited as evidence the cracks on the walls of nearby houses, and the testimonies of those who heard their vessels jingle aloud in their kitchens and felt their cots shake. Another group, environmentalist in orientation, admitted that a mild tremor might have been the immediate trigger, but the real reason was the unscientific construction, filling up wetlands and swamps. The district collector who visited the spot wrote to the government to seek expert opinion on the matter.

As for these things which ye behold, the days will come, in the which there shall not be left one stone upon another, that shall not be thrown down (Luke 21: 6). No one noticed Mathambi, worn out from ringing the bell, utter this verse.

Everyone saw the earth lie split open between the grave of Grandfather Karuppan and the northeastern corner of the churchyard, where he had placed the keystone when they firmed up the land. But no one except Jinsy had dreamed the night before of a short, dark old man wearing just a *torthu* around his waist the colour of solid mud, with an iron hoe on his shoulder, pull off the keystone, and walk away.

Creeping Fears,
Enduring Compassion

In Kerala, the effects of climate change are perhaps most evident on the long coast. Golden beaches, once so common in Kerala, are being steadily eroded; the once-abundant fishing is falling in quantity and diversity. The mindless pollution of the sea has risen manifold, and in addition global climate change now also wreaks havoc on the coast, with massive, unpredictable cycloness which seem to have permanently altered the ways in which local people relate to the sea: for example, in the coastal fishing hamlets of the southern district of Thiruvananthapuram, fisher people seem to divide time into 'pre-Ockhi' and 'post-Ockhi', Ockhi being the name of the cyclone which hit these villages really hard in 2017. A senior fisherman with forty years of fishing experience told me that he could no longer recognize the sea after Ockhi.

The worst sufferers, naturally, are Kerala's coastal people, an extremely resilient community which has weathered many great losses since the early twentieth century. A few generations ago, the coastal people of Kerala, even though subject to the oppressive caste-order, had abundant and free access to marine resources. As many seniors there remembered during my fieldwork, their parents never knew want, even though their life was one of incessant toil. This changed after the mid-twentieth century with commercial interests from outside the fishing sector entered the field and new, ecologically-disastrous fishing technologies steadily gained ground, with the support of government agencies. Overfishing and exploitation rose steadily, but by the 1970s, the traditional fisher community, especially to the south, organized and fought to preserve the ecological well-being of the sea and their access to resources. This brought visibility and some welfare gains, but the ecological destruction of the coast continued relentlessly. And now, the deepening deterioration can no longer be concealed.

Ambiksutan Mangad's deceptively simple story is set in a northern coastal village, among coastal people whose lives are intertwined inextricably with the survival of their visitors, sea turtles who arrive to lay eggs on their beach. The two characters, the researcher Akhil who studies the procreative habits of sea-turtles, and Thankoottan, the fisherman who tries to protect their eggs and hatchlings form an interesting pair of contrasts. Akhil, whose love of nature is shaped by his science, is broken when he finds solid evidence for the disruption of nature's rhythm; shaken to the core, he wishes to retreat into a place away from human violence. But Thankoottan, whose love of the non-human living world is equally or even more powerful, cannot even imagine such a move—for him, caring for the non-human world is part of his very subjectivity. Irrespective of the destruction and uncertainty growing around him, Thankoottan continues to care for wounded beings. Akhil is indeed a stranger to their world. By setting up this gentle contrast, Ambikasutan points to us the nobility and gentle dignity of Kerala's ecosystem people—those who refuse to place themselves over and above the non-human living universe.

Neeraaliyan

'Neeraaliyan'

Ambikasutan Mangad

From the womb of the skies filled with darkness, a *kamalapparunthu*—a white-bellied sea eagle— swooped down to the earth like a flash of lightning. As it circled the hut which stood alone, like the folded palms of the night, it screamed loud and long, sounding like a saw: 'Hey, it's light!'

Akhil, whose heavy eyelids bore with difficulty the sleep of many nights, sat outside the hut and looked towards the east. Behind the black hills that slept under the thick quilts of green, the pale yellow was spreading.

It was not usual for the white-bellied eagle to make its appearance so early in the morning. Akhil felt worried, terrified. Something was wrong. Or did the eagle's long cry mean something else?

Moving closer to the cement tank, he peered in. Both the turtles were alive. Of the two, Bhagawathy was slowly moving in circles. Neeraaliyan—literally, 'The Diver'—was looking at her intently, absolutely motionless. Akhil placed his hand lovingly on her ancient shell, as dark as black iron. She stopped paddling. Neeraaliyan began to paddle towards her with great difficulty, but also great passion. Their lips touched, and they exchanged private messages. Then he tried to mount her. But each time, he failed.

Neeraaliyan's front feet were both gone. They had hit the propellers of seafaring ships. Or maybe the sharks ripped them off. Unable to swim, he lay floating in the far sea; Thankoottan had found and rescued him. Sea turtles that had a hard time on sea or land somehow always landed up with him. He would then bring them to the cement tank filled with seawater set up in front of his hut for the healing. He had healed and released countless numbers of such creatures into the sea. It was Thankoottan who gave Neeraaliyan his name. He allowed his wife Sudharmini the privilege of naming the females.

Poor Neeraaliyan's efforts to mate kept failing. Then a feminine voice arose from behind.

'The poor thing!'

A small shiver passed through Akhil's body. He had not noticed Sudharmini come and stand right behind him.

He did not respond. Who did she mean, 'poor thing'? Neeraaliyan or Bhagawathy?

Pouring a mug-full of jellyfish into the tank from the bucket, she came closer and kneeled behind him, she asked: 'What's up with you, Akhile? You haven't eaten any supper too?'

'Wasn't hungry,' he lied.

Running her fingers through his thick hair, she said, 'I feel so fond of you sometimes, like you were my kid . . . *bhayankara vaatsalyamthonnum* . . .'

He lowered his face, feeling uneasy.

'I feel guilty. Each day . . .'

She noticed his weary eyelids and asked in surprise. 'You didn't sleep at all? Last night too?'

He did not reply; merely ran his eyes on the white sand on the front yard of the hut. Seeing the sand cave in slowly a little away, he shouted in delight. 'Look! There!'

But Sudharmini seemed alarmed by the sight. She slapped her head and called out to the Goddess in sheer pain, 'Oh my Chirumpothy, the egg's hatching now?'

Akhil suddenly noticed that his happiness had been unexpected. It was a week after the expected hatching time. He had waited for it to happen over the past nights, but it was futile. Now his joy had bubbled up seeing the signs of life under the sand. But it should not happen during the day; eggs hatch usually only at night. Is Nature's rhythm failing? Was the untimely, white-bellied eagle's cry announcing this dissonance?

Akhil had been researching sea turtles along peninsular and island coastlines over the past four or five years, but had not seen such a strange phenomenon. He was studying the procreative habits of Olive Ridley turtles. There are eight species of sea turtles in the world; only the Olive Ridley come to the Vanneri beach to lay eggs. Many years back, the large-bodied Leatherbacks used to come too. Each as big as a Maruti 800 car! Thankoottan was fond of telling Akhil about how his father as a child once rode such a huge turtle along with four other kids on this very beach!

Sudharmini screamed again, pointing to the left, 'Look'ere Akhile!'

From there too came the sound of the sand caving in gently. In just minutes, the baby turtles would find their way to the surface and seek the sea desperately.

Sudharmini thought that the darkness was rushing into her eyes.

'Can't make an'thing of this . . . protect us, Chirumpothy . . .'

She remembered the day she had entered this hut, some twenty years back, as Thankoottan's woman. He was so shy, he did not say a word to her when he came to see her, married her, and when they walked hand in hand for a long time—whole nine *nazhik*as— on the beach. But when they stepped in the front of this house, he became alert, instantly, dropping all coyness. He took her on a tour of their yard, giving her clear instructions about where she could or could not step, and the corners where she should be very careful about. The new bride was puzzled. It was his younger sister Karthi who explained things to her.

The sea turtles come to lay their eggs on the Vanneri beach during mating season. Local people dig them up, take them away to make omelettes. Ever since he grew into manhood, Thankoottan would roam the beach at night with the thorny oar made of the *kaaramullu*, to ward off these thieves and protect the eggs. Anyone trying to dig up eggs would be sure to get a solid whack on the back. His skin was as dark as kohl, and so no one would notice him coming. That dissuaded people from digging up eggs, finally.

He would take a second round of the beach when the Morning Star rose, with a bucket and a powerful four-cell torch. He would move the sand carefully, transfer the eggs into the bucket, bring them to his yard and bury them there in holes a foot and a half deep. No one on the Vanneri beach could match his skill in spotting the egg-laying sites of the sea turtles. Once it lays its eggs, the turtle presses down its body weight to firm the earth; then it scatters the sand around to erase its path and other marks, and takes a different route back to the sea to confuse egg hunters.

It would take a month and a half for the eggs to hatch. Because Thankoottan's yard was fenced off, they were safe from dogs and foxes. The baby turtles hatching at night would stay around the house. It was Sudharmini's job to collect all of them in a bucket and take them to the sea. She would scoop them up in her palms affectionately and place them on the shoreline. They would scamper into the sea with great nostalgia. The sea beckoned them with its salty hands, the waves fondling each little one. Sudharmini would wait till the last baby disappeared.

They travel tens of thousands of kilometres through the sea, circling whole continents, growing into adulthood. After ten or sixteen years, the females would return to this very beach to lay eggs. Thankoottan often asked Akhil the secret of how they managed to return exactly at this place, this Vanneri beach, and not any other shore nearby, after so many years. He could not answer it satisfactorily despite being a researcher.

Once Thankoottan asked: 'Is this not a greater wonder than the Great Wall of China?'

Akhil nodded and smiled. Yes, only human feats are counted as wonders. Nature, however, is full of so many greater wonders! We just don't see them, that's all.

Let these hatchlings which have broken out at a strange hour stay beneath the sand till midnight, Akhil prayed; but just then a hatchling squirmed up above the sand, its back gleaming wet and black. It turned to face the sea. It held together its front flippers as though saluting the sea. After a few minutes, four or five more tired-looking hatchlings reached the surface and pressed close to the first. From the other pits, four or five more appeared. They huddled together as though fearful of sunshine.

A great wave of sadness and disappointment rose in Akhil's mind; it spread and moved like a surface current. More than a hundred hatchings should have emerged vigorously from each pit. Now, this—

'Thankoottaa . . .'

Hearing someone call, Sudharmini got up. It was the senior, Karapiriyan *karnnor*, and Dermman.

'Thankoottettan is gone fishing . . .' she said.

They stepped into the yard. Dermman lowered to the ground the basket he carried on his head. A large sea turtle. Seeing it look at them, Karapiriyan said: 'It landed on the shore near my house. Look at its belly? Too big to walk. Thought that if it's with Thankoottan, it will live . . .'

Akhil picked it up. It was heavy, some twenty-five kilos at least. He set it down gently in the water inside the tank. It slowly opened its eyes then. Akhil said: 'It's alive.'

A week before, Thankoottan had brought a pregnant turtle, like this one. He informed the Forest Department—that was the law—and they came with a vet. They were all shocked to see what was inside its belly when a post-mortem was done on it—a heap of plastic, two or three kilos. That was the cause of death, the vet said. The turtles mistake the plastic for jelly fish and swallow them. Thankoottan described how they always found plenty of plastic floating all around the far sea—and said: 'Turtles never spit anything out.'

Akhil waited for another hour. No hatchings appeared. They had buried hundreds of eggs in each pit. To console himself, Akhil said: 'Maybe the crabs were sneaking in at night and eating the eggs.'

No, Sudharmini said, 'If it's the crabs, we'd find their holes . . . the eggs must be going bad.'

Akhil was sure of that after he received the lab reports: 'Yes, they are going bad.'

Akhil managed to eat some breakfast, opened the envelopes and took out the reports again. He had read them many times, but went through them again, quivering within. Sudharmini came over and sat on the doorstep, combing her hair.

'Thankoottettan married me to look after the sea turtles,' she said. 'His sisters got married and left, and he would go to the sea, and then the egg thieves would dig up our yard. He won't let me go do any fish-work! My life is like the female turtle—not in the sea, not on the land . . .'

There was a break pregnant with silence, and then she went on, almost whimpering.

'I so wished to have a child! My luck! All these years I have sent tens of thousands of baby turtles into the sea. But I didn't have my own on the shore.'

Akhil heard her, his heart pounding. But his face buried itself in the bunch of papers. Looking at him, she continued. 'You know something, Akhil?'

He raised his face.

'Of all creatures on the earth and sea, the unluckiest one is the female sea turtle. It is just not fated to know what motherhood is. It can't lay eggs in the sea. The fish will eat it all up! And on land? It has to bury it and rush back into the sea! Or enemies will kill it. It can't hatch the eggs, know if the eggs have hatched, catch a glimpse of that which was born in its own blood, or caress it once! Such luckless creatures . . .'

Akhil looked at her moist eyes with kindness. Her words had seared his heart. He had never thought of this; she had revealed to him a great truth. He withdrew his eyes and began to weigh and measure the babies.

Sudharmini put the comb down there and came up to him.

'There's nothing for you to feel guilty about,' she said. He was silent.

'Thankoottettan would love to see me become a mother.'

Placing the hatchling carefully on the sand, he looked at her, surprised.

'Thankoottettan is very fond of you . . . he told me a month after you came here . . .'

Akhil looked even more amazed.

'What?'

She bowed her head. Said nothing. Her quivering toe drew something on the sand . . . the outline of a baby turtle.

Akhil turned his eyes towards the impassive soft blue that spread above the sea. When a single white-bellied eagle flew up and began to scratch lines on it, the ruthless, burning-coal-like words, which he had heaped in his mind over the past few days, escaped the confines of his mouth:

'I am leaving this place. Have decided. I'm giving up this research.'

Sudharmini looked stunned. Her mouth flew open. Her brows shivered in anger.

'What's it with you, boy? Are you mad?'

'I don't want to go mad!'

'Make it clear, Akhile!'

Without faltering the least, very seriously, he replied: 'The turtles will never come to lay their eggs on this beach again.'

Sudharmini's eyes popped. Day and night, she and Thankoottan were with them. They could not imagine a life without them. If the turtles did not return to Vanneri ... Watching her baffled expression, he continued: 'Can't you see, just ten or fifteen hatchlings, and they are not really healthy, either. There should have been at least four hundred from the three pits. There used to be more male hatchlings earlier—since the past few years, the numbers of female hatchlings have gone up. In cooler weather, more males are born; if the temperature is between twenty-eight and thirty-four degrees, the hatchlings will be all female . . . a wonder, not found among other creatures . . .'

'But what if it gets hotter?' Sudharmini asked anxiously.

'If it rises above thirty-four, they won't hatch at all. They will rot. There will be no babies, male or female. The very race of turtles will disappear from the earth.'

Sudharmini sank down like she was struck by lightning. Akhil gathered the reports quickly and went off to his room. She seemed oblivious of it. When she came to, after some time, she scrambled up and rushed inside. Akhil was packing his clothes to leave. She went up to him and caught hold of his arm with authority.

Her voice failed as she said, 'No, don't go, Akhile. Thankoottan won't let you go away, my son!'

'I can't help it. I have to go.'

'Where are you going? Back home?'

He smiled a sad grey smile, the colour of ashes, of the erikku flowers.

'I have been to tiny islands near the coasts in the places I have visited . . . where the turtles lay their eggs. They are small, just the size of a football field, sometimes . . . with no human habitation. Islands not marked on any map . . . Like Suheli, or Moro . . . and many nameless ones. I'll go live on one of those. When it becomes hotter, the island will sink; I'll sink too.'

Sudharmini was really angry.

'You are totally mad!'

The smile on his lips had not yet faded. He began to roll up the rest of the clothes and stuff them in the bag.

She saw Thankoottan walking towards the house through the beach. It comforted her hugely. She pointed a finger out: 'Thankoottettan is coming.'

He was returning from the sea. As usual, a bucketful of jelly fish hung from his arm. The basket on his head was unusual, though.

He set down the basket on the yard in front of the hut. It contained a big sea turtle which looked dead. Its front flippers were sliced off. Its shell was split from top to bottom; blood had clotted along it. It was blinking its eyes.

Without showing his pain, Thankoottan lit a smile on his lips and told Sudharmini, 'The wound's deep. But we must somehow heal and raise him.'

Akhil leaned out, showing only his head—with the despair of a sea turtle with chopped-off limbs sinking into the depths of the sea.

Settler-Swagger

For centuries, the rainforests of the Sahya mountains on the western edges of Malayalam-speaking regions formed a nearly impenetrable barrier between these areas and the sub-continent. The indigenous tribes which lived there enjoyed control over forest resources and were assigned a position, albeit marginal, to the Malayali social order. This was to change drastically in the late-nineteenth and twentieth centuries: colonial control changed the very understanding of the forests and its inhabitants, but equally important was the substantial migration of settlers from low lands to the forested areas. Syrian Christian farmers were the leading force among the migrants and they were impelled to migrate by a number of factors including changes in population dynamics, repression by the Hindu-majoritarian state in Travancore during the 1930s, and near-famine conditions in the extremely difficult decade of the 1940s. Subsequent waves of migration, often organized by the Catholic Church or even enterprising settlers who carved up the land into parcels for sale, happened in the later decades. By end of the twentieth century, the indigenous population became a minority in their own homelands—for example, in the district of Wayanad. Indigenous land rights were lost forever, it seemed. Settler interests in land are powerful in politics.

A steady narrative on the settler-experience has been available in Malayalam literature and non-literary writings since the 1950s. Some of these have been very celebratory, extolling Settler-Man's persistence against the forces of Nature and their final conquest of the land and underlining the Settler-Man's Burden of 'civilizing' indigenous people. However, by the early years of the present century, life in Wayanad became a struggle for the settlers as well—with agricultural price instability, the shrinking human-wildlife interface, climate change as well as the entry of capital, as granite quarry miners and tourist resorts. Emigration to the Gulf and the Anglo-European-American countries and other parts of India is now an important coping mechanism for settler families. Agriculture is in every sense a gamble, and leasing land for cultivation of potentially valuable crops like ginger across the border in Coorg is common.

Vinoy Thomas's delightful story turns a humorous and critical eye on this narrative. Idaveli—literally, 'Mid-way Fence'—is a fictitious settler-village in the mountainous parts of Kannur district near the border with Coorg. Maani Chaachan displays the cunning and the swagger of the Syrian Christian settler-

leader—swagger which uses the discourse of 'unity' as an instrument of its cunning. Maani Chaachan claims that his card games unite the residents of Idaveli, but he makes a killing from the games, lines his pockets with it. His constant chatter about uniting its residents beyond their caste identities is clearly a lie—clearly, his cultural-political horizon is still of untouchability especially against the Paniya tribal people. No wonder, then, that he and his discourse collapse in a heap when it has to confront feudal power from across the border. Idavelikkaar *represents yet another brilliant instance of the thrust to question the very bases of twentieth-century Malayali pride, and this critique is now an important theme and driving force in Malayalam literature.*

The People of Idaveli

'Idavelikkaar'

Vinoy Thomas

When he sat hunched up in the middle of the sacks of cabbage as the mini lorry came down the Makkoottam pass, Inji-Ravi, smarting from insult and defeat at Shettyppura, clawed and tore at the skin of the soles of his feet. Because the thoughts were thrusting themselves out of his head violently, his eyes would not shut. Last year, the *inji*—ginger crop—failed because the plants curled up and died all of a sudden from the green wilt. And it wasn't much better the year before, either. This year, more than double the land had been leased out for farming ginger, in a daring bid to overcome all the losses at one try. And this had to happen. Yes, one did know that the people of Kodagu were arrogant to their bloody roots, but this was hard to suffer. The ginger plants were only

242

half-grown. Maybe one should've put up with it till the crop was harvested and sold. But then, am I not an *Idavelikkaaran* . . . an Idaveli man?

Lathika smelled the humiliation that pressed down Ravi's head even before he came in through the gate. She, too, was born and raised in Idaveli. Idaveli people marry only each other—outsiders often complained.

As she soaked the mud-streaked clothes that he had brought back from Kodagu and squeezed the dirt off them, she asked: 'Did you go meet Chaachan? Go, tell him all instead of ripping out the skin of your feet.'

Ravi was pulling off the skin from his cracked soles and throwing it away. He looked at her with respect. Yes, he hadn't thought of Maani Chaachan till then! That would have been foolish. They may be anywhere in this world, but for the people of Idaveli, isn't he the most important person?

The house where Maani Chaachan, the most important person in Idaveli, lived, stood on a west-sloping plot of land. Therefore the morning light would wait hesitatingly, finding it hard to enter the house through the front. Now the light plunged on to the plastic mat tied above the cow-dung-hole dug lower down below the front yard of the house, splattered all around, and entered the house upside down. Maani Chaachan was in the veranda lit bluish, reclining on a divan made of fibre, feeling the strength of his thigh muscles, looking as imposing as a warlord. It was then the little chap, his son's boy, began to bawl hanging on to his *kalli*, design mundu. When his patience wore out, Chaachan got up, pulled out some old playing cards and made him some card soldiers.

When the soldiers were lined up, Chaachan scanned the road in front of the house idly. Inji-Ravi stood near the gate.

'Ravi, you've come down from there early?'

'Yes,' said Ravi. 'I came back yesterday.'

Chaachan deployed the soldiers very carefully towards the door and pulled a chair for Ravi.

'Edi, some more black coffee—and wash that glass well to get rid of the fish stink,' he called to his daughter-in-law Justi.

A little wind that bore the scent of cow dung blew in from the compound and toppled the soldiers. The kid began to bawl again. Maani Chaachan rose up again, went over, set up four boundaries, and created a country for the kid.

'Let the kids learn how to fight wars,' he said, lining up the soldiers again.

'Pappa, Pappa,' the kid demanded.

Chaachan picked up a card, tore its edge, and folded it up to make a twisted-headed soldier. 'Here, your Pappa,' he said, pushing it towards the kid.

'This guy is also into card games, huh?' asked Ravi.

'What other toy will Idaveli's *kochunga* play with?' Chaachan said. 'What about a two-hand game for a hundred in the morning?' Fishing out a curled-up note from the mundu-fold on his waist and tucking it behind his year, scratching the rash on his nipple, Chaachan got ready for a game of Rummy.

He pulled out a printed plastic packet from under the teapoy and opened it. Three decks of playing cards, paper to write the points on, a pen—all of this was stored carefully in it. Chaachan combined the cards smoothly and easily like a fortune teller laying cards for his parrot to pick.

'Draw it, Ravi,' he said.

Ravi pulled out the Eight of Diamonds; just then, Justi brought the coffee and held it out to him. She went back in, still smelling her hand for fish stink.

'You deal the cards, Eda,' Chaachan said, pulling his card—the Ace of Hearts.

Ravi shuffled the cards and dealt them thirteen each. The stack was cut and the Seven of Clovers was pulled randomly as Wildcard Joker. Chaachan began the game picking up the first card from the deck. Before he reached the dregs of the cloudy black coffee in the intensely-clean-smelling glass, Ravi had drawn four times. At the fourth draw, he declared, 'Ah! You've hit the full early in the morning, ed!' Chaachan said ruefully, granting Ravi all of sixty-four points. He had been writing the points. Finishing it, he began to shuffle the deck again.

Just watching that smooth shuffling, the marvellous hand movement that has mesmerised the people of Idaveli for decades! Ravi could imagine his ginger fields that covered vast areas of the rolling hills of Shettyppura and the tall, intimidating figure of Maani Chaachan twirling his white moustache looming up in the middle of them.

The truth is that Father Kalathil—Kalathilacchan, or, 'the Master of the Card-Space' or 'Master of the Arena', literally—with his beard as white as the King of Diamonds—was the reason why such a person came to be here in Idaveli. He started the youth club called Yuvajanavedi in 1958, when he noticed that young men here—all migrants from the lowlands, goodness knows from where all—were getting kind of scattered and lost in the hills, generally clueless about things. He created it noting that young fellows needed a place to get together in the evenings and have some fun times. Thoma Saar and Karia Chetan and Kutty Aashaan and Chatta Gopalan and others gathered together, cut trees from their yards for timber, carved out some sandstone, made thatches out of coconut leaves—and constructed a building for Yuvajanavedi. One day, when they were sitting around in the new building and chatting, the idea of playing cards regularly struck Kutty Aashaan. His mother was an enthusiastic card player. In the evening, once the sign of the cross was made, they would go to bed only after two rounds of the game. Kutty Aashaan was so skilled, he taught everyone and in two weeks, all the members of the Yuvajanavedi learned how to play.

When Aashaan came down the hill in the evening, young Maani would be hanging on his shoulder. He would be doing the job of picking up the cards when the card matches were on at the Yuvajanavedi. Before he went back uphill again, Aashaan had to down at least two six-ounce glass-fulls of Sputter-Sankaran's brew. Before Aashaan finished the second glass, young

Maani would receive from him at least two drops of the potent liquid that made your face contort. When those drops gradually swelled and Maani could drink two glass-fulls without distorting his face, someone began to call him Chaachan, Older Brother.

When Maani Chaachan became the secretary of the Yuvajanavedi, its oldster-ish-ness vanished, and the presence of hot young blood became palpable. When it fermented and bubbled up, the Yuvajanavedi began to intervene in everything that went on around. It was when they were strapped for cash to do something they had planned that Maani Chaachan suggested that they hold a card-game tournament—as it was a game that all the locals knew.

In the month of Idavam—June-July—people there planted ginger, tapioca, turmeric, yams, banana and other crops. When the Middle-Idavam monsoon wind hit the hills of Kodagu and the rains began to fall and run down the hills, the people of Idaveli would leave all their crops and prepare to compete in the tournament. The games were Rummy, Auction, Support. The most important of these was Rummy. When it appeared that the tournament might have to be halted because the players got into arguments and even some pushing and shoving, Maani Chaachan decided to write a bye-law. The Rummy's bye-law was written in Malayalam, and it was ridden with spelling errors.

1. Rummy is a game played with one hundred and fifty-one cards and up to nine players.

2. One Rummy with an Ace till King and at least three cards in the order one-two-three. Rummy in the same order with or without a Joker, and a set of cards of the same value but different types—in all, thirteen cards—this is what this game seeks.
3. Cards that can't be inserted into sets will be counted as points.
4. A player who adds up two hundred and fifty points will have to leave the game. The player who stays back till the end is the winner.
5. . . .
6. . . .

When Chaachan reached twenty-six bullet points, the bye-law for the Rummy was complete. At the end was added the following epilogue: The bye-law may be altered from time to time so that the game does not deteriorate—

Even those who used to mock in secret that he could not even write properly were impressed by Chaachan now. All the rules of card games were correctly entered in a ruled notebook with the title 'Bye-Law' carefully written on the cover page—well enough to silence the unruly.

At the beginning the venue of the tournament was the Yuvajanavedi building. Then, as the number of participants grew, it was shifted to the school, with the Father's permission. If the skies promised heavy rain, the school would break early. And on most monsoon days, it would be dark by noon. And even if that didn't happen, Thoma Saar would say: 'We will break, Teachere, the weather is rough.'

But the pupils would not go home. They would hang around watching the card games. Three benches would be pulled close and a black board would be inverted on it; that's how the Rummy table for nine was made. Once they entered the game, everyone needed a smoke—a bidi—to get rid of the mosquitoes. On the veranda, Devasiachan would be selling black coffee, omelettes and buns. He'd get it delivered to the players who needed food.

Many things that weren't mentioned in the bye-law would happen in the middle of the game. The players would wager on money and the organizers would pretend not to know. A good amount changed hands in each game. The first round involved eighty-one games. The second round, nine. The third was the final round; there would be several final rounds.

Maani Chaachan would play only a few games in each round. He would then come and sit, looking very serious, near the table which was the club's temporary office. His very posture made people respect him. Even Thoma Saar would clear doubts with him, addressing him as Maani Chachaa. The tournament is so successful because Idaveli people are so united, Maani Chaachan always said.

Two and a half months after the tournament, when the national flag was raised on the flagpole in front of the Yuvajanavedi building on Independence Day, the prizes would be distributed. The prizes could be full-length mirrors, large vessels or plastic chairs.

After a few years, the card tournament became Idaveli's national celebration. Before the games started, Maani Chaachan would clap and draw everybody's attention. The players were to stand in a circle silently. Chaachan would then begin to speak in a soft voice. In a short speech, he would draw attention to the greatness of the land of Idaveli, the unity of its people, and how card games were instrumental in creating the sense of oneness there.

'Raviye, cut it,' said Chaachan, pointing to the stacked deck.

'Our tournament should've been on, *alle*, Chaachaa?' Ravi cut the deck. They were past the fifth game.

'Oh, I just want it to happen. It's happening in Idaveli, good enough.' The Joker was an Ace.

'But you aren't there in all the rooms, Maani Chaachaa?'

Chaachan coughed and a little phlegm fell onto a card. 'What for? What is mine will come right here for me. See, like you came now? And not just that, if there's a game in Idaveli, a share on the card table is Chaachan's, eda. Our kids respect their elders. They'll bring it in.'

'That'll do. Can the people of Idaveli forget Maani Chaachan? Let me tell you the truth, Chaacha, my ginger farming is exactly like this game which you taught. Kodagu has eaten lakhs of my money. And it has given me an equal sum. I have neither laughed nor cried about it. Because it is all a game. Just a game.' He had drawn a Joker.

'That's all, yes. My boy says, when he stands on the country's border holding the gun, it's like hitting two hundred and forty-eight points in the tournament, close to the ejection bar. That is all! You can be ejected from the game anytime. It's me, this Maani Chaachan, who made Idaveli people so strong of heart!' He said, 'Ah, you're ready to put it face down? Then I am a goner!' He counted the cards.

'Losing the Inji-game of lakhs is not an issue for me. But I can't bear what happened there.'

'What do you mean?'

'I wept, Chaacha. I couldn't help crying when I was slapped on the cheek. And for what, you want to know? I sat with my leg upon my other leg before another man.'

Ravi's eyes had welled; he was beginning to rip the skin off his sole again. Chaachan grabbed his hand and roared: 'Which son of a whore did this to an Idaveli man?'

'At Shettyppura. Bopanna. He's a big landlord there. A big sowcar.' Chaachan's grip eased.

'Doesn't matter where. It's not right that an Idaveli man had to return head bowed. You haven't forgotten Bundummel Kadar and the festival at Poovathumkeezh? That is our legacy!'

Ravi began to deal the cards. The most important player in the district is Khadar, or Kadar, owner of the bus KPK Travels. There was a big field set up as an arena for card games at the Kodambarabu Maqam Uroos festival. Many from Idaveli went there to play, betting large sums. Kadar was the master of the field. One hour into the game, and Khadar had already plucked the feathers and the comb off the Idaveli challengers. Because Chaachan had taught them that they should not let go of the truth while they play, they returned quietly, rubbing their chests.

The big field for the game at the Poovathumkeezh Bhagawati temple's Thira festival at Idaveli was in the revenue land behind the Pazhasshi irrigation project canal. The master of the arena was Maani Chaachan. The players sat in rows in the place lit up by large lamps. Every kind of local card game known there was to be played: the *Chatti* game, Pig-*Malathu*, Underoverlucky, *Katta Marinjhaal Kaanunna Padam*, Elephantpeacockcamel, Luckywheel.

The games began when Chaachan waved his hankie. Bundummel Kadar and his team arrived. Kadar was passionate about Pig-Malathu. He would wager only on the outside cards, but that day, it was the inner cards that were needed for a win. When things went against him, he lost it. He caught hold of the Idaveli boy who was dealing the cards and snarled—dealing falsely, uh? A bunch of cuss words followed. The lights went off like they had all been switched off. There was a lot of screaming and rushing about and yelling. When it was over and it was light again, the Idaveli folk stood there undefeated and without a scratch on their bodies. Who knows where Kadar and his gang had vanished?

'Oh, Chaachaa, those times have vanished,' said Ravi. 'Aren't all the workers at Shettyppura Idaveli people? Did they do anything?' Ravi said, before he remembered that he had drawn a card without a Rummy.

'Ha! All your workers are Paniya chaps? Tribals? What do they know of love for the place?' Chaachan placed his hand face-down.

'Leave those Paniyas. Vengaala Suresh, Keeran Raju, Pachi Baby, these guys too didn't do anything . . . that's what troubles me . . . It's a full . . . write, eighty-one points.'

Maani Chaachan won the next two games in a row. Ravi went out. Handing Chaachan a hundred-rupee note from his purse, Ravi said: 'Just forgive me please, if I am wrong. It was my Acchan who supervised all of my ginger farming in Kodagu. After he died, I am alone, really alone. I am thinking of you in my father's place. Please come with me to Shettyppura. Chaachan there will unite the Idaveli people there again. We have to show them how we play!' Ravi caught hold of Chaachan's hands beseechingly.

'How am I to leave these women alone here?' Chaachan was still reluctant.

'Just think of my request as a plea for Idaveli,' Ravi said, finally.

When he got on the early morning bus that went through the Makkoottam pass to Virajpetta, it was not cold, but Maani Chaachan tied a turban around his head with a towel. Seeing Kodagu yielding to the mist in the turn of the road from Bittangala, he said what came to his mind: 'Like our Wayanad of the old times.

Small slopes with trees on top and fields below, and forests and flowers and stuff on the hilltops. Pretty to see, but not good to settle!'

The bus went some distance ahead on Gonikuppa road. They got off at Bittangala. Then they caught the jeep to Shettyppura and got off in front of a shop. They had to walk the rest of the way.

'Let's drink some tea, Eda.' Chaachan got into the shop without taking off his turban. Sitting on the old bench of wooden planks, the seam of which was showing, he took a look around. There was some stuff, barely enough for a shop. Some rice, in a shade of deep yellow, dried *onthu* fish so aged that it was red in colour, four or five tomatoes, some beaten rice in a box, some stationery items, some stale and broken Madakku snacks in a tea shop jar. When the owner—a Muslim—brought them the tea, Chaachan asked him: 'You're sure that the glasses were washed thoroughly?'

'Oh, yes.'

'What's your name?'

'Oppi.'

'Where're you from back home?'

'Koothuparamba'.

'Oh, so you probably know Bundummel Kadar?'

'Yes.'

'Are you able to make ends meet with this tiny shop in this godforsaken place?'

'Oh, I manage.'

'Ah, you Muslims can do only so much. Hey, Ravi, why're you so silent after coming up here?'

'Nothing, Chaacha,' Ravi paid for the tea.

By the time they walked three-and-a-half kilometres to the ginger fields, Chaachan had begun to pant mildly. Some twenty-five acres of land, divided into blocks and converted into fields. The ginger plants had put out shoots. This was the first crop after clearing the forests. Plastic nets were tied around the fields at the edge of the forests to stop wild boar raids. Idaveli folk were at work bending and coming up, digging the soil from the *cherendis*—the water channels in the middle of the ginger patches—and shovelling it into the fields.

Chaachan went over to an undisturbed, dusty shed to sit down, but Ravi stopped him. He sprinkled some water around to calm the dusty air and laid some heavy sacks on the floor to welcome Chaachan. Lunch was of rice gruel and dry-roasted onthu fish, but Ravi picked some *kanthaari* chillies that grew nearby, crushed it into the fish, and served Chaachan his gruel. All the Idaveli people paid him their respects during lunch time.

When it was evening, Ravi called him to the shed. He took out a half-bottle of liquor from his waist-pocket and taking out banana leaf packet from under the pot, opened it. Chaachan thought that it was the black-coloured gooseberry pickle. Only after he had taken a piece with three fingers and tasted it did he know what it was.

'Eda, this is pork! How come it looks black?'

'Softly! Have just a little of it! Got it for you, Chaachaa. The pork curry of Kodagu. They make it with some masala that looks like our coffee powder and kokum . . .'

'Whatever it is, it tastes great. How did you get it?'

'Oh, I just did.' A smile came to Ravi's lips involuntarily. Chaachan hummed as though he knew it. Just two glasses. Once they got over, the others took the glasses and went towards the forest fringe. Ravi opened his mind: 'The fucking corpses! When I came here and told them about how that Kodagu chap had slapped me, they were busy poking their mobile phones! Not that I can't go back and settle it on my own, but I have put lakhs into this jungle. Do these fellows have any such worries? I can save them and bundle them home in a blink. But they ought to have a feeling that this is about an Idaveli man . . . that's what they don't have!'

'How's that to be expected? Vengaala Suresh is a Chetty—all tangled up with his Chetty-street, and Ganapathy and all that. This guy Paul, he is Christian, but a Latin guy. He won't join with anyone else. And no need to even talk about Baby who's married a second time right on the tail of his wife's death . . . Anyway, you just relax. I am here now.'

Ravi felt relieved. He felt like he was sitting on the veranda of his home at Idaveli. Chaachan's burps seemed to fly over the ginger fields like a whiff of breeze from Idaveli. He was starting to win the game.

'You call all those guys here . . . let's play a hand.' Chaachan opened the end of his mundu tucked into his waist. The Paniya workers did not know how to play. Even if they knew, they had no money to place bets with. But there were nine of the others, and they could play a full table. When they all sat around the table, Maani Chaachan stood up. It felt like the old tournament times. He clapped first and began his brief speech.

'Thoma Saar used to say long back that in some countries they used these cards as currency notes. From the time I heard this, whenever I picked up these cards, it felt like money. And now, these are money for me. They save me wherever I go. Card games are not merely to pass the time. Don't we make a hundred calculations; do all sorts of cartwheels in life, to hang on here? This game is exactly that. The man who knows it is a king in any land. Some kids who went away from Idaveli bring me some fancy things when they come back. Why? Because I am the one who made them players. They control things in the places where they live now. That's how each Idaveli man should be. Our Lord Jesus Christ has said, wherever two or three gather in my name, I am present among them. The card too is like that. When the nine of us sit around a table—there's the Paniya, the Chetty, the Latin Catholic, the Syrian Christian and all among us. But there is something among us which we can't really put our finger on—that's the truth. If we are here holding on to each other like the children of the same womb, that's because we are all from Idaveli. So, my children, we must play, play for Idaveli alone. We must play only for Idaveli.'

Maani Chaachan's words brought tears to everyone's eyes. When they sat together brushing against each other, Keeran Raju remembered how, back then, Thoma Saar would make the children sit together to make the shape of the map of India on Republic Day. When Maani Chaachan ended his speech, he thought he heard someone shout loudly from that isolated shed in the middle of that vast ginger field: '*Idavelikkaar*!'

As they advanced in the game, drawing and discarding, Maani Chaachan threw a couple of pointed looks at Suresh. He saw Suresh repeat the same thing and so spoke up: 'You shouldn't draw the card with spittle on your fingers. Don't the others have to draw them with their fingers?'

'Oh, that's because the cards are stuck together, Chaachaa.'

'For that just sprinkle some powder on the cards? Why use spittle?'

At the end of the game, it was Chaachan who made a killing. He rolled up the notes and thrust them into his knickers, poured some water into the bottle, drank it up, and rolling out the jute sacks, lay down on the floor. The others went back to their mobile phones.

Chaachan got up a little late the next morning. He needed a glass for the black coffee. Baby and Raju were drinking their coffee. He washed his mouth with water from a plastic pot and asked: 'There are no mugs here, Eda?'

Binu came out of the forest quickly with a mug.

'Where did you take it?' asked Chaachan, smelling it.

'There's only one here?' Binu walked back.

'Chaachaa, everyone uses the same mug to brew their coffee,' Ravi said humbly.

'Uh! Dirty! It's not so expensive to buy another mug. This was used by the Paniyan bo . . .' Seeing Binu come close, he stopped at mid-sentence and began to brew his coffee. The others were suddenly struck by the fact that they had not thought about it earlier.

The sun in Kodagu did not make them sweat but instead steamed all their bodies. Chaachan did not pick up a shovel—so what, he filled the whole ginger field with his presence, going up and down the whole day. And so the work on the *cherendis* between two whole blocks was completed that day before sundown. When they stopped work and prepared to get back, it was Chaachan who asked if there was a stream around there. There was one, if you walked through the forest path lined by the kongini bushes and went around the hill. If you get past the lane overgrown with kaara grass, you can get into the stream.

'Not like back at our place, the water here is thicker,' said Chaachan when he rose from a dip. When everyone was back on the bank after a bath and swim, he made another suggestion: 'Why not go off to that Oppi's shop for some tea and also get a cup and a few glasses? Let's all go? Better than staying cooped up here?'

'I am not coming. Have a lot of accounts to write.' Chaachan noticed that the workers were exchanging smiles without Ravi noticing.

'Did this guy find only that low-hanging branch to rid himself of the poison?' Chaachan asked Baby. He had a vague memory of a woman hanging around there at noon. It was she who he referred to as 'low-hanging branch', easy to grab, that is.

Chaachan led the group as they made their way to Oppi's shop. He told the others the most amazing tales from Idaveli. There were not many customers in the shop. Chaachan ordered twelve glasses of tea and seated himself on Oppi-kka's chair.

'Eat whatever you like, it's my treat today! Not because I won the cash in the card game. Idaveli guys are all my kids. Just stay united. Chaachan will do anything for you, *Makkale*!'

He did not take off the turban; instead he tied it tighter. It was then that he noticed that there was a low murmur coming from the thatched shack behind the shop. They found four players engrossed in a card game. Clean card-game-field. Players who looked like fine folk.

'Oho, so this is played here too? Must be Kaakkamaar, Muslims! You fellows brought it to India after all!' Chaachan displayed his knowledge of the world, pulled up his chair behind the players.

'Hey, you, get me a snack,' he ordered, slurping the tea noisily.

'What the fuck have you made this with? It tastes stale!' Maani Chaachan lowered himself firmly into

the chair and began to seriously assess the game of
the fair, short man who sat in front of him. When he
drew the King of Clovers, he discarded the Seven of
Diamonds because he did not have a card to pair it
with. Chaachan sent him a congratulatory smile. It is
easier to find a pair for a bigger card. He drew again.
He's a single-card show now. His neighbour discarded
a Six of Spades. He did not pick it up and drew a card
instead. Chaachan was all fired up now; he looked
at the others. They were just drinking their tea and
paying no attention to the card game. The player now
drew a Queen; he discarded it. His neighbour snatched
it and won the game. Chaachan who was watching it,
completely lost his cool.

'Whose dashed crotch were you staring at when
you played?' he yelled. 'You had the Four of Spades! If
only you picked up the Six of Spades, you'd have made
a set! You'd have won! Player, indeed!'

The short, fair man stood up, slowly. He was no
dwarf, actually. He wore on his neck a gold locket:
two tiny curving swords strung on a tiny gun. It
was a Kodagu symbol. His arm, which looked like
the skinned root of a coffee plant rose up, and they
noticed then that it bore a tattoo of a goddess with
many arms.

The first blow fell on the cheek, while the snack
was still inside the mouth. A yellowish cloud of dust
spread in the air. The second one fell on the neck and
also on the hand holding the glass. After that, no one
could make out if it was a kick or a blow. Many things

happened. In the end, Chaachan was found lying curled up under Oppi-kka's tea shop table.

'Enough, Sowcar, he's old,' Oppi-kka said that, staying well away.

'You dog of a Malayali, come here fer yer work only. If not, don't come—*Illi maathada, bara bendaa, Gotthe*? Goth it? Sonofawhore, teaching a Kodaga man games?'

Chaachan was about to open his mouth and ask, '*Mone*, Son, are you Bopanna Sowcar?' but he decided against it.

'Take away the smelly old fool!'

Vengaala Suresh helped Chaachan up. Except Chaachan, all the others had brought cups and glasses for themselves. In the bluish light of the mobile phones, each of their faces appeared clearly, looking as distinct from each other as different places. No one spoke. When they set back and were halfway through, Chaachan who was a little behind the others began to speak, believing that the others were listening to him.

'It is not right to make these distinctions like Malayali, Kodagan and so on in India. If you think of it, these borders are like ripples that gravel makes when it is thrown on the face of a pond. No one can make out, why it is, what it is!'

Women in Bodies

I am not exaggerating when I say that women in Kerala, despite the continued adulation they receive for their education, better health, fewer childbirths and so on, have been taught for long to devalue and despise their bodies, even fear them. They are constantly reminded that they are nothing but bodies for labour, procreation, and the pleasure of men; and that such bodies deserve no respect. These reminders are served upon, increasingly, not just grown women, but also young and infant girls.

In the recent decades, Kerala have has plagued by a number of shocking incidents that indicate the ubiquity of violence against women and girls. These incidents have ripped off our shared patriarchal common sense about the social world, especially about the sanctity of the family and the dependability of the home as a haven against sexual violence. Even more shocking has been the fact that for the most, the much-celebrated welfare state in Kerala, that points to Kerala's women and children as evidence for its successes, has remained negligent about securing justice to the wronged women and children; to the contrary, in recent times, state functionaries have often actively participated in slowing down and even subverting justice. Political parties that have garnered credit for 'women's empowerment' grow misogynistic day by day. The situation is aggravated by the fact that more and more women in Kerala receive higher education, are exposed to the media, and build their own networks on social media. In other words, even as patriarchy seems to be intensifying especially through sexual violence—that dehumanises women, reduces them to usable bodies, and strips them of social worth and dignity—women seem to be gaining vision and voice that makes them offer dogged but regular resistance to patriarchy.

Shahina E.K.'s hard-hitting story mobilizes the great sense of frustration and anger widespread among women in Kerala today. It is true that 'gender' in Kerala no longer means the male/female divide— there is an active queer movement and much public activism by transgender people. The awareness of the complexity of gender has only sharpened the awareness of both the heterogenity and the omnipresence of patriarchy. Shahina's story is important as the newest fruit of an enduring anti-patriarchal discourse that imagines a world beyond through the eyes of women, inaugurated and fostered in the twentieth century by illustrious women writers, especially Lalithambika Antharjanam and Sara Joseph. She strings together the inner conflicts of people who share the same space, probably in a middle- or upper-middle class urban neighbourhood, drawing actively from real incidents that sent shockwaves through the Malayali public. Her women are united by their awareness of the violence and the indignity and anger against patriarchal authorities. The story reaches a dream-like crescendo as women reject patriarchal protections/ confinement—these women connect, swell and sweep into the streets, leaving behind their homes and clothing, holding hands and joyously embracing their vulnerability. Like, as Shahina's title tells us, the wind or sun or leaves or flowers.

Like Wind, Sun, Leaf and Flower

'Kattum Veyilum Ilayum Poovum Pole'

Shahina E.K.

Joseph, Sriram Lodge, Room No. 3, Street No. 10, Mangala Lane

Daylight, a long stretch like a middle-aged man with a hangover from the previous night's drinking, a loud yawn from a foul-smelling mouth with the bits of onion and buffalo meat sticking to the teeth and the rum, the finger that extends to the eye, digs out the rheum and wipes it on the bed sheet, the long, soundless fart that seems to have anticipated all the unpleasant things ahead that day.

Joseph covered his nose, moved towards the sunshine which had grown warmer, and sat there. Outside the window, the women fussed about by the side of the drinking water tanker. His stomach burned.

Lighting a bidi, he peeked out. There she was, the little slut. Making a big noise. Someone had moved her water pot to the back of the row. She took the filled pot only halfway; her sister took it home, like in a relay race. Following them was the smallest one, like a black puppy.

Someone screams, 'Oh, the squirrel's stopped squeaking!' Someone pushes her pot forward. She bends down.

The muscles on the left of Joseph's stomach cramped. The kick from the little black leg! It still felt raw and tender there; the swelling hasn't yet subsided. With the memory of the half-grown dark-skinned fruit on her chest that he barely got to squeeze, that of the kick which made him keel over and spill his pee!

He moved away from the window quickly, before her eyes which would naturally fall on his window as she swung the pot on her hip, could spot him.

Vahida, 'Dilruba', House No. 11, Street No. 10, Mangala Lane

'I don't know what to do . . . when she used to complain before, I would wonder if it was really true. And I even beat her then, Pushpe . . . But then I began to understand. She's a college student now, our Ruba . . . but her Uppa . . . father . . . doesn't seem to see that when he cuddles her. Maybe it's nothing, uh? Pushpe? Maybe it's because he can't accept that she's grown up now? He wasn't here when she grew up? He's coming home tomorrow . . . As though to get a grip on the worry that grew like hydra inside her as she spoke, Vahida worked in the kitchen at a frantic pace.

Pushpa's voice, flowing from the house on the other end of the street through Vahida's earphones, stopped momentarily, flustered, not knowing what to say. 'Tell *mol* to be careful, Vahida . . . what else am I to say . . . I'll come over this afternoon . . . have some things to tell you . . .' She stopped talking. Vahida cut the call without receiving a single word of consolation.

Ruba who had come into the kitchen to get her lunch box looked intently at her mother's drawn and strained face. She went away quietly.

Watching her walk away, Vahida burned from within. The enemy was inside the house. Those innocent-looking acts; the constant pacing in front of Ruba's bathroom; the nudging, holding.

Ruba complained for the first time when she was a class twelve student. Uppa's trying to touch my breasts for no reason, she had said. She looked like a melting candle when she said that. He was back home on a two-month vacation then. He was then her husband who still desired her with a young man's passion, a loving father who cozied up to his daughter and coddled her, the man who worked his fingers to the bone so that they could have a comfortable life, now home seeking some rest; someone who indulged Ruba's every whim. She was making up things about such a man! 'Watch those filthy movies and spew nonsense,' she had roared, landing a hard slap on her cheek. She broke and fell into pieces. Began to run a fever. Now, when she heard that Uppa was coming home, she became feverish.

Gopika, Medical Student, 'Sayanora', Flat No. C-9, Street No. 10, Mangala Lane

The third day of the forensics department posting.

The professor was explaining the basics of a post-mortem examination.

Suddenly, the sound of boots in the veranda near the class room. The police. Media cameras.

'Come,' said the professor, 'there's a case.' Along with his words, a foul stench that they'd never known before filled the air. A strange fear, hard to turn into words, gripped the whole class.

A small bundle lay on the granite slab in the post-mortem room. A body covered in a blanket.

'The body's decomposed. A child's,' the professor pointed to it.

She pressed her hands hard to prevent herself from being sick. Her head reeled in the disgusting stench, as though she was standing beside a pit of decaying waste. A child, missing since five days. Maggots wriggling out from all over. The lower part, from waist down, was exposed. The genitalia stuck out.

Looked like a male child. Not clear why the journalists took images of the exposed parts again and again; the medical students looked at each other uneasily.

When the bustle was over and after the police and mediapersons left, the professor said, 'Rape and murder. A girl child, six years old.'

A girl child. Girl child.

They were now removing the blanket that covered her.

The unending frenzied writhing of maggots in the swollen bluish flesh; the bite marks; the torn lip, the tongue that stuck out of the mouth; the skin peeling off; the brain that had turned into mush.

The legs that seemed unnaturally open; the arms raised like in a last act of self-defence. Pointing to the arms, the professor started to explain cadaveric spasm.

She collapsed in a heap on the floor; someone held her. The attenders were removing the frock, the necklace of beads, and the little bangles from the body.

Ajitha Teacher, 'Greeshmam', Flat No. D-5, Street No. 10, Mangala Lane

'It was a priest who did it, Thankamme, this great sinner! A man who should have been directing people towards good!'

Ajitha teacher gritted her teeth at the news and invited Thankamma, who was swabbing the floor, to the leaves of the newspaper.

'And to just a kid, ten or fourteen!' A photo on the front page, of him coming out of the police vehicle, surrounded by policemen, wearing a slight smile on his face.

There was more news inside. News that stuck inside you once you softened from the inside; kill-joy news; the body . . . news that was possible only because of acts on the body . . .

'What to say, Teacher-amme,' Thankamma joined her. 'We are all in the same rut, a one-year-old babe and a ninety-nine-year-old crone, rich and poor, actor, politician, whoever . . . last week, my daughter . . . she's small, in the sixth standard . . . some man grabbed her chest and squeezed it hard. The prick lives in that lodge over there . . . just think, Teachere, my girl is so small, there's almost nothing on her chest? Just two little lumps, what else? We're people who don't even have enough to eat, how much flesh our girl will have? It was deserted then, but it's still the open street . . . it's a big case if you attack even a stray dog now . . . but those of us who stay by the road? Aren't the curs given more value than us? Isn't that our fate, Teachere? I wanted to complain . . . Alexander Saar, in whose house I work, is a police, no? He just said, "But nothing happened to your girl, Edi? We are drowning in cases in which things have happened!" And anyway I can barely manage to fill our bellies, how to run after this case and all? I just told my *kunhi* to be careful . . . just be alert whoever it is. Swamiyar or Acchan or Musaliar or Saar or Uncle . . . or saint or whoever . . . their heads are all full of naked women, breasts, bums and such things . . .' Thankamma spat out a whole mouthful of disgust.

Though she tried her best to stuff it in, a memory from months back kept churning in her mind. She had taught hundreds of children, boys and girls. Their faces, fresh smiles, young eyes, tender fingers, classrooms with a whiff of childhood scents in the air . . .

She remembered that picture—with a flower in the middle, and four bees circling it. The one Paaru drew before she shed her petals.

'What's this picture, Paaru?' she had asked, 'Why did you draw it?'

She smiled, looking empty. 'Just felt like drawing it, Teachere.'

Red petals lay scattered below the bough she hung herself; no, the bough on which they hung her body after they killed her. Blacking red-clotted petals. Petals which looked as though someone had crushed them underfoot.

Ajitha was on leave since many months now.

There was a rage boiling in her; an indescribable anger.

Akash, Student, 'Greeshmam', Flat No. D-5, Street No. 10, Mangala Lane

Akash panted as he opened the file in the mobile phone. The bathroom. The sound of the shower. His heart beat hard. Amma was coming into the room, leaving the towel out on the hanger to dry, taking off her sari— from her shoulder, her chest, her . . . He stared at the screen. Something had blocked the view, a shampoo bottle or something like that. He had been so careful! Made a hole inside a large shampoo bottle, slid the camera in and set its camera at the correct angle and switched it on . . . so slyly . . . shit . . . shit . . . he slapped his forehead. Now he had to go through the tension all over again! And Amma is a smart one . . . if she found out . . . then it will be the end of the road . . .

The four of them in the gang had decided to do it.

Sudeep would film his sister changing; Aniruddh would shoot his older female cousin at her bath; Divakar would get one of his mother changing her sari . . . now it was his turn. They had agreed not to send each other the files. They'll just watch it on the phone used to shoot it and then delete. He'd been roving around the house, since many days now. He held the mobile phone in his hand and cursed his luck.

'You should have asked me. I'd have acted the scene well for you!'

Amma's voice.

Akash jumped violently and wheeled around.

He tried to hide the phone, but there was nowhere to hide it.

A whole bunch of petals dried up and fell inside Ajitha Teacher.

'You want to see Amma's boobs? The same boobs you drank from as a baby? The ones you dried up?' she asked. 'Or the place from which I brought you into this world, in endless pain? Tell me, Kanna, my dearest boy!'

She held her son's hand. Planted a briny kiss on his forehead.

He turned a murky shade, like the bee. He buzzed.

A hundred bees buzzed in her head. It throbbed hard with pain. She pulled her son to her chest and held him close, closest she could. Like she used to when he was a scared child. Her heart was racked with pain.

'Now, do you feel lust?' she asked him in a slow, low buzz. He was utterly shaken. Drenched in sweat. She snatched his mobile phone, smashed it on the floor with a single throw, and stormed out of the room.

Women Together, Street 10, Mangala Lane

'I will do it,' Thankamma declared, spine up, chest out. 'For any number of days.'

Yearning to breathe out forever the stench of the little girl's mangled body that simply refused to disappear from her brain, Gopika said loudly, 'I'll be with you!'

Vahida looked on, stumped, open-mouthed.

'I'll come, too,' Ruba joined in with Gopika.

'Me too,' said Thankamma's girl, the sixth standard student. She was still pressing down the pain which refused to fade on her chest. Seeing her spunk, her older sister held her hand out, hesitantly.

Though she was still scared and reluctant, Vahida joined Ruba.

'I've had enough, too,' Fathima said, joining Tessy. 'He claws my body all day and then leers at other women . . .'

'At the shop, on the road . . . we've been taking it for so long . . . and without saying a single word against . . .' The shopgirl Latika and the flower-seller Devi held out their hands.

'He grabs you in the bus when you show the concession ticket and gropes you . . . and the maths sir in class . . . he has to pinch all the time . . . Teacher, count us in,' Pushpa's daughter piped up from among her friends.

Many, many hands, small and big, reached out towards Ajitha Teacher. Their numbers swelled. They went past Mangala Lane and flowed beyond.

Street No. 10, Mangala Lane

Men, caught completely unawares, deprived of their morning tea, hot bath water, and breakfast started trickling out of the apartments and homes in Mangala Lane. Their wives and daughters were nowhere to be found. They were not, like on an ordinary day, at the fishmonger's or the green grocer's. Daughters were not rushing from kitchen to bedroom trying to be on time at school. The sons began to get irked, just like their fathers. Some yearned to bestow a tight slap on the faces of their women. Office travel got delayed; shops opened late. The men gathered near the road trying to find out why. The policeman Alexander, the clothes-store owner Saithalavi Haji, Ajitha Teacher's son Akash and his friends, Joseph, Vahida's husband Ali who had just stepped out from a taxi from the Nedumbassery airport—and many others—looked at it.

A long procession of women, coming up from the extreme end of the lane, very slowly. A seemingly never-ending line of naked women. Dark-skinned, wheatish skin, short bodies, tall bodies, young bodies, ageing bodies—they all walked silently in a line. Not shrinking in shame, not crouching to hide their bodies, not cowering in fear, not bowing their heads . . .

Bellies etched with the spreading branches of birthing pains; scars in mysterious resting places; fall marks; memory marks; dented organs; surgery scars; moles that lie scattered on the skin like mustard seeds; fat legs, thin legs; breasts sucked and fallen, young and risen, unformed and semi-formed, so many kinds of breasts; red nipples, black nipples; female marks between the legs . . .

When the first terrible wave of shock subsided, Saithalavi had an enormous hard-on and turned his burning eye on the body of the salesgirl in his shop. Alexander's eyes fell like a vulture on Thankamma's ebony-coloured skin which he had not yet had a chance to touch. Akash stared at his mother, eyes bulging with fear. Joseph stared at the black marks that his fingers had made on the tiny mounds on Thankamma's girl's chest.

It was in the middle of just rising and burning that Saithalavi spotted his wife Fathima and their three daughters, buck naked. 'Pha! Daughter of a dog! Are you mad?' he bellowed, 'I am going to . . .' He was struck dumb suddenly seeing reddish leers from the crowd fall on their bodies. All other sights dissolved from his eyes.

'Ayyo! Tessy-ye!' Alexander screamed, pulling his eyes off Thankamma's body. Only after did he see his daughter walk beside her mother. Her slim fair body, now grown. He saw thousands of eyes like his own, erect organs like his own, claw his daughter's tender young body. His throat grew parched. Numberless screams and wails of women that had been suppressed and silenced now rose up in him and multiplied with amazing rapidity. When she passed by her Uppa, Ruba stopped for a few moments, looking straight into his eyes. She then strode past him with measured steps, leaving behind his bloodless, terrified face.

Seeing an endless flow of body after body, sick of hard-on after hard-on, the leering crowd began to tire. Then Thankamma's little one began to sing a joyous song, a child's song, endearing nonsense. Ajitha Teacher struck up a rhythm on her thighs and buttocks and began to sing along. Others took it up and carried it forward; the song began to acquire a new tempo. And the bodies began to sway gently to it. They moved ahead as the eyes that watched looked down in shame, weary of lust and excitement. They moved slowly, unhurried, leisurely. Like the wind, the sun, the leaves and flowers, the bodies of women walked on and into the world—a world that was theirs, too.

Acknowledgements

Yama, 'Chudalaththengu', in *Oru Vayanasaalaa Viplavam*. Kottayam: DC Books, 2019, pp. 19–36.

G.R. Indugopan, 'Elivaanam', in *Kathakal*. Kottayam: DC Books, 2020, pp. 276–86.

Santhosh Aechikkanam, 'Roadil Paalikkenda Niyamangal', in *Komala*. Kottayam: DC Books, 2021.

Nirmala, 'Sujaathayute Veedukal', 27 April 2022, https://emalayalee.com/vartha/261465 (accessed 23 July 2022).

Dhanya Raj, 'Green Room', in *Padaprasnam*. Kottayam: DC Books, 2016, pp. 11–19.

K.R. Meera, 'Sanghiannan', first published by Juggernaut, 2018. Original Malayalam: 'Sanghiannan', *Mathrubhumi Weekly*, 6 August 2017.

Shihabudheen Poythumkadavu, 'K.P. Ummer', in *Isayum K.P. Ummarum*, Kozhikode: Mathrubhumi Books, 2021.

Unni R., 'Vatsyayanan', in *Pacchakkutira*, 9 September 2020.

P.V. Shajikumar, 'Asaadhu', in *Sthalam*. Kottayam: DC Books, 2020, pp. 13–35.

Prince Aymanam, 'Pothycchoru Nerccha', in *Samakaalika Malayalam*, 2019, pp. 214–27.

Ambikasutan Mangad, 'Neeraaliyan', in *Ambikasutan Mangadinte Thiranjedutha Kathakal*. Kottayam: DC Books, 2021.

Vinoy Thomas, 'Idavelikkaar', in *Raamachi*. Kottayam: DC Books, 2017, pp. 44–60.

Shahina E.K., 'Kattum Veyilum Ilayum Poovum Pole', in *Kattum Veyilum, Ilayum Poovum Pole*. Kozhikode: Mathrubhumi Books, 2022, pp. 67–76.

Notes on Authors

Yama hails from Thiruvananthapuram and studied at the School of Drama, Thrissur, and the National School of Drama. She is an actor, scriptwriter and theatre professional. She won the State Award for the best actress in the Kerala Sangeetha Nataka Akademi's amateur drama competition of 2008. She also received the Inlaks Fellowship for research in 2009. She has to her credit two short story collections, *Oru Vayanasaalaa Viplavam* and *Paalam Kadakkumbol Pennungal Maathram Kaanunnathu,* and a novel, *Pilpeelika.*

G.R. Indugopan is from the coastal village of Valathungal in Kollam district. An author of over thirty books in prose, he is also a biographer, translator, screenplay writer and cinema director. His translation of the autobiography of a thief, Manian Pillai, into Tamil won the Kendra Sahitya Akademi' translation prize. The televised version of his novel *Kaali Gandhaki* won seven state awards. He has also had a long career as a journalist. He has been awarded the Gita Hiranyan Endowment, the Padmarajan Award, the V.P. Sivakumar Keli Award, the State Institute for Children's Literature Award and the Edassery Prize. The film *Ottakkayyan* which he scripted and directed won two state awards in 2007.

Santhosh Aechikkanam is a full-time writer. A native of the Kasaragod district, he presently lives in Thrissur. Trained as a journalist, he soon came to be recognized as one of the most promising writers of the new century. He has twelve collections of short stories to his credit and has also published several short memoirs. He has also been the screenplay writer for several critically acclaimed movies. He is the recipient of twenty-five major literary awards including the Kerala Sahitya Akademi Award, the Kolkata Bhasha Parishad Award, Delhi Katha Award, Padmaprabha Literary Award, Karur Award, Cherukad Award and so on, and has also won the State Television Award for the best story, *Panthibhojanam*.

Nirmala was born in Ernakulam district of Kerala, and now lives in Canada with her family. She has published three volumes of short stories which include *Aadyathe Pathu* and *Manjha Morum Chuvanna Meenum*. She has won important literary prizes in Malayalam, including the Ponhjikkara Rafi Prize and the NORKA Pravasi Puraskaram, the Takazhi

Prize and the Ankanam Award. Her novels based on immigrant life in Canada have also been acclaimed— *Paambum Koniyum* and *Manjhil Oruval*.

Dhanya Raj works as a higher secondary school teacher. She is a native of Pathanapuram, Kollam district. Her short story collections include *New Woman Beauty Parlour*, *Vaaranthyajeevitam*, *Padaprasnam* and *Pachayute Album*. She has won the Kerala Sahitya Akademi's Gita Hiranyan Endowment, the Muthukulam Parvathy Amma Literary Prize, the K.A. Kodungaloor Short Story Award and many others.

K.R. Meera is one of Malayalam's most powerful literary voices in the new century. Her early reputation as a journalist was soon overshadowed by her literary reputation, built through a series of fine short stories. Later, she produced many notable novels including the much-discussed *Aaraachaar* (translated and published as *Hangwoman* in English) which is an all-time bestseller in Malayalam. Meera has won almost all of the most prestigious literary awards in Malayalam, including the Kerala Sahitya Akademi Award, the Kendra Sahitya Akademic Award, the Odakkuzhal Award and the Vayalar Award. Meera's oeuvre includes short stories, novels, novellas, essays and memoirs. She is widely translated and is recognized as an eminent author outside Malayalam as well. She is based in Kottayam.

Shihabuddin Poithumkadavu hails from Poythumkadavu, in Kannur district. He is the author of several critically acclaimed short stories and novels and his oeuvre includes life-writing, essays and poetry. His short story collections include *Aaarkkum Vendaatha Kannu* and *Malabar Express*. He has also written several scripts for television and ad films. He has won a number of prestigious prizes including the Kerala Sahitya Akademi Award, the Padmarajan Award, Abudhabi Malayali Samajam Award and so on. His stories are part of school and college syllabuses in Kerala. His work has been translated into English, Tamil, French and Arabic.

Unni R. is a well-known short story and screenplay writer in Malayalam. Born and raised in Kudamalloor, Kottayam, his stories often return to this village. His short story collection *Vaanku* won the Kerala Sahitya Akademi award and *Ozhivudivasathe Kali* won the Gita Hiranyan Endowment. His screenplay for the film *Charlie* won the Kerala State Award. His short stories and a novel have been translated into English as *One Hell of a Lover* and *The Cock is the Culprit*. Another volume of translated short stories, *Malayali Memorial*, is forthcoming.

P.V. Shajikumar hails from the Kasaragod district and is a well-known short story writer and scriptwriter. He has won several awards for his literary contributions including the Kendra Sahitya Akademi Yuva Puraskar, the Kerala Sahitya Akademi's Gita Hiranyan Endowment, the C.V. Sreeraman Award, the Ankanam Award and the Bhashaposhini Award. His screenplays include *Kanyaka Talkies* and *Take Off*. He received the Best Screenplay prize at the New York Indian Film Festival (2014); *Kanyaka Talkies* was screened at numerous film festivals around the world. He is a software engineer by profession.

Prince Aymanam, son of V.J. and Thresiamma, hails from Aymanam, Kottayam. He works in the State Goods and Services Tax office as assistant state taxation officer. His short stories and poems have appeared in many reputed Malayalam magazines and literary journals. He is one of the most promising voices in Malayalam fiction.

Ambikasutan Mangad is a renowned writer in Malayalam who has over sixty books, including twenty-five short story collections and three novels. He has won over thirty prizes including the prestigious O.V. Vijayan Award for the short story *Chinnamundi*. His writing is noted for its focus on the non-human living world and he is known as a vocal critic of human violence against it. A leader of the movement against Endosulphan spraying in north Kerala (where he lives and works), Ambikasutan's novel *Enmakaje* was crucial in raising awareness and support for the struggle elsewhere in the state. It has been translated into four language including English (titled *Swarga*). He worked in the Nehru Arts and Science College in Kanhangad and retired as head of the department, Malayalam.

Vinoy Thomas is a native of Nellakkaampoyil, Iritty, in Kannur, Kerala. His first novel *Karikkottakkari* received the D.C. Kizkakkemuri Birth Centennary Prize and also won the Joseph Mundashery Award. He received the Kerala Sahitya Akademi Award for short story for his short story collection *Ramacchi*. Lijo Jose Pellisery's movie *Churuli* was based on his short story.

Shahina E.K. is from Perinthalmanna in Malappuram district of Kerala. She has six short story collections to her credit and has won many prestigious prizes including the Edassery Prize, T.V. Kochubava Prize for Short Story, Muthukulam Parvathy Amma Short Story Prize, the Kamala Surayya Short Story Prize and the Ankanam Award. Her stories have been translated into many other languages.